RED HOT
Roaster

RED HOT Roaster

TALES FROM THE CHOCOLATE LAB CAFE BOOK 1

KRISTIN JEFFRIES

HEA Author Services:
Developmental Editing by Kimberly Hunt
Copyediting by Lisa Carlisle
Proofreading by Emily Laughridge

Cover and Interior Design: Qamber Designs

ISBN 979-8-9923766-0-9 (eBook)
ISBN 979-8-9923766-1-6 (Paperback)

Published by I'll Have What She's Having Publications LLC

Dedication

To my own red hot roaster

About This Book

Red Hot Roaster is a sweet and spicy contemporary romance featuring Rose, an overwhelmed café owner and older mom who's been burned once too often; Rafe, a roaming coffee roaster and army vet with too many secrets; and Princess and her Pirate, their matchmaking pups.

Please be aware this is an "open door" story with explicit sexy times. There's creative profanity too, appropriate to the characters. The story also mentions deaths (off page), illnesses and other topics that may be sensitive to some readers. Intended for those age 18 and older.

Chapter 1

Rose

Goldie took off down the middle of our neighborhood's busiest street, dragging my new chocolate Lab behind her and yelping frantically.

The dog statue was breaking into chunks as the scared old girl ran along, yet she refused to slow down. I needed to reach her—and pronto.

I raced down the street, calling to Goldie and waving at cars to stop. Someone pounded past me, nearly knocking me over. I stumbled, righted myself and kept on going. Then, the sound I dreaded to hear...a drawn-out *screeeeech*.

Oh, no. Oh, Goldie.

Noah ran up and grabbed me around the waist, panting and crying and clinging. I hugged my little neighbor tight and pulled us toward the accident.

A stranger was kneeling in front of the stopped car, his broad back toward us. My breath caught when, in one motion, he unfolded and turned, cradling Goldie in his arms. Blood covered his flannel shirt, and a fragment of the leash dangled from her collar.

Why is he moving her? Did he pick her up without checking for broken bones? Doesn't he realize she's bleeding?

1

What the fido?

By the time we got closer, the guy was rumbling, his face tilted down, "That's my baby girl. I've got you. You're safe now." And again, "I've got you."

Huh. It seemed Goldie was over her trauma of being tied to the dog statue. Instead, the flirt was gazing at her rescuer with those liquid amber eyes, fluttering her impossibly long to-die-for lashes.

I had to know. "Did you even check for injuries before you lifted her? Was she actually hit? Why is she bleeding all over the place?"

That's when Goldie's rescuer raised his head and sent me a cutting glare from cobalt-blue eyes framed by *his* impossibly long thick dark lashes. I may have melted a bit, but his next words left me cold.

"Is this your dog?" he growled. "What were you thinking, tying her to that thing? She could've been run over!"

Before I could get a word in, the jerk went on, "And, yeah. I know what I'm doing. Nothing's broken. The blood's from her paws being scraped raw."

Noah cried even harder. I frowned and slid my eyes down to the boy. The guy finally got a clue and clamped his lips together in a hard line.

"Hey, buddy," I said, hugging him closer. "There's no way you could've known the dog statue was so lightweight. Thanks to this, er, this nice man, Goldie is safe and just a little worse for wear."

I turned to the *nice* man and said, "The café isn't set up for doggy first aid. I'd like the vet to clean her paws and check them for gravel or glass. Could you please carry Goldie a few blocks to the clinic."

It came off like an order rather than a request, so I wasn't surprised when he quirked an eyebrow.

"Or is she getting too heavy?" I asked, half-serious, half-not-so-much.

He narrowed those eyes and shook his head. "Nope, she's fine." And then, "Oh, shit, I should let her know I'm running late. I need to call, or maybe we can stick our heads in the café as we go by?"

I stopped abruptly. "Are you Rafe Amato?"

His face blanked. "Are you Rose Connolly?"

I hope you're more observant when you're roasting my coffee beans, sweetheart.

I pulled off my food prep hairnet so my overdue-for-a-cut hair tumbled out and made a sweeping gesture down my front.

My long apron displayed our logo of a Labrador retriever drinking a steaming cup of coffee over fancy script reading *The Chocolate Lab Café—Where Everybody Knows Your (Dog's) Name.*

"I figured you were into pretty weird rain hats. I also figured you didn't want me staring below your neck." Rafe was quick on his feet—I had to give him that.

Okay, I appreciated the *eyes up here* awareness. I'd gotten enough attention for my curvy figure in the past. Plus, he was going to be working for me. Better to set the tone right from the start.

We'd arrived in front of the café by this time. The old girl was still nestled in Rafe's arms like a seventy-pound baby, and Noah was wiping his tears with his arms. All our customers, dogs and humans, crowded out front to see the action. Noah's big sister, Emma, was there too, wringing a dishtowel between her hands.

"Hey, everyone—Goldie's going to be fine! We're taking her down to Dr. Mica's clinic to get her paw pads checked out. Say 'hello' to Rafe. He's our new coffee roaster, and he's the one who saved our golden girl from getting hit by a car."

Yeah, a lifesaver in more ways than one.

If we didn't get the roaster back up and running, pronto, I was going to lose the chance at the PDX FOODS business and likely the hospital kiosk contract. Then I'd have to close the café and let everybody go. Simple as that.

Shouts of "hi, Rafe" and "thanks, man" filled the air along with "welcome to the Chocolate Lab" and even an "atta boy" or two. Husky mix Louis got the other dogs barking, and Gus joined in with his Basset hound howls.

Quite a commotion, but Rafe kept his chin tucked down, staring at Goldie. A blush—or was it a flush on a guy?—spread up his neck, under his stubble, to his forehead where it met his high and tight dark hair.

To put the poor guy out of his misery (and Goldie had to be getting heavy), I announced, "All right, let's get this sorted."

I grabbed Emma's towel and shoved it toward Noah. "Here, buddy, dry your face. Get a garbage bag from inside and follow Goldie's trail to pick up all the pieces of dog statue you can find. Watch for cars!"

I turned to his sister. "Can you please call your dad, let him know what happened, and ask him to meet us at Dr. Mica's?"

She nodded, and they both dashed into the café.

"Mateo, could you get the kids going again on drinks and food orders? I was just winding up prepping the two salads for tomorrow's menu. You'll see them posted. Can you please finish up for me?"

My manager gave me an "of course, Rose."

I added, "When Noah returns, make sure to give him a sweet treat of some kind, okay?"

So that was sorted. It was time to get on with the rest of the day—I was already feeling behind schedule. I needed to orient the newbie to the roastery, get home to check in with my friend Jen and her crew, and make a few more calls about Mom's party.

And Pirate. My big boy deserved a good long walk before it got too dark.

"Rafe, thanks for being so patient," I said as I led the way down the sidewalk toward the vet clinic. "Bet you weren't expecting all this drama your first day here."

Chapter 2

Rafe

Too fucking right, I hadn't expected all this drama. My idea had been to meet up with the Chocolate Lab's owner, get the lay of the land, and head back to Pete's to settle in. My old mentor had offered us a place to crash until we found our own short-term quarters.

That idea had been blasted to bits when a golden retriever took off running down the road in front of me. Good thing I'd caught up with her in time and popped my knife to make short work of the tangled leash.

What caught me off guard—and I prided myself on being ready for anything—was my reaction to the woman.

Actually, my three reactions.

First, how fast my fury about the dog's safety had shut down—*I was wrong, and this gorgeous woman is handing me my ass.*

Second, how my gut had clenched—*she's the mother of the boy who'd tied Goldie to the statue.*

And third, how my gut had relaxed here at the vet's—*she's not the mother, and she's not married to the guy arriving to claim his dog.*

I needed to get a grip. Yes, there was something about Rose that yanked me right to her, with her heart-shaped face framed by that out-of-control long blonde hair. Her dark-blonde eyebrows

6

arching over those glittering green eyes. Her plump, sculpted lips between those sweet smile lines.

But I was going to be working for her—she was going to be my *boss*. Their roaster Mike, who'd broken his leg in a bike-versus-car collision, would only be out of commission for a few months.

After that, I'd be on the road again, first to a gig in Boise, then on to other temp jobs I was lining up. No need to get distracted from my primary mission: get in, get the job done, get out, get on with the next.

So, yeah, I was dealing with these unexpected reactions, this attraction, these *fucking* sensations.

I was burying them.

The kids' dad (and thankfully *not* Rose's husband, although I tamped down that relief again) walked in the door. Goldie's tail gave a heavy *thump, thump, thump*. Rose introduced me to Liam, who apologized for his son, thanked us for our help, and said he would pay for the statue—an offer she declined.

As we were heading out, I turned back to Dr. Mica, a tiny Asian-American woman who didn't look like she could wrangle a mouse, much less a mastiff.

"My dog Princess is due for her shots soon. I'm new to the area. Would you be willing to see her?"

Rose snapped her head toward me. The biggest smile lit up her face. This time, her eyes were wide and glowing, not narrowed and glaring.

"Rafe, you have a dog? You brought your dog with you?"

I nodded. "She's a rescue, probably four or five years old now. She chose her own name." *Maybe that was oversharing.*

Dr. Mica said, "Of course, I'd be happy to see Princess. I'm assuming you have information on her vaccinations and other care?"

I paused for a beat, not ready to share my history at such short notice. "Yeah, at least for the time she's been with me, the past three years or so."

The vet didn't let up. "Oh, good. Do you know her background before you got her? Sometimes a tough early life can affect health or behaviors later on."

Made sense, so I volunteered a bit more. "She's from Afghanistan, one of a group of camp dogs brought here by a rescue group."

I didn't add *one of the dogs in* my *camp, rescued by me.* Nor did I say *dog rescuing is about all I'm fit for these days.*

Chapter 3

Rose

I couldn't help myself.

As we were walking the few blocks back to the Chocolate Lab, I had a ton of questions for Rafe. All about Princess, of course.

Sure, I should've been asking more about his coffee-roasting background, beyond what Pete had shared. Yeah, I could've been finding out how he planned to get my roastery up and running again. Or I could've been quizzing him on his experience with computerizing inventory.

No, I was peppering him with questions about his rescue pup. Because, well, dogs.

And maybe because I was curious?

How did this muscular beast of a guy end up being a girl-dad? Was Princess as dainty and as demanding as her name implied? Did she bark when she got excited, like he did?

I ran-walked alongside Rafe—I had long legs, but I could barely keep up—and threw my nosy questions at his profile.

"So, where's Princess right now?"

"She's hanging out with Pete at his place."

"Will she be with Pete when you're working at the roastery?"

Rafe side-eyed me. "No….she'll be with me. Not in the roastery, of course. I'll park my pickup nearby, and she'll stay on her blanket throne in the back of the cab."

"Blanket throne? Oh, right, right, she's a princess. I'm picturing cashmere blankets and silk sheets embroidered in gold with tiny tiaras."

He smirked. "Not quite that over-the-top, but still pretty comfortable. That way, on my breaks, I can take her around the block, feed her, and give her water."

I frowned. Typically, Rafe would be working four-to-six-hour shifts, four to five days a week. Would Princess be okay stuck in his pickup for that long with just short breaks?

They'd obviously done this before, so I kept that particular question to myself. But I snuck in a few more before we got back to the café.

"How is Princess with other dogs?"

"Good, as long as there's plenty of time for get-acquainted sniffs. She rat-packed around with a bunch of other camp dogs for her first year or two."

"How about people?"

Rafe grinned, the smile going all the way to his beautiful blue eyes. "Well, she *is* a princess. She's a bit imperious, and she expects you to obey her every command. You have to earn her trust."

I smiled right back. "I can hardly wait to meet Her Highness!"

Chapter 4

Rose

I was all about chocolate brown coupled with hot pink.

Dad used to say the pink was too "feckin' girly" for our café—but that'd been the Irish in him kidding me. My ex, Brent, had labeled the pink as too "unsophisticated" for Portland—but that'd been the lawyer in him judging me. Mom had just smiled as she uncapped the paint can.

So when we walked into the Chocolate Lab, I turned to catch the moment when Rafe spied the walls in all their hot pink glory.

Is he going to throw shade on my choices? Rafe halted and raised his eyebrows, head on a swivel. After shooting me a look, he moved past the pink-painted tables toward the pink-and-brown-striped front counter. His right hand came up to rub the back of his neck when he clocked the pink boards slanting overhead with all our food and drink offerings written boldly in chocolate-brown chalk.

"Did you paint the roastery—" he started to say, but was interrupted by Emma and Noah rushing over.

I assured them Goldie was okay—a few scrapes and cuts after being chased by the scary, mean dog—and turned back just as Mateo walked out from the kitchen prep area.

"Hey, Rafe, meet Mateo Flores, the Chocolate Lab's manager. Mateo, meet Rafe Amato, our new temp roaster and Goldie girl rescuer."

Rafe and Mateo both did the chin lift thing.

Since we'd all be working together, I'd shared Rafe's info with Mateo to get his take. With someone new coming from outside the area, even for a short time while Mike recovered, it was important to have a good fit.

Rafe could get acquainted with the kids on the café crew later. Anyone in their teens or twenties was a "kid" to me. He'd meet my "real" kid too when Finn came home from college for his grandma's party this weekend.

"Everything under control, Mateo?" If it was worth checking once, it was worth checking forty-seven times.

"Yes, Rosita. No worries." He so knew I'd be asking again before the day was out.

I motioned for Rafe to precede me. "Let's head back to the roastery and get started on orientation."

Wait. Oh, shih tzu.

Rafe had those bloody smears from Goldie's scraped paw pads all down the front of his plaid shirt. Plus on the no-longer-white T-shirt where it showed through his unbuttoned shirt.

"I am so, so sorry," I blurted out. "I'll take your shirts home and get the blood out. If I can't, we'll replace them, of course."

I asked Mateo for a garbage can liner and whirled around to the shelves holding our branded gear right by the front counter. Diving into the pile of Chocolate Lab T-shirts, I snatched the largest unisex size we had—XXL, for the soccer team we sponsored. Hot pink with our logo and lettering in chocolate brown, of course.

By this time, Mateo and Rafe were both looking at me like I was crazy. Didn't matter. I was on a roll, places to go, things to do.

I tossed Rafe the new T-shirt and shook out the liner to accept the bloody clothes. He looked around for a moment, rumbled something like "thank you, Rose," and shrugged off his plaid shirt.

He loosened his belt and did that thing that guys do—grabbed his T-shirt behind his neck and pulled it off over his head in one swift motion.

So here's the thing. I tried not to stare, and I succeeded. For the most part.

But in the short moment Rafe tugged on the Chocolate Lab T-shirt, I took in a lot.

His broad chest lightly furred with black—and silver—hair. His sculpted pecs narrowing to a defined six-pack tapering further into his jeans. His shoulders and biceps bulky enough to put the stretch into the XXL T-shirt.

And his entire right arm, from shoulder to muscled biceps through corded forearm to thick wrist, fitted out with a sleeve of tats.

One or two other customers were there for the show, but I had a front-row seat.

It'd been too long.

Rafe turned his back, unzipped his jeans partway, tucked the T-shirt in using quick jabbing motions, zipped and re-belted. All done. He stuffed his bloody clothes in the plastic liner and held it out to me. After a beat, I took it—time to get on with the orientation.

"Thank fuck," Rafe muttered under his breath when we walked into the roastery space at the end of the hall.

"I'm pretty sure I have some pink paint left over from the café if you…" I trailed off when he shook his head.

"I'm good, thanks."

"Well, if you change your mind," I teased, seeing if I could get a rise out of him.

No-go. He ignored me and slapped his big paw on our spanking new Diedrich commercial coffee roaster—an upgrade from our first roaster in terms of size, output, noise, everything.

"What's this monster doing in the back of a café?" He quirked an eyebrow my way.

And by *a café*, he meant *your little old dog-friendly hot-pink-painted neighborhood hangout spot.*

Nope. Not me. Not defensive at all.

It raised my hackles when people—especially newbies to my life—questioned my ability to make decisions, run my business.

Yes, I'd upgraded to the big-girl roaster because I planned to grow my coffee-roasting business beyond the pink walls. I'd also just made a breathtaking investment in green coffee inventory, now stacked in burlap bags in the corner of the space.

To put coffee cupping on the same fancy level of wine tasting, I'd even found a vintage oak table that spun on its pedestal. Potential retail clients could sit around the table sipping our different signature blends—and clearing their palates with elegant water crackers—before making their choices.

Did I share any of this with Rafe? Uh, again, a big nope. No need for me to get all offended—he was just a short-timer.

Instead, I quipped, "We tried putting her out front, but she was so loud she started all the dogs barking."

Rafe snorted and left it at that.

Last surprise on the roastery tour was the industrial sink or, really, the mirror above it. Jam-packed up and down, side to side, with my Post-it Notes—not one sliver of mirror showing through.

Those notes were my to-do list, my organization out of chaos, my security that I wouldn't forget anything. *If I kept busy, I'd be okay.*

I'd been drowning, and my girl Jen had thrown me the Post-it Notes life preserver. She used them all the time in her business of organizing, downsizing and moving.

Each Post-it featured one "to-do" item—yellow for an errand, orange for a phone call, blue for an email, green for an action, purple for paperwork, and so on. I arranged them in columns, each headed by a topic, all written in black marker.

Like the "Temp Roaster" Post-it that Rafe was staring at right now.

I hadn't planned for Rafe to see the crazy that was my business life here at the Chocolate Lab…quite yet. Of course, no need for him to catch a glimpse of my crazy at home, where mirrors in the bathrooms, front hall and utility room were crammed with Post-its of my personal "to-dos."

"Sorry. Here, let me get those out of your way," I said, pushing past Rafe to reach up and start peeling off the notes. A large, warm hand immediately engulfed—and stilled—my fingers.

"Whoa, Rose, slow down. I don't need a mirror to powder my nose. Are those things we need to do to get me going and get the roastery running again?"

Wow, three complete sentences in a row. I nodded, momentarily speechless.

Rafe released my hand, and I pulled it back down. Luckily, he stepped back, too, since we were a little too close for my comfort, boss-employee-wise.

We spent twenty-five minutes going over each Post-it Note under "Temp Roaster," starting with me explaining my color coding. Points to Rafe for being patient with my system, although he did grunt a time or two when I lingered over "to-dos" he likely already knew how to do.

Some we did right away and trashed the notes. Rafe signed his contract and filled out a 1099 tax form as an independent contractor. I walked him through my three-ring binder with recipes for blending different coffee beans for our signature coffees. I showed him how to log into our laptop and find the spreadsheet with the current coffee bean orders for our daily café needs, online sales and any catering jobs.

He cut me off when I tried to show him how to update the spreadsheet. "Already know Excel, Rose—thanks." We were back to short and sweet.

Other Post-its we left on the mirror for later, at Rafe's insistence. My biggest need—I'd been too busy to do it—was to set up formulas for calculating how many pounds per coffee bean origin to roast per day to fulfill our orders. Origin being where the beans came from, like Brazil, Ethiopia, Kenya and so on.

Then we could project when it was time to buy more green coffee so we'd always have enough on hand. Enough inventory would be super important when, not if, we snagged the grocery store and hospital accounts.

When I started my deep dive into details, Rafe waved me off. "Got this, Rose—no worries."

Pretty soon, we'd cleared a smidgen of space on the left side of the mirror.

"Hey, you may have to duck," I declared, "but now you have room enough to see when you comb your hair."

He lifted his arm, biceps flexing under the T-shirt sleeve, and rubbed his hand over his tight cut, bending over to peer in the mirror. "Works for me," he said and shot me a small smirk.

If I'd had a tail, it would have gone *thump, thump, thump. Down, girl.*

Instead, I said, "That about does it for today. Any more questions for now?"

Rafe shook his head.

"Let's meet here tomorrow morning at six so I can let you in and you can get started. Oh, fido, I need to get you a set of keys." I grabbed the pad of green Post-its, wrote *Retrieve keys for R* on the top one, peeled it off, and stuck it on the mirror under "Temp Roaster."

"Did you call me 'Fido'?" Rafe sounded...horrified? Puzzled? Entertained?

Argh. Got to remember I had *new guy* here, not someone familiar with my...quirks.

"Yes, yes, I came up with all sorts of creative swear words when my son was young," I shared. "Kept using them with so many little ones in and out of the Chocolate Lab. They just stuck, I guess."

With that, I turned out the roastery lights, made sure I had my phone still tucked in my back jeans pocket, and snared the sack of Rafe's clothes. Since Mateo was closing this week, I didn't need to worry about locking up and setting the alarm.

We went through the outside door to the sidewalk, where a few people sitting on our covered deck glanced up curiously. There was a wave here and there, and even a hopeful bark from Tessa, a poodle always on the lookout for a treat.

We said our goodbyes and headed in opposite directions—me toward my house and Rafe, I assume, toward his pickup.

At the last moment, I remembered and turned around to shout, "Looking forward to meeting Princess tomorrow morning!"

I got no words, just my very own chin lift in response.

Chapter 5

Rose

I slowed as I got closer to my front porch.

In the past, I'd been thankful our house was just a few steps down the side street and right behind the Chocolate Lab. After a day at the café, I'd rush home to share every newsy bit and dog tale with my family. I'd find Mom cooking up a storm, Dad grappling with the books, and Finn frowning over his math homework.

Now I was in no hurry to get home.

At age thirty-seven, I'd never lived anywhere else, aside from one cut-short year at college. I'd always lived with my family, other than a roommate that one semester. I'd never lived alone...until now.

That was unless you counted the latest in our line of Labs—any color you chose as long as it was chocolate. And most days, I did count Pirate. Most days.

Other days, I was starving for human, not canine, companionship. I craved a loving and loyal relationship—one where you could count on the guy to never leave you in the lurch.

Where you could ask the guy to sit...and stay.

And the only person who knew about my dream of love—and my doubts and fears—was gone. Even Finn and my besties would never suspect I had dreams that didn't revolve around the futures of my son and the Chocolate Lab.

Mom, sick as she was, had prodded and pushed me until the end.

Sweetie, you cannot give up on your dream. Yes, you've had two bad breaks on the love front. But you have to keep hoping for love, fighting for love.

You have to promise me.

I did, of course, but I wasn't sure I could keep that promise. I wasn't sure I could trust myself to go there again—even if six feet of temporary temptation had walked in my café door. I shook off my depression—physically, from head to tail, much like a dog shakes off rain. It was good none of my neighbors were outside to see me.

I had to catch Jen before she finished for the day. She and her team from Movers&Shakers were helping me clean out all Mom's and Dad's clothing and other accumulated "stuff." And by *helping me*, I meant taking the lead to save me the time—and heartache—of doing it myself.

But first things first. I veered off down the driveway and peered over the backyard gate.

Pirate was lying on the brick patio, his big, blocky Lab head resting in his empty kibble bowl. With eyes closed, ears drooping and tongue lagging, he could be sleeping...or passed out from hunger.

After all, I was fifteen minutes late with his dinner.

"Hey, Pi-Pi," I called softly. "Are you a hungry boy?"

The moment he heard my voice, he sprang to his feet and went all wiggle-butt. I hit the latch, walked through and pushed the gate closed. By this time, Pirate was running in circles around his dish. Then he took off to do his zoomies around the perimeter of the fenced-in backyard.

I had time to toss the sack with Rafe's clothes over to the sliding glass door and snag the food dish before Pirate arrived back on the patio. After he ate and had a big slurp of water, he crowded me to see who could get in the back door first. News flash, he won, the command to "wait" long since ignored. A walk down to Dogwood Park to play ball before it got too dark was on the agenda, and Pirate knew the routine.

But first, I untied my Chocolate Lab apron, put it, along with Rafe's dirty-slash-bloody shirts, in the laundry room, and went upstairs to find Jen.

My girl was a miracle worker.

In the five weeks since Mom had died, Jen and her team had gone through the entire house, attic to basement, plus the apartment converted from our old garage. They sorted clothing, furniture, décor items and other accumulated "stuff" from close to eighty years into mountainous piles—what to keep, donate, recycle or dump.

The clean-out would free up the apartment to be rented again as an extra source of income to support café growth and college costs.

We had moved Mom to the ground-level apartment in the last months of her colon cancer...and surrounded her with the things, people and dogs she loved most—namely family photos and Elvis memorabilia, friends and neighbors, and Pirate. This love, coupled with me sleeping on her couch and the daily visits of outpatient hospice, made her wish to die at home come true.

I found Jen in the main bedroom upstairs, moving the last of my things over, and threw my arms around her for a massive hug. We were big huggers in my family, so she was braced for it and hugged me right back.

We separated and stood grinning at each other for a moment.

"Well, girlfriend," she demanded, "are you ready to let loose this weekend?!"

We were putting on a party for Mom at the Chocolate Lab Saturday night. Not a memorial service, not a wake, not a celebration of life—but a party. It'd be like she was there but had stepped out for a moment. There'd be plenty of food and drink, plenty of laughter and storytelling, plenty of music and singing.

And we, the four of us, were getting the party started early. Jen, Mica, Lauren and I were gathering at Fay's Bar tomorrow night for burgers and Manhattan toasts to Mom. My bestie, Lauren, was staying with me this time, rather than in a hotel like in the past with her soon-to-be-ex. She'd bunk in my old bedroom since I'd moved to my parents' bedroom…or, I guess, *my* bedroom now.

Jen grabbed me by the hand and pulled me into the attached bathroom. She placed me in front of the mirror and said, "Ta-da," motioning wide with both arms.

Arranged in orderly fashion all over the double mirror, my personal Post-it Notes celebrated their escape from the smaller mirror in the hall bathroom. Jen had left a little oval in the middle clear so I could wash my face, brush my teeth, do my hair, put on my makeup—or even powder my nose.

At that last thought, I smiled and pulled in Jen for another, this time "thank you," hug. She knew I'd be lost without my Post-its making order out of the chaos in my head.

"Rose, I gotta get going," she said. "The girls are coming home soon from soccer practice, and it's taco night. Those puppies aren't gonna make themselves."

Jen lived in the neighborhood with her twin middle schoolers, the center of her life. With her corgi, Pants, being a close second… or was it third?

"Everything's good to go in the apartment," she added. "All spick-and-span for a new renter. I locked up and left the key on your kitchen counter."

Oh, shih tzu—I needed to add *search for a tenant* to my Post-its on the laundry room mirror, or maybe the front entry one.

We said our goodbyes and promised to meet up Friday night. I turned back to the little clear spot on my bathroom mirror. Staring back at me was a bedraggled creature—untamed hair, shadowed eyes, and face without a speck of makeup.

What did Rafe think when he met me today? Wait. Why on earth would I care?

It had started to pour when I got downstairs. Pirate was jumping back and forth at the front door, collar jingling. I grabbed his leash, his Frisbee and my rain hoodie—Dad had always claimed umbrellas were for amateurs in Oregon—or Ireland, for that matter.

We headed out the door and down the sidewalk toward Dogwood Park. Once we got there, I threw the Frisbee for the first of a bazillion times on the big soccer pitch. Pirate took off to snag it before it hit the ground, and I pulled back the hood of my jacket to gaze directly up into the rain.

And cry in perfect privacy, except for one oblivious dog.

Chapter 6

Rafe

I sat in Rose's driveway and stared at the house to my right. Princess stood up from her pile of blankets and gave a good shake, her ID tag jingling on her collar. She shoved her head on my right shoulder, and we stared together.

"Quite a place, huh, baby girl?" I grunted.

With its colorful paint job, wide front porch and lush rose gardens, the bungalow called to me. Flat-out appealing…as appealing as the woman living inside.

The places where I grew up in Oakland had been nothing like this. They'd been shabby apartments or falling-down tract houses with no yards or flowers or brightness at all. Army quarters had been even uglier—old barracks stateside or flimsy tents in the sandbox.

Yeah. If this place were my home, I'd do everything in my power to protect and take care of it—and the family living there. *And I'd be thankful every day for the privilege.*

Rose had called last night, said her name and apologized for the late hour. Funny on both counts—she was already in my phone's contact list, and I'd been up because I couldn't get her out of my mind. She said I was welcome to park in her driveway when I was working since she lived right behind the Chocolate Lab.

She assured me, *Rafe, it'll be safer for Princess. You can pop over during the day to check on her, take her for walks, feed her—things like that. I won't take* no *for an answer.*

Rose had a knack for making an offer sound like an order, but I'd yielded to her this time around.

We'd arrived at zero five forty, earlier than scheduled so I could scope things out. I didn't like to be caught by surprise. Rose wanted to meet Princess, and then we'd walk to work together.

I scrubbed my hand down my face and leaned my head against the driver's door. My eyelids drifted shut—not sleeping, just…resting while we waited.

After I'd left the café yesterday, I hadn't been able to let it rest. I'd had questions.

Why did Rose's eyes, as beautiful as they were, look so tired, with smudgy circles underneath? Was she married after all? She had a son— although, apparently, not the boy who tied the old dog to the statue. *Where was her husband—I hadn't clocked a ring—or son or other family, and why weren't they helping her with all those Post-it things?*

I'd also wanted to kick myself in the ass. *Why did I care? I'd be moving on soon enough.*

On my way back to Pete's house, I'd picked up groceries for dinner. He wouldn't let me pay rent while we stayed with him, so I helped with food, home repairs, fixing meals, those sorts of things. Since Pete was the one who'd called me to help out his old family friends, he'd be sure to have the answers to my Rose questions. And he wouldn't give me crap about my curiosity.

I could always count on Pete. He'd taken a chance on me a few years back when I'd retired from the army. At thirty-eight, I'd been the oldest student in his roaster training program. Afterward, he'd put me in touch with his network of roaster buddies for short-time gigs.

So yeah, whenever Pete called me for a favor, I came running.

A sharp *rap-rap* sounded on the passenger side window at the same time that Princess gave a short *woof.* Caught off guard, I jumped a mile. I'd been chewing on the info I got from him last night and must have spaced out.

Rose peered in and started giggling. She gave a little wave, stepped back and held up a large brown paper bag. Today she had all that wild streaked-blond hair bunched up in a knot on the back of her head. Her smile stretched all the way to her gorgeous green eyes. Tight jeans wrapped her long legs down to her pink sneakers, and her pink T-shirt proclaimed her a *Hot Dog Mom* in fancy script.

Oh, fuck me. Am I going to start dreaming in pink tonight?

I told Princess to chill for a minute. She was eager to get out and investigate—and by investigate, I meant *sniff*—the stranger. I jumped down from the driver's side and swung around the front to come up close to Rose.

"Looked like you were asleep at the wheel there," she pointed out. "Now I'm sorry I kept you up late with my call."

I didn't let her know I'd stayed up even later thinking about her and what Pete had shared.

"Here are your shirts, nice and clean and blood-free." Rose thrust the bag at me.

I stood frozen for a second before grabbing it. And another second before I pushed out "thanks" from my too-tight throat.

Why was I so surprised? Rose was a woman of her word, and she'd done something nice for me. When you're on your own, you get used to taking care of yourself, taking care of *everything* yourself.

So this one time, I should enjoy it. *Just don't get used to it.*

"Oh, and I stashed one of our private-label chocolate bars in there too," she went on. "A new local shop makes them for us. I went pretty vanilla with our rich milk chocolate version since I don't know what you like. Hope you're not allergic or anything."

I opened the bag and looked in. I saw a big-ass chocolate bar sitting on top of my folded—and ironed?—tee and flannel button-down.

What was the woman trying to do here—give me a heart attack? I rubbed the center of my chest where it'd started to ache. *Calm down, man.* Obviously, it wasn't a big deal to her, but it was a big *fucking* deal to me.

This was my first gift since…well, since I was little, real little. *So, a big fucking deal.*

"Yeah, I'm okay with chocolate. Thanks," I mumbled, turning to tuck the bag under a tarp in the pickup bed so that rain and the baby girl couldn't get to it.

Rose smiled at me for a few seconds before she clapped her hands. "Before we get our days started, can you introduce me to your pup?"

"She's pretty wary of new people so don't be disappointed…." I trailed off when Rose looked over my shoulder and started laughing again. I turned to find Princess ramming her muzzle against the passenger window and wagging her tail like crazy.

"Oh, what a darling girl you are!" Rose crooned, backing up a few steps and sinking gracefully to her knees. "Rafe, would you please let Princess out? I'll stay still while we get acquainted. Is it okay if I give her a treat—a piece of dental dog food?"

She plucked a big kibble from her jeans pocket and showed it to me. The woman walked around with dog treats on her person.

Why did this not surprise me?

I nodded, and Rose fisted the treat. I opened the passenger door, and Princess leaped down, prancing over to her.

Yeah, pranced. Despite—or maybe because of—being a camp dog of definitely mixed heritage, Princess was forty pounds of pure elegance. Creamy white fur with honey-colored spots covered her from graceful long legs to delicate pricked ears. One look into her amber eyes when she'd danced into camp that day, and I'd fallen hard.

Rose held perfectly still, smiling without showing her teeth. *Smart woman.* She murmured, "What a sweetie, what a pretty pup, what a good baby girl."

Princess barked one sharp demand. Rose turned her hand and opened it flat. After hoovering up the treat, Princess dropped and rolled over on her back.

"Belly rubs are the best, aren't they, sweetheart?"

Ahhh...she had a soft touch when she wanted.

"Guess I was worried for nothing," I muttered.

"Whaaat?" Rose protested. "You were worried? I'm an old dog wrangler from way back."

I cocked an eyebrow. "You mean whisperer, right? Dog whisperer, like that guy on TV?"

"Well, both, if you get right down to it. I need to be for a dog the size of our current chocolate Lab. Pirate weighs in at 103 pounds, even more soaking wet. And believe me, he's wet most of the time, what with our Portland rain or swimming in his pool or diving in the river down at the park. He's also never met a mud puddle he doesn't like."

"Wait, wait...he has his own pool?"

"Well, sure, one of those round kiddie ones. Does Princess like to swim?"

"Yep. Sometimes I take her camping between gigs, and she likes to dip her toes in a lake or stream."

Rose continued to stroke Princess's belly. The easy girl's eyes were closed in bliss.

"Maybe we can introduce these two a bit later," she suggested.

On cue, a deep "woof" sounded from behind the backyard gate, and sniffing started at the base of the fence. Princess rolled to her front and sat up on her haunches, looking first at Rose, then at me.

"Or maybe a bit sooner than later," whispered Rose. "Oops, sorry, I was going to leave Pirate in the house for the morning. How do you feel about a meet-and-greet right now?"

"Depends. How does your *behemoth* get along with other dogs?" I grumbled before I could curb myself. I didn't want Princess steamrolled by some dog three times her size.

Rose stood slowly and narrowed her eyes at me. "Behemoth? Really? You're judging him for his size without knowing anything else about him? Like idiots who claim all pit bulls are aggressive just because some were bred for fighting?"

Oh, fuck. I should've trusted Rose to know her own dog. The contempt in her voice struck me square in the chest.

Luckily, Princess ignored us both. She trotted to the fence and stuck her muzzle at ground level where there was a gap. Once her nose met Pirate's, she did the play bow thing. Next, she yipped twice and sat down facing the gate.

I couldn't have gotten the message more clearly if she'd suddenly spouted English.

Rose looked at me and smirked. "I guess Her Royal Highness has spoken."

Yep, I was clearly outmatched. When both Princess *and* Rose ganged up against me, they were impossible to resist.

Rose pulled me to the fence gate and puckered her lips to make a kissing sound. Directed at me or Pirate—I wasn't sure.

"Hey, Pi-Pi, meet Rafe." The behemoth looked up at me and snorted, not impressed. I'd have to earn his trust.

I picked up Princess and motioned with my head to open the gate. Rose caught the cue and unlatched the gate to slowly push in first, backing Pirate up as she went. She got him to sit down—a treat bribe may have been involved—and I followed with my girl in my arms. The minute we were all in, Rose shut the gate behind us.

I sat Princess on her feet and stepped back. Rose said, "Okay, Pirate," and he scrambled to his feet. The two circled each other and then took turns sniffing each other's butts. I slid a glance toward Rose but she didn't seem put off by typical dog shit.

And just like that, they were off.

Pirate burst out running across the yard with Princess on his heels. They reversed direction at the back, and Pirate chased Princess around the perimeter. After a few minutes of this, they collapsed back at our feet. Panting, puffing, grinning. Yes, grinning at each other.

Rose turned to me, and *she* grinned. "If you're okay with it, let's leave them here together for an hour or so while we get started at the café. The yard's fully fenced, and I just filled Pi's water dish."

I hesitated for a second, and she picked up on it.

"Oh, right, you might be smack-dab in the middle of a roast. If you trust me, I could come back and check on them?"

I jerked my chin up in a *yes*.

We left Princess and Pirate stretched out on the grass, tongues lolling from their mouths. We were, clearly, surplus to requirements.

Don't let the gate hit your asses on the way out.

Chapter 7

Rose

When we got to the Chocolate Lab—only ten minutes later than normal, even after all the dog drama—I let us in the side door to the roastery and hustled to turn off the alarm while Rafe moved purposefully around the space. He flipped on the lights, pulled out the coffee blend binder and switched on the roaster.

He was getting right down to it—not needing my help or time, thankfully.

Still, I had to double-check. "You okay with starting on your own?"

He looked at me and rumbled one word. "Rose."

"Well, you know where to find me if you need anything," I said, thumbing over my right shoulder toward the front of the café—like he couldn't find his way. Rafe gave me a chin lift, and I got out of there before I embarrassed myself further. *No hovering needed.*

I headed down the hall, switching on lights in the bathrooms and the meeting room as I went. Mateo had done his usual sterling job, with the help of the kids on the evening crew, of "closing" the café last night. Tables and chairs, wiped down and straightened—check. Coffee carafes washed and draining on the back counter—

check, check. And finally, the espresso machine, cleaned and ready for action—check, check and triple check.

The first shift, three kids on a busy Friday morning, was due to arrive soon. We unlocked the doors promptly at seven, and usually folks were there waiting to get their morning beverage of choice and bakery treat. I snagged my Chocolate Lab apron from its hook in the kitchen and got the day started.

I quietly closed my backyard gate, still smiling. As promised, I'd gone down to check on Pirate and Princess after the morning rush. I'd found them sleeping on their sides, facing each other, close as close could be, totally drenched.

Evidently, the kiddie pool had been a hit. It was a warm late summer day, and they'd dry soon enough. I'd refilled the water dish and scooped a poop or two. Now I was walking back to the Chocolate Lab to make my report on the doggy duo.

Trust me, Rafe. You didn't need to worry about my pirate carrying off your princess.

When I stepped through the side door, the smells, sounds… and sights of roasting coffee ambushed me. With the machine going at full speed—probably on the fourth or fifth roast by now—the space had heated up. The roasting beans were releasing hot steam, fragrant with a sweet, nutty aroma. Sharp pops, like popping corn, also filled the roastery.

Rafe stood in the midst of it all, tatted skin glistening from the humidity and damp T-shirt sticking tight to his chest and biceps. Even his close-cut hair was slick.

He was listening to the "crack"—that popping sound that signaled the stage of the roast.

I gave myself a moment to steep in all that was this man. I wasn't going to go there, since acting on this insta-pull was wrong on so many levels, yet I *could* soak up the moment.

After a few minutes, as the sounds changed, I edged around the room so I'd be in Rafe's sight line. He didn't startle when I gave my little wave, so he'd probably already sensed I was there. He nodded and started to wind the roasting process down.

Once it was quiet-ish, I launched into my updates, talking my usual mile a minute.

"So it looks like all is well in Doglandia. They ran, they swam, they dug—don't worry, only a bit in my rose bed—they collapsed. Here's a pic of them sleeping it off in the sun." I handed my phone to Rafe so he could see my snap of Princess and Pirate lying by the kiddie pool.

"Hopefully, your girl will be dry by the time you're ready to go home. If not, I'll get you a towel to give her a rubdown."

I paused, and Rafe handed my phone back and stared at me.

So I moved on with my updates. "Later today, my friend Lauren is flying in from California. I'm going to take off about two or so to pick her up at the airport. Mateo is coming in then for the rest of the day. In the meantime, if you need anything, just let me know. I can always free up one of the kids to fill coffee bags for the café or online orders. Oh, and please help yourself to any drinks, pastries or lunch—on the house, of course!"

Another pause, and this time, a barely visible chin lift from Rafe.

So I proceeded to my final update. And took a breath. "Pete may have shared with you that my mom passed away a few weeks ago." No pause since I didn't want to hear any condolences, and to his credit, Rafe didn't open his mouth to offer any.

I plowed on. "We're closing early tomorrow, around one, to get ready for Mom's party later that afternoon. It's just a party, not a memorial service or anything…formal or serious like that. We're getting people together to enjoy her favorite things—lots of food, wine, coffee, drinks, dog stories, laughter, and singing, definitely singing."

I did pause there, thinking of Mom and her love of all things Elvis.

"Anyway. Rafe, I told you all that to tell you this. If you're planning on roasting tomorrow, could you possibly wrap it up by noonish? We need to set things up, bring in stuff, make food, decorate. You know, get ready for the party. We've got about seventy-five folks coming."

I stopped to catch my breath and waited for Rafe to comment. It'd be fine if he only said "okay," since he was a man of few words.

"Okay," he said, as expected.

Then he added, "I could be your dogsbody."

Chapter 8

Rose

I raised my eyebrows and queried, "Did you just call yourself a 'dogs-body'?"

The corners of his lips quirked up, and he informed me, "Yeah."

"Okaaay…you do know that 'dogsbody' means you would be kinda like…my servant, taking my orders, doing all the drudgework for the party? I was counting on my son for all that when he gets home from school tomorrow morning."

He surprised me with the longest string of sentences I'd heard from him yet.

"I'm fine with you bossing me around. I don't want to intrude on this family thing, but maybe you could use some extra help with all those Post-it Notes I'm sure you have?" He smirked and went on. "I could carry the heavy stuff in, move tables around, run any last-minute errands. Then I could stick around to replenish food, make coffee drinks, clean up, do whatever you need. That way, you and your son can focus on the party and all your friends. I'll be behind the scenes."

I stuttered, "Oh, th-th-that's nice of you, bu-bu-but…."

"Please, Rose. Let me help."

How could I turn down that kind offer? I could hear Mom in the back of my mind:

Needing help is not a weakness, sweetie. Giving people a chance to help you is a sure sign of strength. Just say 'thank you.'

So I did. "Thank you, Rafe. You are now my official dogsbody."

"Whatcha doing, girl?" I called to Lauren, who was standing on our side deck with Jean-Luc's Bernese mountain dog.

"I'm gettin' me some lovin' from this handsome boy," she called back.

As often happens with Berners, Cab was a leaner—in his case, one-hundred-thirty-or-so pounds worth. The grand-sized dog was leaning into the petite-sized Lauren, whose normally sleek, curled-under do was all mussed up. Somehow, she stayed on her high heels by curling over him and looping her right arm around his neck.

They gazed adoringly into each other's eyes, having a moment.

I'd left Lauren outside when I went into the café to talk with Jean-Luc about the wines for Mom's party. He'd brought down a few sample bottles of reds and whites from Dogwood Wine Merchants for my choice.

Cab, short for "Cabernet," had accompanied him, off leash and on his best behavior. It was the neighborhood mystery how Cab could wend his way around Jean-Luc's crowded shop—shelves of wine lining the walls and crates of wines stacked around the floor—without knocking over the valuable inventory.

So by the time Jean-Luc and I had completed our negotiations (meaning he wanted to give me the wine for free and I wanted to pay him for it, with the final agreement that I would pay at cost, although I was sure he was fibbing about the cost), Cab and Lauren were renewing their acquaintance.

Jean-Luc followed me out the door and stopped when he saw Lauren. He looked around for a quick moment, as if expecting to see Oliver, her soon-to-be ex. They'd met once before when Oliver picked up Lauren from our girls' wine-tasting outing last February—and had taken an instant dislike to each other.

Oliver had been his usual snooty "my family owns a vineyard" self, and Jean-Luc had been his usual superior "how can Californians possibly think they make better wine than the French?" self.

I hadn't had a chance yet…or a reason…to let him know Lauren and Oliver were divorcing.

With no Oliver in sight, Jean-Luc smiled tightly, white teeth against his close-cut dark beard, and said, "Bonjour, cherie. I see Cab has attached himself to you. Push him away if he's too heavy."

Lauren straightened up and gave one final ear rub to Cab. "Oh. Hi Jean-Luc. It's good to see…your pup again."

"Pup? Puppy?" He raised one eyebrow, like he was trying to get Lauren's casual English term right. Or *pretending* not to get it, since he spoke perfect English. "Yes, but I rescued him when he was already full-grown. Some imbécile dumped him when he got too big…and too scared of loud noises."

"Their loss, your gain," Lauren agreed. "What a total love bug! I don't have Baby with me right now, so I'm getting in all the pup cuddles I can. I'll tell her Cab says *bonjour*."

Rafe stepped out the door behind Jean-Luc. "We're going down to the shop so I can help Jean-Luc bring back those wines you decided on. After that, I'll pick up Princess and head back to Pete's. Looked in on them a couple of times while you were gone—hope that's okay?"

I nodded, pleased that Rafe was pitching right in. *I hadn't expected that from somebody just passing through.*

He finished with "thanks again for letting my girl hang out with your boy."

When Lauren and I had come home from the airport earlier, Rafe's pickup had still been parked in my driveway. We'd peeked over the fence at Pirate and his new friend before heading into the house. Lauren, being my snoopy bestie, had started quizzing me.

So while we'd settled her in my old bedroom and changed into clothes more girls'-night-out friendly, I'd filled her in about Rafe. Because it was Lauren, she'd gotten the unedited, uncut, unabridged version—as fast as I could talk.

And once she'd heard me out, she'd cut right to the chase. "Girlfriend, I can't wait to meet your hot roaster, pup rescuer and man of few words."

Not mine, I'd protested, to no avail.

So Lauren was prepared when I introduced them outside the café. Of course, I couldn't trust the little traitor. She turned her back to the guys and gave me "big eyes"—the ones where you raise your brows high, widen your eyes as far as they can go, and curl your lips together in an oh-so-wide smile.

She wiped the expression from her face before turning back around. We all said our goodbyes so the guys could get on with the wine-porting and we could get on down to Fay's.

I adored two things about Fay's.

First, their cherry-garnished rye Manhattans hit me just right—sweet *and* spicy with a bitter undercurrent.

Second, for five bucks, I got ten toothpicks to blow through a straw at their ceiling—pretending I was stabbing the dog butts in my past.

Jen and Mica had already claimed a tall table in the middle of the bar. Shot glasses crammed with frilly toothpicks in a rainbow of colors were set at our places.

Thanks to our good aim, we'd had very few, if any, stab-by-toothpick-related emergencies in the past. We took out our male-dominated frustrations on Fay's ceiling with bragging rights as the only reward.

Charities were the real winners, chosen to receive all the proceeds from the frilly toothpick sales. This month, the local chapter of Guide Dogs for the Blind had secured that coveted spot. The girls and I were happy to do our bit since the pups-in-training often stopped to sit outside the Chocolate Lab and practice being "on duty" while people and their pets walked by.

We waved at Kurt behind the bar as we made our way to the table. Kurt had taken over from his grandmother Fay, who'd opened the bar in the 1930s.

After hugs were traded all around, I eyed our group and announced, "Drinking and chitchat first."

Our chitchat time was anything but. Sure, some of our catching up was trivial and lighthearted. Lauren hadn't visited in a while, and Jen, Mica and I had been busy with our businesses. But we also touched on the heavier stuff—family stuff—at least as much as talking in a public place allowed.

When I received no protests, although I hadn't expected any, I queried this time, "The usual?"

After nods, I waved to Kurt, who was apparently watching for "the signal." I held up four fingers, followed by two fingers. In turn, he gave a thumbs-up—four rye Manhattans with two cherries each were on their way.

Even though Kurt knew to make them on the rocks, it was a good thing we all lived within walking distance.

We held off on chitchat until Vera—who was almost as old as the place itself—bustled over with our drinks a few minutes later. Lauren led the toast with "to Ellie!" and the rest of us raised our glasses in response—"to Ellie" and "to Mom."

We heard echoes of "to Ellie" around Fay's—from Kurt, Vera and many people there. If you were from the neighborhood, you likely had known Mom and would be coming to the party tomorrow.

Mica started off with questions about Finn, no surprise there. They'd all known my son since he was born, and Mica, being a few years younger than the rest of us, had even babysat him early on. And they knew he'd adored his grandma, his one and only.

"How's he doing?" Mica asked. "Has he settled in at school? Is he answering your texts with more than three words?"

This was a standing joke among my girls. He'd answer my long texts—to make up for the lost art of emails—with two, three, or if I were lucky, four words.

"Yeah, he's kinda okay, I guess." I shook my head. "He's still worried about me. He texted again about taking a gap year—just staying home when he comes up for Mom's party."

Gasps broke out around the table.

Jen said it first. "He'd lose his scholarships—right?"

"Yep, along with support for room and board. We could maybe swing some more loans if he returned to school, but we're already maxed out with the roastery expansion." And extra for Mom's care, although I didn't need to say that. They knew.

Everyone was silent for a moment, remembering. Finn had worked hard to get scholarships and work-study grants to an out-of-state school known for its mechanical engineering program. Summers and after school, he'd put in time at the café and roastery—all for the same wage as the other kids on the crew.

As we were gearing up for expansion—bam!—the pandemic had hit. We'd closed the café and roasted coffee for online sales only. Then Dad had his fatal heart attack, and Mom had been diagnosed with colon cancer. By the time we'd reopened, she was in her final months, and Finn…Finn was fighting me about going to college at all.

You'll be alone, Mom. You'll be living in our big house all by your-self. You'll be running the Chocolate Lab on your own. I don't like it.

Turned out, my son was just as stubborn as me. Luckily, his grandma had been more stubborn than the two of us combined. Even in her weakened state, she'd pushed us out the door and into my packed beater for the long drive to California. And she'd made Finn promise he'd come home for her party this fall. As if there'd been any question.

Finn knew, like my girls, that we couldn't count on any money, support or even contact from his father. I'd been careful to never set up false expectations—I hadn't wanted my son to be hurt the way I'd been.

The man—dog butt number one in the stabby-toothpick sce-nario—had never acknowledged Finn's existence. The moment I'd told him I was pregnant, he'd ghosted me.

And what was worse? I hadn't learned my lesson. I'd let Brent get too close to me...too close to my young son, and then he'd bailed at the last moment. He'd earned the dog butt number two spot for the stabby toothpick.

So, nope. I didn't expect anything from guys, didn't trust they'd stick to their word. Or just plain stick.

That's why, despite Mom's urging, I'd put away my dream of finding a true—and true-to-me—relationship.

I clapped my hands to break the pensive mood. "Finn will get here tomorrow, and you can see for yourselves how he's doing. He's found a rideshare and will arrive in time to help set up for the party."

"Guess who else is helping get ready for the party?" Lauren put to the group.

"Besides us and half of Dogwood?" Jen asked, pointing out the obvious.

Annnd before I could stop her, Lauren blurted out, "Rose's new red-hot roaster!"

"Yes!" shrieked Mica, never one to hide her enthusiasm.

"Wait, wait," said Jen. "Who is this guy, and why haven't I met him?"

"Okay, ladies, everybody take it easy!" I glanced around us while making calming motions with my hands. "Rafe arrived yesterday, and he's going to be my temporary coffee roaster while Mike's out with his broken leg."

"Well, he seems super nice," Mica declared. "I met him when he carried Goldie down to the clinic, and he's already called to schedule a time for his dog to get her annual vaccinations."

"I met him just before we came here," added Lauren, fanning her face. "He couldn't take his eyes off our girl."

I snorted. "He was shocked to see me in something other than my usual getup."

I'd traded in my pink T-shirt and sneakers for a pink scooped-neck sweater and pink patent-leather flats.

Jen turned to me and said one word, "Spill."

So I shared my observations regarding all things Rafe. He *seemed* to be a nice guy, albeit a bit grumbly and short on words. He *appeared* to be competent and hard-working, based on one day's evidence. And my beloved Pete had recommended him, after all.

He was *definitely* a proud—and protective—papa to sweet girl Princess, who had Pirate wrapped around her dainty paw. I paused for the *ahhhs* from around the table.

Last but not least, he was *more than* easy on the eyes, what with his muscly and tattooed goodness—an understatement according to pointed looks from Lauren and Mica.

I stopped and said, "Down, girls. Down. Don't get too excited."

See, I knew my girls. They were already getting…ideas.

They knew my "love" life since dog butts one and two had consisted of blind dates forced on me by well-meaning people, a couple of hookups I'd rather forget, and secret shower sessions with my favorite toy.

I'd made Finn and the Chocolate Lab my priorities...and I was *so* not in a hurry to place my trust in a man again.

Sorry I can't keep my promise, Mom.

"Ladies, need I remind you that Rafe is only our *temporary* coffee roaster, until Mike can return in a few months? In fact, Pete told me Rafe likes the rootless life. He's been traveling from gig to gig ever since he finished training a few years back. He's probably got his next jobs already lined up."

"And the problem with that is...?" asked Lauren.

"Yeah, we're talking about a no-strings-attached fling here," Jen added.

"You can't tell us Mister Vibrato is doing it for you!" Mica prodded. *Again, I wished she'd keep her voice down.*

"Ladies, enough!" I whisper-shouted. "I am *not* looking for somebody here today and gone tomorrow. I am *not* looking for a short-term fling-thing. I am *not* looking for a real-life Mister Vee." *I am* not *looking for love.* "Been there, done that, got the T-shirt... actually, the kid."

That was enough to get my girls to fall silent, at least for now. Then, as one, we picked up our Manhattans and hoisted them in another toast to Mom and her love for us—and to Finn—and to all things doggo.

After that, we finished blowing our frilly-stabby toothpicks into the ceiling, ordered another round and asked Vera for the menus. We had some serious planning to do for Mom's party to-morrow, including the choice of which Elvis songs we wanted to claim for the karaoke part of the fun. "Hound Dog" and "Return to Sender" topped the list.

Chapter 9

Rafe

What got me was the level of hubbub from all the people jammed in the Chocolate Lab.

From the moment the party started mid-afternoon, people began pouring in the door. Now the level of noise—chatter, laughter, even shouting—was off the charts.

Yeah, there were breaks when somebody or several somebodies stepped up to the mic to sing—usually an Elvis tune since, apparently, Rose's mom had been a big fan. There was a quiet moment when Finn read one of his grandma's favorite poems, about dogs, of course. There was another pause when Mateo called for help in pushing tables and chairs back for dancing, and at least half the men groaned. I suspected dancing—and singing—were spectator sports for most guys like me.

Otherwise, hubbub.

From my vantage point behind the counter, back to the wall, safely out of the way, I could keep an eye on everything. Spy what needed to be done. Replenish food platters the kids brought up. Make foo-foo coffee drinks on demand.

Watch Rose without seeming like a stalker.

Now, I'd only met Rose two-and-a-half days ago. But by the time of her mom's party, I knew a few things to be true.

She was a knockout who couldn't be any less conscious of her looks. Her honey-colored hair was tied up in a high ponytail with strands falling all around her face. Her creamy cheeks were flushed, bare of any makeup as far as I could tell. Her T-shirt and jean skirt hugged her curvy body, yet were covered by a Chocolate Lab apron. Her long, toned legs ended in scuffed pink sneakers.

She was hands-on, not only in overseeing the party, but like... literally. Hugging shoulders, patting backs, stroking cheeks, ruffling hair. Even handing out kisses here and there to older people like Pete or kids like Noah.

She was kind and generous, not only to a stranger like me but to everyone and everyone's dog. You could see that people were here not just to pay tribute to her mom, but also to show affection and support for her and her son Finn.

Another thing I knew to be true. Rose could not sing worth shit.

Earlier, when she'd linked arms with her girls in front of the crowd and karaoked the hell out of the old Elvis hit "Hound Dog," it hadn't been noticeable.

Now, she was crooning "Love Me Tender," which she dedicated to her big boy Pirate, and it was evident.

But to give her credit, Rose owned it. She hammed it up, clutching her hands over her heart, gazing skyward—or at least to the ceiling—and putting her all into it. No half measures for this woman.

As she was finishing up, Mateo came out from the kitchen to stand next to me. We exchanged smiles. Because, well, Rose and singing.

We'd discovered earlier, when we were puzzling over Rose's Post-its for the party, that we had something in common. He saw one of my tattoos and quietly shared that he'd gotten an early discharge from the army to take care of his mom and little sister.

Now, Mateo had my six and said one word, "Incoming."

As a stranger, the only stranger amid all the friends and neighbors here tonight, I stood out like a sore thumb. Even though I stayed safely out of the way behind the counter, people kept coming up. Maybe with the excuse of asking me to make a latte or mocha. Maybe with no excuse at all, only to check out the newbie and ask what he was doing at Rose's café.

Generally, I could give short, practiced, just-the-facts answers. Like "Yeah, I'm the temp coffee roaster while Mike is out." Or "No, I don't live here. I'm staying with a friend." Or—and this came up more often than I'd expected—"Yeah, I have a dog. She's a mix, and her name is Princess."

Yet with Rose's girls, I sensed they wanted more than my short on-the-border-of-abrupt responses. More about my background. More about my reasons for taking temporary gigs. More about my personal life.

Lauren couched her questions in humor, Jennifer was subtle, and Mica was direct. Mica even gave me the "I'm watching you" sign by pointing V-sign fingers first at her own eyes and then at mine.

I got it. They were being protective of their friend who was going through a vulnerable time. They wanted to scope out the new person around her and make sure she wasn't being taken advantage of. They wanted to make sure she was safe.

I just wasn't ready to share my life's story quite yet. If at all, since I was only going to be around for a few short months.

Hence, the warning from Mateo, who saw Jennifer approaching...again.

This time, though, it was different. She nodded at me, looked over and said, "Hey, Mateo, can you spread the word about Rose's apartment? It's all cleaned out and ready to rent, but I know she's gonna drag her feet about finding somebody. She's got so much on her plate."

"Sure thing. If Rose's okay with it, maybe I can check at Reed or Lewis and Clark. See if they have any students looking for housing next term."

"Oh, good idea! Let's ask her in a week…after things settle down." Jennifer turned, as if getting ready to ask me yet another question. Luckily, Finn walked up with his own.

"Hey, you guys interested in a pickup match tomorrow morning over in the park? Thought I'd try to squeeze one in before I need to catch my ride back to school in the afternoon. You, too, of course, Aunt Jen," he added and grinned big-time—like he knew she'd say no.

Finn and I'd had the chance to shoot the shit while setting up big tubs of ice for soft drinks and beer earlier today. Good kid, outgoing, obviously sad about his grandma's death, also obviously, watching out for his mom. Full of questions, hidden behind smiles, for me.

Since he had a right, being Rose's son—and only family left?—I revealed a bit more, mainly about my time overseas. One thing had led to another, and I'd shared how we'd used to kick a soccer ball around and play shirts and skins with the village kids.

Jennifer rolled her eyes and said, "No, thanks, young man. And don't be asking my girls to join you—you guys are older and too rough for my taste."

Finn had the grace to laugh and then looked at Mateo and me. "You in? Mom said some of the kids are okay staffing the café alone for a few hours. I'm thinking we'd get over to the park about ten. Rafe, you could drop your pickup and Princess off at our place, and we could walk down together."

Mateo said, "Sounds good to me." And just like that, three pairs of eyes turned to me.

What could I say without sounding like a total antisocial asshole? Nothing. So instead, I replied, "You bet, thanks for asking me. I'll get to your house a bit before ten, Finn. To get Princess settled and all."

Adam, the keyboardist and karaoke guy, saved me from further talk by blowing into his mic. "Hey, folks, Rose and Finn want me to thank you all for coming out to Ellie's party. Now, grab a partner and dance while I sing one of Ellie's favorite Elvis songs named—you guessed it—'Party'!"

I slipped around the counter, through the crowd and out the side door to go check on the dogs. Only so much singing and dancing and hubbub a man can take.

As I walked down the sidewalk, the music swelled up. I smiled to myself. Rose was one lucky woman. Even with her mom gone, she was surrounded by people who loved her, and she was safe.

What led me to enlist in the first place—the guarantee of decent work, food on the regular, clean clothes and a safe place to sleep (war zones, safe?...but there are different definitions of safe)—had pushed me out in the end.

I'd had nobody of my own, no woman or kids or family or friends. Nobody to see me off, and nobody to welcome me back from my deployments. Nobody to be thankful I came back in one piece. Alive.

Now out of that life for going on three years, I was still on my own, still alone. Yeah, I had Pete in my corner. Nope, I had no worries about getting my share of hookups. Yep, I could count on the loyalty of my best girl.

But I was a loner at this stage. Maybe it was too late—I was too old, too guarded. Maybe I wasn't worth it, given my history growing up and the people I'd let down.

Why would anybody trust me to keep them safe?

On that happy thought, I walked down Rose's driveway to the backyard gate. I put my hand on the latch...and stopped.

A woman's voice sounded, low yet honeyed in its warmth, clear yet edging into huskiness as though tears were taking over.

Singing "Love Me Tender" again, yet this time...hitting *all* the notes.

She drew a ragged breath and continued. I peered over the gate. Rose sat on the lawn near the patio, Princess and Pirate cuddled up close with their heads in her lap. She was stroking down their backs as she sang, and then she broke off and started sobbing into Pirate's neck.

My throat clenched, and I didn't, couldn't call out. She didn't need me, didn't need a stranger intruding on her grief. I turned around and headed back toward the café. I'd have a quiet word with Finn to let him know where his mom was. After that, I'd duck behind the counter and start cleaning up.

Chapter 10

Rose

"You should have seen the look on your face when he took off his shirt." Lauren was doing her famous giggle-snorts and falling off her bar stool at the same time.

We were now well into the after-dinner-drinks phase of our evening—did somebody say "limoncellos all around?"—and we were perilously close to feeling no pain.

All our laughing was just what we both needed. It was only the two of us this time, out for dinner at my favorite Italian place before Lauren flew back to California—and her unraveling life—tomorrow.

We'd spent the entire afternoon together. Lauren had dragged me out of the Chocolate Lab early, with Mateo waving goodbye, and Rafe looking mystified. After my initial protests, after I'd agreed to "chill the fido out," she'd treated us to a salon-and-shopping spree. An early birthday gift, she'd said—although my birthday wasn't until next April. Also, she knew I'd never do this on my own. Because, well, money and time.

The new day spa across from Fay's had been our first stop, where Lauren's charm—and, I suspected, her pocketbook and an earlier call—had gotten us in the door. A fresh cut and style, a green tea facial and a pink-painted pedicure later, we'd strolled out and down the street to a tiny boutique that Lauren had spied.

One look, and I'd turned to go. My bestie had grabbed my arm and propelled me backward.

"Uh-uh, girlfriend. You need to wander out of your comfort zone. Trust me!"

An hour later, we had poured ourselves into our new outfits—tight, clingy skirts, silky camisoles, short flirty sweaters and strappy sandals—and had set out for the liquid portion of our day.

The neighborhood around Limoncello's was usually packed, but I'd squeezed into a spot on a side street. Over our first Manhattans, we'd agreed on one rule for the rest of the evening—only funny, happy, lighthearted talk. We'd already dissected the sad stuff in both our lives ad nauseam. Enough.

During another round of Manhattans and a bottle of red, with a "side" of pasta, Lauren had shared more stories from the dance fest that'd wrapped up Mom's party.

I'd gone missing in action by that time—it had gotten to be too much for me.

"You nailed it, Rose," she informed me with glee. "Most of the guys took one giant step back when Adam asked everybody to find a partner and dance.

"Luckily, your good boy pulled his Aunt Mica out into the cleared area, Jen and I joined them, and we got things started. Pete asked Mateo's little sister to dance—or really just swing hands together. So cute! Scott convinced his twins to come out and rock with their old man and proceeded to embarrass the hell out of them—on purpose, I'm sure—with all his crazy moves. Even Jen was laughing."

Scott was Jen's ex. They'd split a couple of years ago under sad circumstances—anytime we saw her being lighthearted was a win.

He still lived in the Dogwood neighborhood and saw his girls all the time.

"By that time, most everyone had gotten into the spirit," Lauren continued. "People were dancing like you hoped—even if they were dancing by themselves. And here's the sweetest thing. Mateo had asked his mom to dance when one of the slower songs came up where they could two-step. After a couple of minutes, Pete tapped his shoulder and cut in to dance with Liliana...and *they* slowed it down even further, basically to a waltz, I guess. So sweet."

"From what I could see when I walked back in, you knew how to waltz too," I pointed out. "You've been hiding your talents from us!"

"I was just following Jean-Luc's lead. It would've seemed rude to say 'no' when he asked me to dance. He has elegant, smooth movements, I think. Don't you agree?"

She trailed off and looked at me. I raised an eyebrow.

"Not a word about this to Jen and Mica," Lauren begged.

"Of course not." I was *so* going to pass along her opinion of the handsome Frenchman.

"Well, speaking of really being able to move, what did you think of Rafe at the soccer match?"

By this time, we'd settled our dinner bill and were seated at the bar with our house-made limoncellos—my treat this time. I let the abrupt change of topic pass because I was that type of friend. And because we'd eventually come back to it.

It was Lauren's turn to rib me about the new guy on the scene. Before she even started in, I blushed—or was it *flushed?*—the sizzle sweeping from the tips of my breasts, up my throat, over my face and under my hair to settle in a heated *pulse, pulse, pulse* inside my head.

Was I under the influence of too many Manhattans? Or was I ready for a distraction after this week?

Even though we'd put them on hold for this evening, my deepest and darkest emotions had overshadowed my week.

Grief had hit me anew after clearing out the apartment where Mom and I had spent so many weeks toward the end. Melancholy had struck next after sorting through memories from Mom and Dad's lives while moving into the main bedroom. Even loneliness replaced the joy of welcoming Finn home when I'd had to literally push him out the door to catch his ride back to college.

Being long sensitive to what made me tick and with the *bestie* of intentions, Lauren launched her diversionary tactics. "So when did you start to notice all the *fine* that is red hot roaster Rafe? Was it when he flexed his muscly kindness to pull the soccer supply cart all those blocks to the park?"

Rather than trying to jam everything into my car, we'd loaded my garden cart—aka soccer supply cart. Its rollability had been tested with an ice chest crammed full of waters and juice, bags of oranges, a first aid kit, orange cones, towels and extra T-shirts. Rafe had won the right to haul the cart while Finn had wrangled the excited dogs. We girls had been left to carry nothing heavier than our phones.

So I smirked at Lauren and said, "Check."

"Or was it when he tugged his T-shirt over his head and revealed all those muscles upon muscles?"

See, Rafe was real-life—not some guy in a book or a movie I used to get off with Mister Vibrato. I was sure my jaw had dropped a mile with the big reveal. Well, the encore reveal, because I *had* caught a peek before.

Still, I had to stop myself from drooling over his broad chest narrowing to his compact six-pack, his bulging biceps leading to his corded forearms, his ridged muscles at the dip of his spine crowning his tight rear and muscular thighs.

So, yeah, Lauren had caught me looking. I again said, "Check."

"Or, finally, was it when he ran the ball all the way down the field—and passed it to Finn to make the winning goal, rather than shooting it himself?"

Hotness was not just the physical goods, and my girl got that too.

So, "Yes, Lauren. Yes! Check, check and double check!" I all but shouted. "Rafe is *FINE* in some and several ways."

Doggone it. Now I was speaking, not just texting, in shouty caps.

At that, we broke into giggle-snorts, hanging on to the bar so we wouldn't pitch off our stools. Obviously, our drinks—and our girls' day-slash-night out—had done the distraction-from-our-lives job well. So well that I knew I couldn't drive us home safely.

I shared this fact with Lauren, who nodded, and continued to nod and nod and nod.

Case closed.

"Here," I said, digging around in my purse for my phone. "Nature—or rather, our liquid dinner—is calling. Why don't you use my app to call for a ride while I hit the ladies'?"

She took my phone and nodded again—it was getting to be a thing. I hoped she'd still be upright when I got back.

Thankfully, when I returned a few minutes later, Lauren was sitting where I'd left her. And she had a big Cheshire cat grin on her face.

"Okay, what's going on?" I squinted my eyes at her. "What have you been up to?"

She wiggled off her stool while her grin got even bigger, if that were possible.

"I called Rafe to give us a ride home. He—and Princess, I guess—are gonna be here in a couple of minutes. Oh, and I changed his name to 'Red Hot Roaster' in your contact list."

Oh, no, no, no. I grabbed my phone from the bar and checked my "recent calls." Yep, there was a call to Rafe. I hit the phone icon, but the call went to voicemail. Guess he was already on his way here.

I was going to kill Lauren.

We hurried out of the restaurant just as Rafe's pickup pulled up to the curb. Rafe jumped out while Princess was pacing around in the back of the cab, ready to help.

I immediately babbled, "I'm so, so sorry. Lauren overstepped." Yeah, throwing my girl right under the bus. "We could've called a taxi or ride service."

He held up his hand in a stop-it-now motion and nailed me with those dark-fringed cobalt eyes. "Not a problem. Appreciate you not driving when you've been drinking. Rather drive you home than have you ride with a stranger."

What could I say to that? Nothing, except "thank you, Rafe."

"Did you leave anything in your car that we need to retrieve? I'm assuming the car's locked up and parked in a safe place?"

Lauren and I looked at each other and grinned for two reasons. First, we were wearing all our new gear, with the old stuff stashed in the trunk. Second, on a scale of zero to ten, it was minus ten that anyone would want to steal my old clunker.

"Nope and yeah," I answered back, figuring he'd get my drift.

Rafe opened the passenger side door of his pickup and paused, eyeing—not in a pervy way, but in a frowny way—our short, tight skirts.

"Okay, Rose, you first," he rumbled. "Turn your back to the door, and I'll lift you up."

I didn't argue, because I realized I had no chance of climbing up on my own without everything showing. And by everything, I meant my panties, heinie and hoo-ha. When I was situated, Rafe did the same thing for Lauren.

He went around and climbed into the driver's seat. The three of us were squished together on the bench. Luckily, manual transmissions were a thing of the past. I was pressed into rock-solid goodness, my left shoulder, arm and thigh right up against Rafe's. Evidently, Princess was in pup heaven since she snuggled her muzzle on my left shoulder and sighed.

We made it back to Dogwood and my house in under twenty minutes, Lauren chatting all the way. And me? I was silent, holding it together. Rafe parked in my driveway, told us to sit tight and came around to open the passenger door. He lifted us both down and closed the door so Princess couldn't follow. I repeated my thanks, trying to tamp down the effusiveness.

Then Lauren capped the evening.

"Rafe, thanks again for coming out to give us a ride," she said. "And just think, it's like one of those billboards. If you lived here in Rose's apartment, you'd be home by now."

I was so going to kill that girl.

Chapter 11

Rafe

What. The. Fuck.

I drove down Eighteenth toward the Chocolate Lab where two cop cars and a city ambulance crowded the curb in front of the café.

The last time my heart rate had spiked this way was two weeks ago when I'd gotten the call to pick up Rose and Lauren from the restaurant and take them home. Well, Rose's home.

Yeah, my heart had beat double time when I'd learned they were planning to text a total stranger to give them a ride. At least, until Rose's girl had decided to call me instead—on the sly, as it turned out.

Once back here, Lauren had followed up with her flip suggestion (or not so flip, hard to tell with that girl) about me living in Rose's garage-turned-apartment.

I'd frozen because...how had she read my mind? Rose had seemed surprised, probably embarrassed, by the idea—if her red face had been any sign. Rather than saying anything, we'd both looked at our feet, then the garage, and then back at the pickup where Princess was sticking her head out the window and grinning. Obviously enjoying her part in the rescue mission.

I'd jumped into the breach, throwing out commands like I was back in the army.

"Rose, let me have your house keys. I'll go in first, switch on some lights, and make sure everything's okay. Is Pirate in the backyard?" I briefly paused until she nodded. "Good. You can let him in while I'm inside. And don't call a taxi tomorrow morning to take you to your car. I'll pick you up early, around five thirty, and take you over there."

Okay, I'd been so far over the line, I couldn't even see the line, it was so far in the distance.

I'd been lucky Rose hadn't handed me my ass right then and there.

Instead, she'd looked stunned, and her girl had snorted. She'd stuck out her hand with the keys dangling. I'd grabbed them. Then we'd done everything I'd suggested.

In the last couple of weeks, our exchanges had been pretty much "just-the-facts-ma'am." That was after Rose had again apologized for the late-night call, and I'd given her a look. Princess had continued to hang out with Pirate when I was working. We'd even taken the dogs out for a walk around the neighborhood a couple of times, shooting the shit as we went.

But when she'd asked me to join her, Mateo and some of the café kids for pizza last Monday night, I'd replied thanks but declined, saying I had something to do with Pete. No use getting (too) attached.

Now it was a Wednesday morning here at the café—super early since I wanted to get a head start on a jam-packed roasting day.

Flashing lights in the dark. An ambulance with its rear doors thrown open. Two police cruisers angled into spaces in the front of the Chocolate Lab, blocking part of the main drag.

What the fuck was going on? And where the fuck was Rose?

I pulled into the side street, parked opposite the café's deck and launched myself out of the pickup. Pirate was howling in Rose's house across the street, throwing his big self against the front door. Princess started barking too, but I ignored her and ran across to the front sidewalk.

And immediately stopped. Broken glass had shattered *everywhere* along the front of the café. Some fuckers had smashed the hell out of the two plate glass windows on either side of the entry. Jagged shards jutted from the bottom sills. More glass fragments covered the floor beyond the windows.

Inside, Rose huddled in one of the chairs, wearing a T-shirt, shorts and what looked like bedroom slippers. *Goddamned slippers.* A medic knelt in front of her, his jump bag beside him on the floor. She twisted her head down, watching him clean and bandage the bloody cuts on both her knees. Thick white dressings already wrapped her hands.

An old wooden baseball bat, scarred and mottled with age, laid on the table within her reach.

I pulled a fast breath in. *Stand down for now, soldier. Stand down. She's safe. No thanks to you, but she's safe.*

I started forward, crunching over glass in my work boots, to get to her. A patrolman stepped in front of me and stuck his arm out.

"Stop right there. This is a crime scene. Who are you?"

I was getting ready to swat his arm out of the way—not thinking too clearly at this point—when Rose looked up.

She said one word—"Rafe?"—in a tentative voice and swallowed a sob.

I shoved my way past the cop and stalked through the door to Rose. She must have seen something in my face. She grabbed my hand, winced and offered, "Rafe, it's okay, no harm done. I'm okay. I got by with a few scrapes and bruises."

Shit. *She* was trying to comfort *me.*

"What happened?" I managed to growl out—limiting the swear words to zero since I didn't want to upset her any further. I walked to her side, angled close, squatted and got my right arm around her shoulders. I may have squeezed a bit.

Rose turned her face to me and drew in a shuddering breath. Her skin, always pale and creamy, was now stark white. Her green eyes filled with tears, and she looked up as if to keep them from falling.

"I was asleep when the alarm for the Chocolate Lab went off in the hall outside my bedroom. I fumbled for a moment, got my phone off my nightstand and called 911. I grabbed Dad's bat and ran over here."

She side-eyed me, still trying to keep the tears in check.

"I could hear yelling and laughing, and I came around the front. Some guys took off running down the street after I shouted. Broken glass was scattered across the sidewalk, so I was careful. I really was!"

I must have made some noise for her to feel the need to reassure me.

"I could hear sirens in the distance, so I figured it was okay. I'd forgotten my keys, so I cleared some of the glass pieces off with my bat and climbed over the sill. And that's when I slipped and fell on the glass."

I didn't know where to begin. Other than planning how to strangle the person who set Rose up with an alarm that only sounded in her house. She needed the right sort of system that rang not only in her fucking house, but also on her phone *and* at the café *and* at a security company. Plus, signs posted everywhere blaring "these premises protected by…."

Maybe it was a matter of money, not being able to afford a real commercial system. But, still, someone had jerry-rigged this excuse of a system, and I wanted to find out who.

Time for that later, maybe when I'd cooled off.

I hugged Rose closer. She looked down at me again, and the tears finally spilled out of her eyes.

"I was so stupid not to wait," she whispered.

Well, shit. That was it. She did *not* get to beat up on herself when she was already hurting. And her place was a shattered mess. I hugged her again and shushed her.

I hadn't been a platoon sergeant for nothing.

The medic, who'd overheard our exchange, finished and stood.

I raised my eyebrows at him and said, "Will any of these wounds require stitching?"

He shook his head.

"How should I take care of them, and do you have some extra supplies for me?"

He nodded, explained what to do, and left some bandages and antibiotic ointment. He also advised Rose to take some acetaminophen or ibuprofen when she got back home—not aspirin since that could cause more bleeding. Plus see her doctor for follow-up. And take it easy for a few days.

By this time, Rose was frowning, appearing ready to push back on the instructions and enforced rest. So I stood and thanked the guy. Even hurting, she realized he was just doing his job and thanked him too.

Another police officer—an older guy and luckily not the youngster who'd tried to prevent me from getting to Rose—stepped up next.

He must have already taken her statement since he smiled and said, "Looks like you're feeling a little better, Ms. Connolly, now that your husband—or is he your boyfriend?—has arrived."

I may have been reading into it more than I should, but it sounded like the word "finally" was implied.

But Rose jumped in before I could say anything. "No, no, Officer Brennan, this is Rafe Amato. He's the coffee roaster here. He was coming in early to work. He lives across town."

Brennan smiled again, noting my arm still around Rose, and moved on to share, "I wish I had better news for you, Ms. Connolly. It's unlikely that we'll catch these guys. They smash windows, maybe spray graffiti, then take off. No fingerprints. Even if there are cameras, no dice. They usually wear beanies and masks."

I butted in there. "Is this common in these neighborhoods now? Do they ever do more than break windows?"

"Nah, it's usually the thrill of vandalizing. However, in one or two recent cases, they moved further into the premises, looking for cash or valuables. So, Ms. Connolly," he said as he looked Rose square in the eye, "please, in the future, should this happen again, *wait* for the police."

I kept my mouth shut this time. Rose nodded, asked for a police report for her insurance and thanked Brennan. He left through the front door.

Right on cue, Mateo opened the side door with his key, walked in and said, "Princess is going crazy in the pickup, and I can hear Pirate barking up a storm at Rose's. What going on?"

He stopped when he saw us. "What the fuck?" He had the morning shift this week, with Rose taking the afternoons. We hadn't thought to call him in all the chaos.

Mateo rushed over at the same time that Rose and I both yelled, "Watch the glass, watch the glass!"

He put the brakes on. When he saw Rose's bandages, he let loose with a soft string of Spanish swear words—some even I couldn't make out.

"Rosita, are you okay? What happened?"

By this time, Rose was fading—and fast. I needed to get her home and give her some pain meds so she could nap.

I raised my eyebrows at Mateo, and he immediately got my message.

Rose launched into an explanation of what happened and what we should do next. I pressed my fingers against her lips and said softly, yet sternly, "Rose. Shut it."

She stopped and narrowed her eyes.

Before she could start up again, I informed her, "Mateo and I have got this covered. Right now, I'm going to carry you home so you don't slip in those stupid slippers."

I reached down, put an arm under her knees and tightened my arm around her shoulders. I'd never let go from earlier. Picking her up, I cradled her in front of me like a hurt dog, like a tired child. Or like a bride.

"Once we get you settled on your couch or bed with some pain meds, I'll deal with the dogs. Then I'll come back and work on things with Mateo."

At this point, Rose was staring at me like I'd lost my mind. Maybe I had, starting when I'd clocked her white face and bloody red knees.

"Please, please, Rose, let me help." I wasn't afraid to beg.

She nodded slowly and rested her head against my shoulder.

I nearly spoiled it all by saying, "Princess and I are gonna get our stuff from Pete's and move into your garage apartment tonight."

Chapter 12

Rose

"Jen, this is blackmail. Don't pretend otherwise!"

I glared at her—and her partner-in-crime, Mica—from my "jailhouse" on the couch. Granted, it was a pretty cushy jailhouse, with pillows plumped behind my back and Grandma's quilt tucked carefully around my bandaged legs. My e-reader sat close at hand on the coffee table, along with my phone, the remote control, a glass of water, chocolate bars from the café and a box of tissues. Princess was curled up at (or on) my feet, and Pirate lay on the floor, wedged between the couch and the table.

But still, a jailhouse. Just with benefits.

Rafe was no help. In fact, he was part of the problem. He leaned against the doorframe to the dining room, arms crossed with flexed biceps stretching his T-shirt's sleeves. He watched me impassively while Jen worked her blackmail magic.

"Rose," Jen said patiently, with a sprinkle of mom-splaining, "you know you can't wait any longer to call Finn and let him know what happened."

I nodded, grudgingly. I'd slept for hours, and it was late afternoon now. While I'd tinkered with the idea of *not* telling my son, a little voice that sounded suspiciously like Mom's whispered *that's not fair, sweetie, that's not right.*

"And you know," Mica continued, "he is truly going to lose his shit and want to come home immediately unless—"

Before I could get a word in, Jen finished up the tag team act, "—Unless we have a plan, and that plan involves Rafe moving in to your apartment until Finn comes home for the holidays."

See, that was where Rafe was part of the problem. Because after *announcing* that he was moving into my garage apartment early this morning, he'd *already* carried out that move by early this afternoon.

Even before I dropped off to sleep, I'd regretted falling apart on Rafe. *What a scaredy-cat. Get it together! You've dealt with worse than this.*

But by the time I'd woken up, he'd returned with two duffel bags stuffed full of the necessities—whatever those were—for him and his pup. He'd claimed he'd only stay a few days until I recovered, adding he didn't want me on my own if the bad guys came back. I may have rolled my eyes at that, because…I needed to get used to being on my own.

I agreed that his staying would free up Jen, Mica and Mateo to return to their families this evening. It would also prevent Lauren from hopping on the next plane back here in the midst of her divorce and custody difficulties.

Now my girls insisted that "just a few days" with Rafe on board—and all up in my space—should turn into more than two months. They demanded that he stay until mid-December when Finn came home for winter break, Mike returned to the roaster job, and Rafe left for his next gig.

Jen and Mica swore—on the heads of their firstborn dogs—that they'd hunt down a permanent tenant for the apartment by the time Finn went back to school in late January.

So, yeah, I got it. My friends and large-and-in-charge Rafe didn't want me to be on my own after what happened with the break-in. And if my safety were in question, this would be the tipping point for Finn. He knew I was feeling lonely after the loss of Mom, and he'd use this as an excuse to quit school and move home.

I was *not* letting that happen. That was a promise to Mom I could keep.

I needed to suck it up and accept help. I needed to accept that Rafe was part of the solution, not part of the problem. I'd even accept the bossiness from Rafe, which, I had to admit, came with a generous dose of sweetness.

He was the one who'd set me up with my jailhouse benefits and made sure I took some painkillers. He'd checked all my bandages twice since I'd woken up, gently blotting off the blood, and replaced them on my hands. He'd fed and watered the dogs, along with taking them out back to do their business.

And, apparently, Rafe staying at my place was just part of the plan.

The Plan-with-a-Capital-P had emerged right after I'd left the café this morning. While Rafe was getting me situated, Mateo had called in the troops—our crew, my girls, other friends and neighbors—and started things rolling.

Thankfully, everyone had agreed *not* to text, call or email Finn before I had a chance to talk to him.

I hadn't been in charge, like usual, since I was sitting on my heinie. But surprise, surprise—things had gotten done without me, as I learned later.

While I was lounging at home, the kids had swept up every speck of broken glass and mopped the floors and sidewalks. Rafe and Mateo had nailed up big sheets of plywood to cover the gaping holes. Jean-Luc had picked up lunch for everyone, and Liam had called in favors with his suppliers to rush the replacement windows order.

Don't get me wrong—I appreciated all the help. I just wasn't quite sure how I was going to pay for the things the insurance wouldn't cover. But I'd stress over that tomorrow when my hands, knees and head weren't throbbing so much.

After Mateo's mom had heard what happened, she brought a hot dinner to my house—her famous and fabulous enchiladas. I could look at it as another form of blackmail...or maybe a bribe, since Jen and Mica insisted I wait to eat until *after* I'd made the difficult call to Finn.

Once I got over myself about not being in charge, I hugged and thanked my girls, as well as Liliana. She promised to pass on my thanks—and a hug—to Mateo. I even briefly considered adding a hug for Rafe. My better angels prevailed.

Everybody left—my friends to their homes and Rafe to the kitchen—to give me some privacy to call my son.

"Finn," I said, when he answered his phone, "first off, everything's fine."

What everybody wants to hear as the opening to a call. As in, never.

I went on to share the unemotional facts about the break-in and quickly followed with the Plan. As any mother would, I downplayed the scary bits—like the bad guys still being there when I ran up with the bat, like scoring my cuts and bruises when I fell on the broken glass, like losing it on Rafe's shoulder.

When I got to the part about Rafe moving into the apartment *just for now until you come home for Christmas,* my son said one word, "Stop."

He went on, "Mom. I'm so glad you're okay. Now, hand the phone to Rafe. Please."

I wanted to resist, but the "please" got me. After calling Rafe to come take the phone, I parked myself on a dining chair. I could only hear one side of the conversation. But from Rafe's customary short answers, it appeared Finn was verifying my side of the story—and asking what I'd left out. After a couple of minutes of this back-and-forth, he grunted his agreement with *yeah, I'll make sure your mom sees her own doc this week.* They exchanged numbers, and Rafe handed my phone back to me.

Finn informed me that he loved me (I already knew this). That he was going to call all three of his honorary aunts tomorrow—they'd have more to tell. And that he was driving home for Thanksgiving weekend, no argument, since this was a change from staying on campus to study. After extracting a promise from me that I'd call immediately if-slash-when the *next* emergency reared its ugly head, he ended the call.

Huh. Evidently, I had two over-protective males watching over me now—one my still-a-teenager son and one my brand-new employee.

As my son used to say as a toddler, *you're not the boss of me.*

Rafe walked past me to the living room, carrying two plates loaded with enchiladas, along with forks and a roll of paper towels tucked under one arm. He frowned when I tried to clear a space on the coffee table with my bandaged hands.

Yeah, it took a moment, but I managed fine, thank you very much. Rafe pushed Princess to the floor and nudged Pirate over so he could create a spot on the other end of the couch. I clicked on the TV to watch some rom-com on Netflix—he didn't protest—and we ate in silence.

After we finished our meal, Rafe checked a piece of paper on the coffee table and walked into the kitchen. I snuck a look while he was out. He'd been keeping track of the times for my meds. He returned with a fresh glass of water and two more ibuprofen.

We sat for a while more to watch the rest of the movie. By the ending credits, I was slumping sideways. Yeah, I needed to call it a day.

Rafe let the dogs out back one last time. Then he rattled all—and I meant all—the doors and windows on the first floor to make sure they were locked tight. He grumbled around the rooms, muttering something about needing more security here and different locks there. As if I had the money...

Grabbing my phone from the coffee table, I pushed myself upright and took a couple of steps toward the entry hall and stairs. Did I wobble? Yep. Did those stairs look daunting? Double yep. Would I end this horrible day asking for help in my own home? Nope.

Rafe made a move my way, like he was going to scoop me up again.

Shaking my head—*fido, that ached*—I waved him off and clomped over to the foot of the stairs. He hovered right behind me, like a guard dog afraid I'd collapse at any moment.

That's what happened when you showed any sign of weakness. I didn't want to rely on his help when he'd be gone at any moment.

Grasping the handrail, I pulled myself up the stairs, one step at a time. Rafe tracked my progress sooo close behind me—if I fell backward, we'd both tumble all the way down.

Or, more likely, he'd catch me. But I wasn't counting on that.

The doggos followed us into my new bedroom, Pirate to settle in his huge bagel bed in the corner and Princess to snuggle against my leg for one last ear rub.

I was no fool. Since I was a smidge shaky, I asked Rafe to wait by the door while I brushed my teeth—awkwardly – and did my business—even more awkwardly. I left off the face-washing for now, because, well, bandaged hands.

Anyway, I'd never put on any makeup, given I'd started my day by running out of my house like a madwoman.

When I stepped out of the bathroom, he had my phone in his hand. I raised an eyebrow, and he said, "Sorry. Checking to see if your battery is charged up." He didn't sound that sorry.

He walked back to the door while I kicked off my slippers and climbed into bed.

"Rafe, please, hang on a moment." I drew in a deep breath. "I couldn't let today end without telling you how relieved I was to see you walking in the door this morning. I was hurting, and I looked up...and there you were. Thank you for everything you did for me today."

The sides of his mouth quirked up. He turned out the light and said, "Good night, Rose."

I turned on my side and burrowed under the covers. "Good night, Rafe, sleep tight," I murmured as I was drifting off to sleep. *Wait, wait,* I thought to myself. *What did I say?* But then my exhaustion dragged me under.

Chapter 13

Rose

My gratefulness had a short shelf life.

It was Saturday morning, a week-plus later, and I was back in the roastery space, arguing in heated whispers with Rafe.

Whispers, because one of the kids was over at the worktable weighing and packing coffee blends into our custom bags.

Rafe and I faced each other in a furious standoff. He demanded that he pay rent for the apartment. I refused to accept any money since he was doing me a favor by staying close to me.

Plus, he was only going to camp there for a couple of months, three at the outside, before he took off for his next job. Wherever that would be.

Of course, Rafe didn't see it that way. In fact, he seemed a little insulted—not my intent at all—by the implication that he'd expect to stay for free in exchange for helping me out.

How could I tell?

He stood all tense, towering over me, with his arms crossed, biceps flexed, corded and veiny forearms on display, staring me down.

Now mind you, I wasn't intimidated. But I was a little distracted there for a moment by all the muscly gloriousness that was Rafe. I came out of my trance and met his glare head-on.

"Okay, okay," I hissed. "If you insist on making a deal out of this, I will allow you" —*he growled*—"Er, rather, ask you to pay some rent. Let's say five hundred bucks per month."

I slid my eyes to the left. Rookie mistake.

Rafe barked out a laugh. It was so loud that the kid at the worktable jumped and jerked his head around.

"I don't think so. I talked to your girl Jennifer yesterday."

Uh-oh.

He pulled out a wad of what looked to be one-hundred-dollar bills rubber-banded together. He reached over and tucked it into the pocket of my Chocolate Lab apron before I could do anything.

"Yeah. No," he grumbled. "She said that the going rate for a one-bedroom apartment in this part of Portland is at least fifteen hundred a month. So here's thirty-five hundred for the rest of September, October and November. I'll get you the rent for December when I know my schedule."

My jaw must have dropped, because the next thing I knew, Rafe used two fingers under my chin to gently close my mouth.

When I tried to take the cash out of my pocket to give it back to him, he rested his hand on mine. "Rose. Please. You will be making *me* feel better if you take this. I *always* pay my own way."

What could I say to that? I totally understood. My family members, from my grandparents down to Finn, had always worked hard for everything we'd gotten. We did *not* believe in free rides.

Plus, Rafe—unlike some dog butts I could name in my life— had shown up and stuck around when I'd needed help. He hadn't run off when the going got tough.

In my book, that alone deserved a lot of gratitude…and a little treat.

So I stepped back, clapped my hands and said, "Thank you, Rafe. Happy that's all settled."

He looked puzzled at my sudden amiability. Before he could say anything, I went on to inform him, "Now *you* are going to make *me* feel even better by accepting my invite to Sunday supper tomorrow. I'm making my grandma's Swedish meatballs on mashies. You'll love 'em!"

Rafe stopped looking puzzled and smiled instead. "Are you always this bossy?"

I probably should have paused there, but Rafe had to know. "Oh, no. Usually I'm pretty easygoing."

Did I hear a snort?

"You're getting the friends-and-family special."

Before he asked *which am I?* I twirled smartly around to head down the hallway to the café.

Chapter 14

Rafe

I hadn't turned on the bedside lamp yet, so it was still dark, being five thirty and early October and all.

I didn't need the light to recognize that the life-sized cardboard figure in the corner was Movie Elvis, not Vegas Elvis. I'd been going to sleep with and waking up to the damned thing the last few weeks.

He flaunted that sophisticated look I'd never aspired to—polished boots, black slacks, brown linen sports jacket, black tie, crisp white shirt, gold cufflinks (shit, *cufflinks*).

Frozen in time, maybe caught at the *best* time of his life, Elvis strummed his guitar, smiling that confident smile, flashing those bedroom eyes, singing directly to you.

Well, not me. I didn't see the attraction of the music or the man.

But I wasn't a woman…or a bitch. And by bitch, I meant the female dog type. I may have been growling under my breath, but I swore Princess had the hots for the King. At bedtime, I'd find her lying in front of the Elvis cutout, muzzle nestled between her front paws, gazing in adoration.

Females.

Without Rose's permission, I wasn't going to move cardboard Elvis into a closet, over to her house—or out to the garbage can. It might've been some too-sensitive reminder from her last days with her mom in the apartment. Why else would Jennifer have left it here when she cleaned out the place? And why hadn't it made a guest appearance at her mom's party?

I figured I'd ask Rose about it, maybe hear more about the Elvis backstory, when I went over for supper later today. I already had so many questions I wanted to ask her, things I wanted to find out about her.

But, fuck, I'd need to rein it in. I could tell she was still tired from her injuries, even though the cuts—hell, gashes—on her hands and knees were healing. And the dark circles under her eyes were fading.

With all she had going on, Rose was asking me to supper. Sunday supper. A first for me.

Sure, I'd eaten with my foster families, prepared meals with Pete, gone out to bars with army buddies, taken girls on cheap dates. But this was the first time I'd been invited by a woman for dinner at her home.

And not just any woman. Rose, a woman who was claiming more and more of my waking thoughts.

Yeah, I shook my head over her stubbornness, but it was her giving nature that drew me in. That and the physical impact of the sweet slant of her cheeks under those green eyes, the lushness of her lips, the soft fullness of her body.

No doubt I was imagining more than was good for me, or her, given that I'd be moving on in a couple of months.

Still, I needed to do this invitation up right—I wasn't some raw recruit. Buy some flowers for her. Go by Jean-Luc's and get him to choose a bottle of wine. Call her to see if it was okay to bring Princess, although I suspected I already knew the answer to that one.

Yeah, today was a first. My gut was aching as I laid there, twisting the top sheet in my hands. It was only supper—right?

It was the first time I'd seen Rose flustered. I was standing at her front door Sunday afternoon, a big-ass bundle of flowers in my left hand and a bottle of red in my right. Princess was sitting at my feet, no leash and on her best behavior, looking past Rose at her buddy Pirate.

We were right on time, if not a minute or two early. I knew Rose was still expecting us since I'd talked to her earlier in the day. She was even wearing a Chocolate Lab apron with a kitchen towel slung over her shoulder.

Yet she was flustered to the point of blushing, fluttering her hands, stuttering her welcome…and blocking the doorway. I pushed forward gently so she had to back up. Then Princess and I walked through, and Rose closed the door behind us.

I turned to her and pushed the flowers into her arms.

"Rose, these are for you." *Smooth, Rafe, who else?* "I brought you some wine too." *Obvious, Rafe, what else?* "Is everything okay?" *Are you okay?*

She dipped her nose into the flowers, took a deep breath and then raised her face with a breathtaking smile. "Rafe. This is the first time a guy has brought me flowers. They're beautiful. Thank you!"

What about past boyfriends? What about recent dates? What about Finn's father before he'd…what? Died, disappeared, flaked off?

Yeah, I had so many questions, but—thank fuck—I didn't spew them all out on the spot.

Instead, I zipped it and followed Rose as she swayed her way through the dining room in her tight jeans, throwing comments over her shoulder all the while.

"I'm going to find one of Mom's pretty vases for your flowers. Oh, you brought wine too? That's too much! There's a corkscrew in the drawer there—can you open it? I put some beer in the fridge to chill for you. I got a ton of choices. See if there're any you like."

While I opened the wine and chose a brown porter, she put the flowers in a big glass vase and the vase on the dining table. A long, dark wood table with curvy legs, surrounded by fancy matching chairs, already set for supper—yeah, we were eating at the dining, not the kitchen, table.

She then made her last comment, or I guessed, question, "May I borrow your muscles for a while?"

I had all sorts of answers to that, but being a smart guy, I kept my mouth shut and cocked one eyebrow. Rose laughed a little self-consciously and, damn, blushed again. Rose held up her still-bandaged hands on either side of her face, like she was surrendering, and then tilted her head toward a row of peeled, boiled, semi-crumbling potatoes on the kitchen island.

"Normally, I'd mash these bad boys myself, but my palms are still too sore to grip the masher hard enough. And to apply pressure."

Again, I shut it and gave her a chin lift instead. She stepped over to the stove where the meatballs and cream sauce simmered in a big skillet, richness wafting into the air. Some sort of vegetable was cooking in a pot, and a small saucepan was steaming what turned out to be milk, butter and garlic.

"If you can move the potatoes back to their big stockpot over there on the counter, I can pour in the milk mixture while you mash."

So that's how I ended up with Rose tucked close to my side, holding my left shoulder to steady herself while she slowly streamed the milk-butter-garlic into the pot and I plunged the masher down again and again.

We both were a little heated when it was all over.

We stepped away from each other. Rose pulled up her apron to blot her neck and fan her face while I ran my forearm across my forehead. I hated to admit it, but she was the first to recover.

She grabbed serving dishes from her cupboards and issued orders disguised as requests. "Rafe, would you mind dishing up the mashies in this bowl while I get the broccoli ready? Rafe, would you mind ladling the meatballs and sauce onto this platter? Rafe, would you mind putting out this lingonberry sauce while I spread the pickled cucumbers on a little plate?"

I didn't mind at all.

After the dogs were fed and directed to sit—and not beg—in the kitchen doorway, after our drinks—even my porter—were poured into nice glasses, and after Rose turned on some music—no Elvis, thank God—we sat down to supper.

We filled our plates, and then Rose declared, "You should be thankful it's not Thanksgiving."

"Why's that?" I asked, taking the bait like a sucker.

"Because before you can eat, you have to present a three-minute, memorized speech detailing what you were thankful for in the past year," she replied with a perfectly straight face.

"Each and every person at the table has to do this?"

"Oh, yes. We have a huge family-and-friends-giving here at the house." She hesitated before adding, "So the speeches may last over an hour before we can dig in."

Rose frowned and stopped talking, maybe thinking about the first Thanksgiving without her mom. Bet her mom had been one of those who made a big deal out of all the holidays. Bet she'd gone overboard in the best possible way—feeding everyone and their dog within shouting distance.

Rose looked sad, and I wasn't going to allow that. Not that she didn't have a right to be sad or to take as long as she wanted to grieve.

77

I wasn't going to avoid asking Rose about her mom like people often did when somebody you loved died. I'd get her to talk and share stories.

When my mom died, nobody ever talked to me about her again. Nobody asked me what she'd been like. Nobody asked me if I missed her. Nobody even said her name again. And I'd been a kid, just seven. I didn't even have one photo of my mom—before smartphones and too poor for cameras. And my mom's family and my sperm donor had deserted us, so nobody was there to help.

Rose had photos all over the place—living room bookshelves, dining room buffet, even the kitchen counters. Framed pictures of her at all ages—with her mom, Finn, a gray-haired guy I took to be her dad, an elderly couple holding hands, her girl crew. Photos of Pirate and earlier generations of chocolate Labs filled an entire wall.

So, yeah, I was going to go there. I was going to talk about the elephant in the room. Or, in this case, the Elvis in my bedroom.

"You know, Rose, I had to promise Princess one of your mom's meatballs to get her out of the apartment this afternoon."

"Wait, what? Why?" I understood her shock—Princess always wanted to come over and hang out with Pirate in the backyard.

"I may be exaggerating a bit, but she loves that Elvis in the corner of the bedroom. Anytime we're there, morning, evening, whenever, she lies pointed toward the guy, worshipping him with her doggy eyes. What *is* it with you women and Elvis? Why did your mom love him so much?"

"Oh my dog, I forgot he was there. I got that for Mom as a joke when she was sick. Jen must have left him behind when she cleared out the place. I can come get him out of your way!"

"No, don't you dare. I think it would break Princess's heart to see him go. But tell me more about your mom, about Ellie—why did *she* love Elvis so much?"

A grin lit up Rose's beautiful face. I got distracted for a moment and then caught up to what she was saying.

"He was the entire package! Elvis could sing, dance, act—all wrapped up in those shaking hips, sensuous lips and hooded eyes. Mom was a teenager in the sixties, and that was pretty racy stuff for those times. She bought the records, watched him on TV and went to his movies. I'm surprised my grandparents permitted it, but Grandpa usually went along with what Grandma said. And it *was* pretty innocent compared to *these* times."

She kept going, and I was happy to see her talk about her mom. "Elvis didn't disappear entirely when Mom and Dad got married. He kinda took a back seat for a while. Grandpa was gone by then, Dad was busy setting up our first roastery, and Mom was helping Grandma in the coffee shop."

Rose paused and ladled some more mashed potatoes, meatballs and sauce onto my plate. She popped up to push past the dogs and grab a couple of small saucers from the kitchen. As she came back to the table, she continued talking a mile a minute.

Mission accomplished.

"Now you'd think my dad would've been jealous—after all, they'd played 'Love Me Tender' at their wedding, and Elvis albums were background music in the coffee shop—but he was a wise man. He knew he was always number one on Mom's hit charts. Dad even took Mom to Graceland a couple of years after it opened—I still have the photos somewhere around here."

Princess and Pirate stood, tails and hind ends wagging hard, as they watched Rose spoon two meatballs each on the saucers along with a little sauce and broccoli. No mashies because…garlic. She set them on the kitchen floor just over the threshold, and the dogs gobbled their treats up. In five seconds flat. Like they hadn't had *their* supper a half hour ago.

We smirked at each other and settled back into finishing our meal. Rose continued telling me about her mom and her lifelong crush on Elvis.

"After I came along—she was an older mom at thirty-nine, they'd tried for years before they had me—she'd moved on to collecting Elvis CDs and his DVDs. So I guess I grew up listening to Elvis and watching his movies. Even though"—Rose grinned at me here—"by the time I was in my teens, I was more into Beyoncé and Justin Timberlake.

"But Elvis was always our 'thing'—especially in those final months. That's when I found the Elvis cutout. That's when we'd cuddle on the bed like a slumber party and watch movie after movie on an old DVD player connected to the TV."

She'd turned inward, humming a little and singing under her breath. "Love Me Tender," if I wasn't mistaken.

She looked at me, her green eyes glassy, and said, "Thank you for asking, Rafe. She was a wonderful mother, and I miss her every moment."

Rose paused, seeming to gather herself. "You've probably figured it out—I was a *younger* mom when Finn was born. As in, still-a-teenager young. And single, with his father not in the picture. I was so lucky to have my mom there. Dad was great too. Yet it was Mom who taught me how to be a mom. But that's a story for another time."

She stood abruptly and clapped her hands. The dogs jumped up, and I jumped a little too at the sudden change of direction. So immersed in her story—and in her—I guessed.

"Let's clear the table and put any leftovers away. I'll do the dishes later on," she directed.

I started to protest, but she shook her head. "No worries. This way, we can take Pirate and Princess for a walk around the neighborhood, maybe down to the park, while it's still light outside."

We returned to Rose's front porch about forty-five minutes later, after a leisurely amble around Dogwood's streets—or as much as you could amble when the dogs stopped every two feet to sniff— and through the park. I offered, again, to come in and help her clean up the kitchen.

The stubborn woman smiled and shook her head. "You've been so sweet, Rafe, I really appreciate it. It made me happy to spend this time together."

She stepped closer and rose on her tiptoes to aim a kiss at my cheek. Steadying herself by gripping my shoulder with one hand while holding Pirate's leash in the other. At the last moment, I lifted my free arm and slid my hand around her cheek to the nape of her neck, my fingers weaving into her thick hair. I pulled her head toward mine and kissed her sweet mouth. Gently, gently, I kept my lips on hers and touched my tongue to the seam of her mouth. She let me in.

Meanwhile, the dogs wrapped their leashes around us, getting tighter and tighter.

Chapter 15

Rose

"Then he apologized!" I whisper-shouted into my phone, glancing around to make sure I was alone in my backyard. Except for the two pups, of course.

"He what?" Lauren just plain shouted back.

I winced and jerked the phone away from my ear for a moment. It was early Monday afternoon, and I was filling Lauren in on the sweet ending—or so I'd thought—to my supper with Rafe.

"He said he was sorry. He didn't want to take advantage of me. Forget he ever did it, won't happen again." All these bull-shih tzu excuses delivered while we were still wrapped up in the leashes.

"Well, did you kiss him back?" Lauren demanded.

"Yes!" In fact, I'd leaned into it.

"Was it as hot as it sounds?"

"Hotter!" In fact, I'd melted into it, my first kiss in ages—years, actually.

"So what did you say to his sorry-ass apologies?"

"I said it's too late for take-backsies. I said I'm not some shy teenager. I said it takes two to tangle...er, tango!" At least, I hoped I'd said "tango."

Lauren snorted.

I pointed out, "Girl, I was so *not* going to let him get away with it. Here we'd had a wonderful afternoon together, he'd been kind about Mom, and we'd topped it off with a perfectly sweet—hot—kiss. Then, he'd had the nerve to pull back. Anyway. Something I said must've struck him funny, because he burst out laughing."

She snorted again, the little traitor.

"So, of course, I got all indignant, but only for a moment. I was laughing too. And the dogs started barking and leaping around us. By the time we got the leashes untangled, I managed to extract two promises from Rafe."

Lauren inserted a "you-go-girl" here before I could continue. I rolled my eyes but realized she couldn't see me, so I went on.

"One, I got him to swear that he didn't regret kissing me—or me kissing him back. Two, I got him to agree to walking the dogs together in the evening since it's getting dark so much earlier."

I heard another "you-go-girl," so I had to stop and tell her, "You know—I'm usually so tired at the end of the day that Pirate gets short-changed in the walk department. This way, I can guarantee him a decent outing around the neighborhood each evening."

Yep. That was my story, and I was sticking with it.

Lauren was my girl, so she was willing to swallow my lie, er, story. We ended our call after she shared she'd decided to drive, rather than fly, for the holidays. Her marriage was winding up for its sad finish, and she wanted to be with friends to start the new year.

I doled out treats and ear rubs to Princess and Pirate and headed down to the café to relieve Mateo.

The first thing I had to do when I got to the Chocolate Lab was break up a fight.

No, it was not what you'd think. This was not a coffee bar brawl where I had to call in the brawny bouncers, meaning Rafe and Mateo, to drag apart two over-caffeinated seniors.

Oh, no. Chloe and Zoey, long-haired mini-dachshund sibs, were at it again. Skilled at raising a racket, they yapped and lunged—on their leashes, thank dog—at the two-foot-tall Doberman skeleton in a corner of the café. As was their custom, they turned on each other to continue their high-pitched battle. No blood was shed, other than from busted eardrums.

"Ladies, ladies, leave it!" I said in my sternest dog-trainer voice—while pulling two bribes, aka biscuits, out of my hoodie pocket and waving them overhead.

I used my other hand to help their person, Miss Ada, ancient and ninety-two pounds soaking wet, pull her beloved doxies away from their bony foe. I led all three, using the dog biscuits as lures, out the side door to a seat at one of the tables on our covered deck. I promised Miss Ada I'd send one of the kids out with her coffee and favorite scone in a few minutes.

After that, I did the baton-passing thing with Mateo, where I got all the updates from the morning shift and touched bases about the upcoming catering jobs. He also graciously agreed to stay to meet with Katt about finalizing the sign-painting she was doing tomorrow on our new plate glass windows. Surprisingly, or maybe not, it didn't take much arm-twisting.

I stepped into the kitchen prep area to peruse my Post-its on the sink's mirror and hold my usual internal monologue—the one where I berated myself about trying to do it all on my own in my quest to grow the Chocolate Lab.

This time was different though. This time, I argued back. Maybe the fighting doxie sisters had the right idea.

Girl, you've got plenty of help—look at the last few weeks. You don't need to do it all on your own. Mateo has really stepped up to manage the café. Lauren's been using her marketing superpowers to give advice. Some of the older kids are taking over the food prep duties.

Even Rafe has been coming in early and sticking around late to cover all things coffee-roasting-wise. He's even stayed to help close the place.

He'd kept everything very businesslike since our supper last night. Except…except a time or five today when he'd brushed close to me when we passed in the café, heat radiating from his body. Just recalling those times sent tiny puppies zooming around my stomach.

So to combat those, I grabbed a couple of businesslike Post-its off the mirror and walked down to talk to the gentleman in question.

Later that same day, a little after nine, I stood on my front porch reading the Post-it I'd plucked from my front door. It wasn't one of mine that I'd discussed with Rafe this afternoon. No, this one was printed in Rafe's bold hand, letters upright and in all caps. Not shouty caps—he wrote everything that way. Coffee bean orders, coffee bag labels, even his signature.

And, apparently, Post-its for me. This one read:

> ## MEET RAFE & PRINCESS
> ## ON DRIVEWAY AT 9:30
> ## FOR PROMISED WALK

I smiled, unlocked the door and stepped into my front hall. Nails scrabbled on the kitchen floor, and I just had time to slap Rafe's Post-it on the mirror by the door before Pirate ran his big ole Lab head into my stomach full force. He dropped on his side, rolled on his back and groaned his approval of my belly rubs.

Too much time later—or too little, depending on your point of view—I hurried upstairs to get ready for the walk.

First, I changed my clothes into something warmer—*sure, the nubbly emerald sweater was soft for the dogs' head rubs.* Moving to the mirror in the bathroom, I unbound my hair from its knot and shook it out around my shoulders—*of course, my knitted beanie would fit better.* Finally, I powdered my face and swiped mascara over my eyelashes. *Okay, okay, those efforts were for my own vanity.*

Not thinking of that kiss last night. No. Nope. Not at all.

Back downstairs, I grabbed my hat and Pirate's leash from the coat-tree. I tucked my phone in one hip pocket and, at the last moment, my keys in the other. Usually I left the front door unlocked for our walks. By this time, Pirate was barking and jumping in the entry, knowing something was up with all my rushing around. After I clipped the leash on his collar, we headed out the front door...and ran smack-dab into Rafe and Princess standing on our front porch.

And by smack-dab, I meant Rafe had to grip my shoulders so I didn't topple over. And Pi yanked my arm right around Rafe so he could greet Princess in the time-honored doggo manner. Yes, sniffing was involved.

Rafe rumbled, "Everybody, stay!"

Yes, he did, and we all did.

I queried him, "I thought you said driveway?"

He answered, "Yes, I did. I also said nine-thirty. It being nine-forty, I thought we'd see what the holdup was."

I threw back, "Impatient much?"

"Yes, where you're concerned," he returned.

I had nothing to say to that and was quiet for once.

He said, "Rose? Keys."

"What?"

"Keys. You got your keys to lock up?"

Yep, here we went again. I nodded, and Rafe put his hand out for the keys. I shook my head and reached around him to lock my front door.

He muttered "stubborn" or something similar, just as the dogs lurched forward, dragging us down the porch steps to the sidewalk. We headed left toward the park.

After making slow progress for a couple of blocks, with Princess pausing every two feet to sniff something in the parking strip and Pirate doing the same in each front yard, I decided to break the silence. Plus, I was determined *not* to talk about the café or the roastery or business.

So, instead, I came out with, "How long has it been since you carved a pumpkin for Halloween?"

It was Rafe's turn to say, "What?"

"It's a valid question," I claimed. "We're having our annual competition at the Chocolate Lab this Sunday afternoon, and I need to know if you developed crazy pumpkin-carving skills in the army."

"Wait, is this for kids or adults?"

"Both, actually. Two categories with prizes—kids age eighteen and under, and kids over age eighteen. Our most senior kids serve as the judges—people like Pete, Miss Ada, Mateo's mom, Mica's dad."

"Sounds like you take your contest seriously. Is there any trash-talking or pumpkin-seed-slinging involved?"

"Oh, yeah—the littlest kids can be the scariest." I winked. "For the Chocolate Lab's part, we spread newspapers on our tables, supply the pumpkins, and fuel the contestants—and spectators—with apple cider, coffee and bakery treats. Everyone who enters gets a prize too."

"Any rules?"

"Yep, just two. Bring your own knife or carving tool and leave your pup at home." As we crossed to the path leading into Dogwood Park, I added with a grin, "Just so you know, I'm pretty competitive."

Rafe quirked his lips and shot back, "Well, no worries from this quarter. You're right—skill training on pumpkin carving was *not* offered in the army. In fact, I can count the number of times I've even touched a pumpkin on one hand, with three or four fingers left over."

Pirate chose that moment to grab a twig and start chomping on it. Of course, he interpreted my command to *drop it!* as *chew faster!*

While I leaned over to yank the thing out of his mouth, I said, "Didn't you carve pumpkins as a kid, go trick-or-treating, dress up as a superhero?"

When I straightened and glanced over at Rafe, he was staring straight ahead, lips clamped together.

Shih tzu. Open mouth, insert foot. I started to say something, anything, when he commented matter-of-factly, "I was in and out of foster care from when I was little. So my history with Halloween was pretty spotty. And the families I stayed with usually weren't the warm and fuzzy, pumpkin-carving, costume-wearing types."

I knew better than to offer sympathy, so I kept looking ahead as we made our way around the park. Sometimes you could talk about more difficult things when you weren't looking at each other. I learned this from countless times driving Finn to and from various activities. Our best convos were often the best because we *weren't* staring into each other's eyes.

So I clutched Pirate's leash a little tighter and murmured a noncommittal "mm-hmm."

There was silence for a beat. Then—thankfully—Rafe went on to say, "I do have a memory, a *good* memory." He said this with emphasis, like good memories were hard to come by.

"I remember my mamma getting a pumpkin from somewhere. Not a lot of spare change in our household. I was only five or six, I think. She cut off the top around the stem and scooped out the innards. We giggled and giggled because they were so slimy and gross. She had me draw a smiley face on the pumpkin using a blue pen from her purse. She handled the knife, of course, and sliced out the eyes and nose and toothy mouth. Following my lines, more or less.

"Afterward, Mamma begged for a candle stub and matches from one of our neighbors. We lived in an old apartment building, so no place to put the pumpkin except on the fire escape outside our window. An open flame was definitely a no-no, but she took a chance. We waited until Halloween night, until it was dark. I remember staying up late, or at least late for me.

"Mamma finally put our pumpkin out on the fire escape and lit the candle. We stood by the window, hugging each other, watching until the candle burned itself out. Yeah. Good memory. One of the best."

I looked straight ahead, my eyes filling. Vowing I wouldn't look at him, wouldn't take his hand. I cleared my throat and asked, "Your mom, what's her name?"

"Her name was Angelina. She died when I was seven. She was beautiful."

At that, I reached out and squeezed his hand. I let go, and we both kept looking ahead as we walked out of the park. Under the streetlight, my tears spilled over, but I turned my head away. Rafe didn't need to see that.

We took a different street toward home, the dogs stopping us for treats a couple times along the way. Then, when I had it together, I quietly shared, "You've got another chance to carve a Halloween pumpkin this Sunday. So, are you in?"

I glanced over to see him nod. Still looking ahead.

"In fact," I continued, speaking a bit stronger now, "I'm going to pick up the pumpkins at the farm stand behind Reed College on

Thursday morning. I called ahead, and they're putting a bunch aside for me. Wanna come along and help me stuff 'em into my car? It's like a clown-car exercise but with pumpkins instead."

By now, we'd reached the steps to my front porch. I quickly wiped away the wet from my cheeks with the back of my free hand. Rafe finally turned to me. His whole face was rigid, his eyes dark and intense, his lips pressed into a straight line.

Oh, fido. Did I bring up bad memories? Did I get too personal? Did I hurt him? Did I make him sad? Or maybe, sadder?

He stared right into my eyes and said, "Yes, Rose."

Yes to what? I'd forgotten the question in the midst of my concern.

His face relaxed, and one side of his mouth quirked up. "Yes, Rose. Yes, I plan to come on Sunday to show off my mad pumpkin-carving skills. And, yes, I will take you to pick up the pumpkins on Thursday. We're going to use my pickup, since, frankly, your car is a tiny beater on its last legs. Plenty of room in the bed of my pickup for pumpkins. And that way, the dogs can come along with us."

I didn't argue because he was right…about everything.

We climbed up the stairs to the front door. Holding out his free hand, he said, "Keys."

I smiled up at him and handed over my keys. He unlocked the door, pushed it open to see I'd left on some lights, and handed my keys back. He tilted my chin up with his fist and pressed a hard, closed-mouth kiss on my lips.

"Rose. So sweet. Remember to lock up. See you tomorrow at the café." He pulled Princess down the steps, walked around to the driveway and headed to the apartment in the back.

Chapter 16

Rafe

"That's harsh, man!"

I'd called Mateo on his bullshit, and he had the nerve to act all offended.

We'd been celebrating our win at the local pub, Hair of the Dog, and the server was clearing the table of empty glasses, pitchers and pizza pans.

Most of the guys had already left after a round of fist bumps and shoulder claps. I'd waited until it was just Mateo and Jean-Luc still sitting there to start my sham rant. I had my reasons, and I didn't want the rest of the soccer team listening in.

Nice guys, but this was about Rose. So, discretion required.

"Yeah, Mateo, you pulled a con on me." I scoffed. "You told me it was an over-forty rec team. You claimed you only needed me for a sub. You said there were a couple of matches left in the season. Shoulda known I was being bullshitted."

Turned out it was an over-thirty team, which I should've copped to since Mateo was in his early thirties. Plus, there were two guys out for the rest of the season from various injuries, so they needed more than a sub to fill out the team. And I would be here in

Portland just long enough for the remaining five—count 'em, five—matches before the rec league moved indoors for the winter.

Earlier this evening, over at Dogwood Park, I'd been on the pitch most of each forty-five-minute period—plus the stoppage time. Thank fuck I was in decent shape and had some fast footwork for midfield.

In the sandbox, we'd played pickup games with other units and the local kids. I'd always been a runner—needed to be in times past—and still ran four, five miles every morning. These days, I hefted coffee bean bags—one hundred and fifty pounds at a crack—for a living.

Still. I was going to take advantage of the fact that Mateo, aka "the bullshitter," owed me.

"So, brother, I'm going to need a favor in return," I informed him.

Mateo raised his eyebrows, and I could hear Jean-Luc huff out a laugh on the other side of me. Maybe he knew where this was going.

I wanted to give Rose a getaway. When we were picking up the pumpkins this morning, she'd let drop that she hadn't taken a fun trip for ages, what with her mom sick, Finn busy with school and, of course, operating the café.

Not complaining, not her style. She was just remembering when she and her parents used to take Finn to pumpkin patches and petting zoos in the countryside outside Portland.

I figured Rose was due for a day off, or at least, part of one. And I had a selfish reason for taking her on an outing. We'd have more time together—more time *alone* together, if we didn't count the dogs.

"Here's the thing," I continued. "One day soon, while the weather is still good at the beach, I want to take Rose for a day trip. The only way that's gonna happen is if you take her early shift so we can get on the road first thing in the morning.

"I'll get us back by early evening so we can relieve you and close up. But I have to present this to her as a done deal. Otherwise, she'll never go for it."

Mateo got a big shit-eating grin on his face and said, "No worries, man. Take Rose out for the whole day—I'll cover it."

At the same time, Jean-Luc smirked and said, "*Present* it to her? You sound like you're proposing a business deal, not asking her on a date."

Fuck. Was that what I was doing?

Well, yeah, maybe. But the idea of "dating" when you were in your thirties or forties was bizarre—like the terms "boyfriend" and "girlfriend." So "dating" didn't begin to describe my irresistible desire to make Rose's life better.

My longing didn't stop there. I craved finding out more about her, craved getting closer to her.

Was that fair to Rose? Was I being selfish in wanting more with a woman for the first time in my life—given who I was and where I'd come from? Was that fair given that my plans hadn't changed—get in, get the job done, get out and on to the next?

So, no, not fair to her. But, yeah, irresistible to me. And did that make me a bastard for wanting Rose, even in the short-term?

Too late. I already was.

I shook my head at Jean-Luc, nodded my thanks to Mateo and tossed some bills on the table. Their laughter followed me out the door.

The fuckers knew I was hurrying to go on my nightly walk with Rose.

Rose was laughing so hard she was in danger of choking on her dad's Irish whiskey...or snorting it out her nose.

I sat my tumbler on the coffee table and was reaching for her to somehow help when I stopped. Maybe she'd forgiven me for over-stepping earlier today.

I was okay with Rose laughing at me. In fact, that was my new fucking mission in life, since she seemed to be so serious or sad or just plain swamped most of the time.

I'd gotten an entirely different reaction this afternoon when I'd announced—her word, not mine—that I was taking her and the dogs to the beach next week. She'd been pissed. To make it worse, it'd been obvious that Mateo was in on the scheme—again, her word, not mine—to cover her entire day off.

I should've listened to Jean-Luc.

In the army, being direct was a good thing. Being a man of few words was good too. In the interests of time and lives, you often need-ed to give or receive orders without a lot of explanation. Apparently, being direct was not so good in civilian life. And especially not with the woman you wanted to make happy or, even better, laugh.

Could an old dog learn new tricks?

Luckily, I'd regrouped and turned my almost-order into an invitation.

Please join me on a trip to the beach. It'll be good to go while the weather's still warm and sunny. Pirate and Princess will get a chance to run and chase seagulls. We can take off our shoes and walk along the shore-line. Bet we can even find some seafood for lunch. Maybe even watch the sunset before heading back home. Please say you'll come with me.

I was pretty sure I'd had her at "take off our shoes." Plus, she'd looked a little glazed over at the fact that I could string so many words together. She'd smiled big-time and said, "Yes, I'd love to go to the beach with you. Thank you, Rafe."

She'd thanked Mateo again and again for taking on her shift and promised to do the same for him another time. She'd even jumped forward and hugged me—a little PDA that I didn't mind—it'd been just Mateo and us in the roastery, after all.

Now it was Saturday evening, and she'd invited me in for a nightcap as a reward for walking the dogs so late. The Chocolate Lab had hosted live music, and I'd stuck around after working in the roastery to do closing with her.

Tucked in our respective corners on the couch, we'd been talking about funny dog names. I'd shared some crazy nicknames from my army days, including my own. Which set her off.

Thankfully, Rose got it together enough to stop laughing and gasp out, "Angel? Angel! I thought *Rafe* was your nickname in the army, short for your full name. How did they come up with Angel? Oh!"

The penny dropped.

"Yeah, my mother named me after the archangel St. Raphael," I shared. "She'd been raised Catholic, I think, and maybe it brought comfort to her, some connection to her faith. We never went to church."

Rose stilled for a moment and asked, "When did you shorten it to Rafe?"

"Oh, Mamma did when I started first grade in public school. She figured out that Raphael wasn't going to work in our inner-city Oakland neighborhood. Bullying was alive and well even back then. 'Rafe' served me well through high school."

And during my teenage gang years, too, which I *wasn't* going to share with Rose.

"Smart woman, your mom." Rose smiled while looking into my eyes.

"Yeah, she was," I said shortly and moved on. "I enlisted in the army when I was eighteen and had to use my full legal name. On the first day of basic training, the drill sergeant took one look at my tough mug and reckoned I was the ugliest angel he'd ever seen. The name stuck for twenty years until I got out."

"Wish I could've seen you at that age. Do you have any photos from back then? Snapshots with your buddies or maybe your military ID?"

"Nope, thank fuck. You get a new ID each time you advance in rank. And I was issued a final ID card with a current photo when I got out."

"Huh. Not sentimental, are you?"

"Nope, not about my history." I almost said, *not* with *my history.*

Rose was like a terrier. Once she got ahold of something, she wouldn't let it go.

"I bet you looked like your mom. Except for the stubble, of course." She reached over Princess, who was curled up on the couch between us, to rub the back of her right hand lightly along my jawline. "Oh. And, I guess, the scar."

She paused and frowned, like she was puzzled, and drew back. I didn't volunteer anything, didn't want to tell her anything about that part of my life.

Instead, she asked the unexpected. "Do you have any pictures of her?"

I stayed frozen in my corner. I hadn't anticipated her sudden touch—she hadn't said a thing about the old knife scar until now. But the scars inside? Did I want her to know about those, about what'd happened to my mamma and me?

It was only fair if I expected to learn more about what'd happened to her.

"Nope. No photos. Mamma didn't wake up one morning—I couldn't wake her up, no matter what I did. I hugged her and held on to her, thinking maybe she'd gotten too cold overnight."

I'll never forget rubbing her cheeks—they were like the ice cubes in our freezer.

"Nothing I tried worked. I piled on blankets from my bed. I turned up the heat as high as it would go. I was responsible for her, and I couldn't get her to wake up."

"Rafe, you were only a little boy!"

"No, Rose. I was responsible for my mamma, and I let her down."

I sucked in an unsteady breath. *Why was this so hard to tell?*

"I finally got scared enough to run to the next apartment. The neighbor lady called 911, and they came. There was nothing they could do either—she was already gone. She'd been sick a lot, but we didn't have the money for a doctor or medicine. Barely had enough for food."

Rose let out a pained *ohhh*, but I shook my head and plowed on.

"When I couldn't give them any family to contact, the medics took Mamma away in an ambulance. The neighbor stayed with me and called my school. I found out later the school counselor called Child Protective Services to say I was alone. Later that same day, one of their people showed up at the apartment. She put my clothes in a plastic garbage bag and took me to a temporary foster home. I guess the landlord sold or dumped the rest of our stuff."

Rose's eyes were glistening, and I knew what she was going to say.

"Why were you so on your own? I get that your father wasn't around. But what about your grandparents? On either side?"

So, I gave her the full story. At least, the beginning of the story. I'd leave the darker details of my years in foster care, gang activities and war zones until later. Or never.

"When I was about six, I started asking Mamma where my dad was. Why I didn't have a dad like the other kids at school. She played it cool—although it must've hurt. She said he'd loved me very much but had passed away when I was a baby. She also said all my grandparents lived far away and that we couldn't afford to visit each other. She even mentioned a younger brother—I got the sense he was still in middle school—my uncle, that I might get to meet someday.

"This all made sense when I was little. But I figured things out later. My mother must have gotten pregnant when she was young—so innocent and naïve. She probably thought she was in love, and then the guy took off on her. Her family was Catholic, so abortion was not in the cards. They probably wanted her to put me up for adoption. She must've refused, and they disowned her, cut off all ties. It's as cold as it sounds."

Rose got up on her knees, pushed Princess off the couch and scooted up to my side. She stroked my jaw again, gently, and laid her fingers on my lips to silence me. She looked into my eyes for a moment and leaned in to wrap her arms tightly around my shoulders and put her cheek on my chest.

We sat there, close like that, quiet like that, for some time.

Chapter 17

Rose

It was Sunday morning, and I was trying to sleep in. And by sleep in, I meant stay in bed until at least seven, not my customary five thirty. Even when I wasn't opening, my internal alarm clock roused me at that time.

I'd been wide-eyed awake for a good part of the night, obsessing over everything Rafe had revealed. After he'd shared his story, I'd invaded his space before I'd even thought about it. Rafe'd gone rigid—not in the good way—and then finally hugged me back. We'd hung on to each other, not kissing, just quiet, until we'd said our *goodnights.*

So yeah, this morning, I'd granted myself permission to indulge in a bout of "sleeping-in."

I flipped to my left side, snuggled under the comforter and squeezed my eyes shut. Color this picture *woman snoozing.*

It didn't work.

First, I couldn't actually fall back to sleep because I'd restarted the whole thinking-about-Rafe obsession.

Second, Pirate was huffing and grunting right in my face, poking his muzzle on mine.

Third, something was making a dog-awful metallic *screech, screeech, screeeech* right outside my bedroom window. The occasional *fuck* or *shit* convinced me it wasn't a giant crow or squirrel trying to break in.

Wait a minute. *My bedroom was on the second floor.*

I sat bolt upright, swinging my legs to the floor and nudging the pup out of the way. Sliding over to plaster myself next to the window, I pulled back the curtain and peered out.

I squealed—not ashamed to admit it—and jumped back, letting the curtain go. Another *fuuuck*, except louder and longer this time. Luckily, no new sounds followed, like *loony hot guy falling to his doom on my thorny rose beds.* That was, until my own loonball started barking.

Rafe had been right outside my window on a ladder, stretching overhead to clean out the gutter with a long-handled scoopy thing. Good thing he had nerves of steel, or he could've pitched over backward at my sorta-scream.

But hang on a minute. What the fido was he doing up there in the first place?

I moved to stand in front of the window and threw open the curtains. Rafe was continuing to scrape at the gutter, dragging out leaves to fall in clumps to the ground.

Hmmm. Guess it'd been a while since I'd done that. Or Mom or Finn or who knows?

I shook myself, undid the window latch and pulled up the lower half. He paused and looked down at me. At least I didn't say, "What are you doing?"

However, I did say something only marginally better, "Why are you cleaning my gutters?"

Did he answer me? Nope.

Instead, he said, "Nice T-shirt" and went back to work.

I looked down and realized I had on my XXL sleep T-shirt that hung down to my knees, covering my private bits.

It read *Can I Pet Your Dog?*

"Rafe," I started, but he interrupted me.

"Rose, I probably should've checked, but I thought you were already up and over at the café. I cleaned out Pete's gutters yesterday and asked if I could borrow his ladder for your house since yours looked stuffed full."

He kept babbling, which was pretty rare, so I let him go for it.

"I know this probably falls in the category of asking before doing—or telling, kinda like the beach trip. Look, I'm sorry. I didn't mean to assume you weren't going to do this yourself."

I held up my hand, palm out—the universal *stop talking* sign. "Rafe. Please don't apologize. I had completely forgotten about cleaning our gutters, and a lot of other house stuff for the last couple of years. This falls in the category of being super thoughtful. Thank you."

He rumbled something like, "Oh. Okay, then. You're welcome," without looking at me.

"I'm going to pull on some clothes and come help you," I informed him. He turned his head and frowned at me. "No, no, not on the ladder. I'll rake the leaves and put them in bags. After that, I'll fix us some coffee and breakfast—maybe treat you to my infamous dog-head pancakes. Do you like eggs? I make a mean puffy scrambled dish."

I was the one babbling now, and Rafe was staring at me. I turned and stumbled into Pirate who was parked right behind me. He had that big loopy grin that Labs get, and his tongue lolled out. No doubt, he was expecting Princess to join us for breakfast.

As if dogs could have expectations like humans. As if.

I turned back, slammed the window down and closed the curtains. Before I could say anything more.

Busted.

Rafe caught me in the act and paused to quirk an eyebrow my way. Of course, my face burst into flames at once. I was surprised I didn't set my hair on fire.

See, I should've been helping Mateo and his mom fill the carafes with hot cider and coffee or putting out the boxes of applesauce doughnuts we got every Halloween from our favorite fruit orchard.

But was I? Nope.

I was perving on Rafe as he flexed his biceps and hoisted our big boy pumpkins from my garden wheelbarrow onto the café tables.

Worse yet, I was putting it out there for anybody with twenty-twenty to see.

Since my previous disasters, I'd kept any yearning, dreaming, *hungering* for love a secret from everyone except Mom.

Get a grip, girl. Was I so starved for love that I'd mistake a short-term friendship with benefits for the real thing? Would I trash my resolution never to trust a man again in favor of my promise to fight for my dream?

I ripped my gaze from Rafe and grabbed my phone to take more snaps to post. We'd spent the time since we'd closed early turning the café into the kid-friendly-not-frightening setting for our annual Howl-o-ween Pumpkin Carving Contest.

Sparkling strings of white dog-bone lights and black cat-head lights ran rampant around the walls. Glow-in-the-dark dog skeletons—at least two dozen—crowded every corner of space, from a tiny Chihuahua to a jowly bulldog to an enormous Great Dane. Even a few cat and rat skeletons tip-toed around the place—I suspected Katt's influence there.

Old Chocolate Lab aprons waited on a side table for those who wanted to protect their clothes from pumpkin innards. Behind the counter, I'd tucked a box full of little prizes and gift cards for the winners of our contest.

And by winners, I meant every contestant—young or old—won a prize. We had umpteen categories for pumpkin originality, and our grand—in age—judges had fun deciding who got which award.

Friends and their families would start rolling in the side door soon, toting their own knives, pumpkin-pulp scoopers, fancy sculpting tools and all manner of embellishments. Jen's twins even bedazzled their pumpkin with beads and sequins last year.

This was the first Halloween without Mom and Finn, and I missed them. Yet at the same time, I was distracted by my hunger—yes, I'd admit it—for Rafe.

Too soon, the angel on one shoulder advised me. *You just met him a month ago. Seize the day*, the devil on the other shoulder urged me. *He'll be gone before you know it.*

The friendship zone could be fantabulous, don't get me wrong. I was already basking in his kindnesses at home and in the café, our long talks about everything under the rain clouds on our dog walks—even our frank exchanges about our mothers.

If you added *benefits*, then I could give in to those cravings that consumed me. I'd start by yanking off his tight T-shirt and stroking my palms down his sides, over to his flat abs and back up his chest. I'd hook my arms around his neck, press close to all that heat, and pull his head down for a kiss. Not the semi-innocent ones we'd shared a couple of times this past week—no, nothing innocent about the wet kisses I had in mind.

And in this daydream, *my* T-shirt had disappeared too, along with my bra.

Just then, our Halloween mixtape cued up "Devil in Disguise." Rafe must have felt my eyes back on him because he lifted his head and pierced me with his cobalt gaze. He didn't smile, and neither did I—we stared at each other.

Was he the devil, or was I? And what were we hiding from each other?

I startled and wrenched my eyes away when Ana came up and slipped her arm around my waist for a hug.

"Tía Rose, Tía Rose, do you want to guess what Mateo and I are doing for my pumpkin?" she demanded. I was lucky enough to be an honorary aunt to Mateo's little sister.

"Hmmm," I said, tapping my chin and squinting off into the distance. "Is it a tyrannosaurus rex?"

"No," she giggled. "Way too big!"

"How about a giraffe?" I countered.

"How would I carve the neck?" she demanded.

"An elephant is kinda round like a pumpkin," I suggested.

"Where would I get the trunk *and* the ears?" she quizzed me.

"Oh, I've got it—a Sasquatch," I declared.

"Too big *and* hairy! You're not even warm, Tía Rose," she chortled.

"I'm fresh out of guesses—you'll have to surprise me!" I surrendered.

I suspected I already knew though. In the manner of chatterbox ten-year-olds everywhere, Ana had been talking of nothing but kittens for the past few months. Which was hilarious, since they already had a humongous husky named Perrito—who, in the manner of huskies everywhere, talked all the time. But I also happened to know that Liliana had asked Katt for places to adopt a kitten and for tips on all things feline.

I gave Ana a hug back and glanced up to see Rafe rolling the now-empty wheelbarrow down the hall to the roastery. At that moment, the side door burst open, and in danced Noah, followed by his sisters Emma and Meggie and their dad Liam. Other staff, friends and neighbors poured in behind them.

Pete waltzed through the door wearing a big grin and a headband of flashing pumpkins on springs. Jen came next, bringing her twin girls, as well as Miss Ada. She'd agreed, reluctantly, to leave *her* doxie girls at home. Katt waved as she walked in, a tote bag of art supplies slung over her shoulder. Mateo emerged from the kitchen just in time for Ana to tug him to a table.

We'd even lured Jean-Luc to the dark side with the promise of an adult beverage—mulled spiced wine—*after* all the carving implements were safely set aside. Halloween was not a "thing" in his native France. Gentleman that he was, he'd stopped by the vet clinic to help Mica walk her dad down to the Chocolate Lab. Mica's mom was long gone, and she'd moved in with her dad when he'd developed memory problems.

In Halloweens past, Dr. Tanaka had always been one of our contest judges. Today, we made sure he had a comfortable chair at a special table alongside the current judges, Pete, Liliana and Miss Ada.

I saw Rafe coming back down the hall. He paused to take in the boisterous crowd. Even though I'd told him everybody showed up in high spirits for this party, I don't think he believed me. Unless you had kids, I doubted the army celebrated this holiday in quite the same way. And the way he'd alluded to the foster families made them sound more frightening than friendly.

Rafe started to turn away and head back to the roastery. *Not so fast, sweetheart.*

I clapped my hands and whistled for attention—it wasn't for nothing that I was a dog mom. Rafe paused again and looked back my way. I caught his eye and gave him a smarty smirk.

"Hey, everybody, welcome to the ninth annual Howl-o-ween Pumpkin Carving Contest! Before we get going, I want give a shout-out to a few people who made this possible. A hand, please, for our panel of judges—you all know their names! Thank you to Liliana, Mateo and Ana for getting the place ready. And a nice welcome to Rafe, a newbie to the Chocolate Lab, who not only helped set up but also graciously volunteered his pickup—and himself—to pick up the pumpkins."

People craned their necks to see the newbie, and then applause and cheers and hoots broke out.

"Now you all know the drill—you have forty-five minutes to scoop, carve and/or decorate your pumpkin. When you've finished, line up your pumpkin in the meeting room and put one of the LED candles in it. Our judges will tour the table and decide on the winners in the different categories. Remember—every entrant will be a winner, and everybody will go home with a prize!

"You can enjoy treats after you've finished your pumpkins— hot cider, coffee, mulled wine and applesauce doughnuts await. We'll be taking plenty of pictures, too—plus a group shot around the table afterward. Any questions?"

"Yeah," I heard from Jean-Luc back in the corner. "Am I going to be the only guy carving a pumpkin solo or is Rafe going to get in on the action?"

Trust Jean-Luc to stir shih tzu up. But I was ready for him... and for Rafe.

"I'm glad you asked! You all know my usual pumpkin-carving partner is off at college this year." (People ahhhed and ooohed about Finn being gone.) "So, I'm asking Rafe to team up with me so I won't miss out."

I stopped and motioned him toward me, before I continued, "Rafe?"

How could he deny me? He couldn't, didn't and moved to my side.

I smiled up at him and turned back to the group. "Now, everyone—find a table with the pumpkin of your choice."

While people were selecting their tables, I looked at Rafe again and gestured with my head toward a nearby table I'd already set up with some supplies.

Not that I'd planned this all out in advance or anything.

He peered at the mini-pumpkins sitting next to the big pumpkin, one already fitted out with a halo and the other with devil horns, and quirked his lips. He got the picture, er, pumpkin.

"Ready, set, scoop!" I shouted.

An hour and some change later, I took pics for the Chocolate Lab's social media. Group shots, individual shots, one of our judges with their own "face" pumpkins (carved by Katt beforehand), and even a special shot of Ana and her award for Best Scaredy Kitten.

Yes, I did get a photo of the Team-Rafe-and-Rose entry. People were a little puzzled about the theme of the pumpkin, but I just shrugged my shoulders and tried to look mysterious. Rafe was his usual stoic self, not giving anything away.

But I had to say, he'd gotten into the spirit of the thing. When I'd shown him a quick sketch I'd made of my idea, he'd winked at me and pulled out his knife. *Not* a dinky Swiss Army knife with all those teeny attachments—a big folding knife he kept in a sheath on his belt.

We'd divvied up the tasks—Rafe carved, I scooped, and we assembled together. After we'd carefully moved our work of art to the meeting room, we stood back and grinned at each other. Rafe grabbed one of the LEDs, turned it on and stuck it in the middle pumpkin. The middle pumpkin was one of three—the largest with carved-out, bugged-out eyes and a round mouth. On a tiny, attached sign, it shouted out, "Oh, noooooo! Who do I listen to?"

A mini pumpkin perched on one shoulder, carved with an angelic face and embellished with equally mini white wings and gold halo. Another mini pumpkin floated above the other shoulder, carved with a devilish face. Two pointy red peppers stuck straight up for horns.

I loved that Rafe got my idea and the others didn't. Or maybe Jen and Mica did—they kept shooting me suspicious looks.

What could I say? The Elvis song "A Little Less Conversation" kept coming to mind. Especially the parts about "more action" and "satisfying."

Anyway. Our Halloween party was winding down, and people were leaving. For many, it was a school night. For most, it was time to head home and get dinner going on this chilly October evening. The sky was already deepening to blue-black at five thirty.

For others, it would take a little longer. Jean-Luc, after a mug or two of mulled wine, was helping Mica walk her dad home. Pete had to drive back to his house—he'd stuck with hot cider.

Finally, after saying *goodbye* and *remember to take your pumpkins* and *don't forget your certificates and prizes* and especially, *no thanks, we'll clean up after we take the dogs out,* Rafe and I were alone in the café.

Chapter 18

Rose

I plucked my moist T-shirt away from my breasts, flapping it to cool myself.

From across the now not-so-crowded room, Rafe caught the motion, his eyes narrowing as they glided down and then back up. Taking their time.

He couldn't have missed my hard tips swelling against the clingy cotton.

When I wiped my damp hands on my jeans, I found the wet heat between my thighs had seeped through. So instead, I snatched my hands up near my head, shaking them to dry. The fanning eased my flaming cheeks too—but only for a second.

Was my current state of steaminess due to the two courage-building mugs of spicy mulled wine I'd chugged in quick succession?

Or was I all hot and bothered because I wanted to pitch the angel act and play the devil? Was it time to yield to temptation when I'd been good for so long?

"Rose," Rafe rumbled. "Are you okay? You look a little...a lot flushed."

"How can you tell?" I tossed back to him. "I'm burning up over here, and you're hiding out over there."

He growled at that insult and crossed the café in three strides. I held my ground, not backing up—or down—an inch. We glared at each other before we moved at the same time.

It was another contest—one where we both could be winners. Who could melt into the other the fastest? We tied for the prize, and Rafe was just lowering his face to mine when he muttered, "Fuck. Windows."

He backed up and let me go—*oh, no*...only to grab one of my hands again and take off down the hall toward the roastery. *Oh, yes!* He opened the door and reached in to turn on the lights. Too bright, evidently, and he turned them right off again.

"We'll have enough light from the hall, don't you think?"

"Barely." I panted, ready to get a move on. "But barely is all we'll need this time."

"Yeah." Rafe smirked. "Let's save candlelight for another time and place. The fire marshal tends to frown on open flames."

He tugged me into the roastery, spun me around and started backing me toward the pallets of coffee bean bags. When my thighs bumped up against the stacks of bags, I stopped—and had second thoughts. Not about getting closer to Rafe. That train had already left the station.

No, I had second thoughts about getting horizontal on bags of coffee beans—*scratchy burlap* bags of beans—versus on my *velvety-cushiony* couch.

Especially given the next step in dealing with our now-mutually steamy states—the stripping and shedding of T-shirts, jeans and even silky underthingies.

Was burlap burn any different from beard burn?

Again, Rafe rescued me from being lost in my head. He did this by dropping my hand, stepping even closer and gently cupping my cheeks with his palms. He pressed his fingers into my hairline and tilted my chin up.

The heat of his stare scorched my skin. His calloused hands ignited a fire that raced from my face straight down to my core.

"Rose, I want to kiss you and touch you everywhere," he rumbled. "Is that okay with you?"

At that, I just nodded, although this was hard since he was now clasping my face even tighter.

"I need words. Please."

I reached up to grip the back of his neck and caress the corded muscles. "Yes, Rafe. It's beyond okay. I want you too."

His eyes flared and closed as he angled my head and leaned down to press his lips against mine. My eyes closed too, as I sighed—*at last, a little less talk*—and opened up to his tongue licking into my mouth, dancing with my tongue. We continued for a few minutes, changing angles, exchanging wet, open-mouthed kisses.

When I gasped for breath, Rafe pulled us apart. I followed his lips, and the devil just laughed. He reached up with both hands to unravel my messy bun, throwing my hair tie and hairpins behind him. He dug his fingers deep, gently unraveling the waves to fall around my shoulders.

Gripping the bottom of my T-shirt on either side, he paused a scant second to arch an eyebrow in question. When I responded by raising both arms, he peeled off the now super-snug T-shirt in one quick move. It disappeared over his shoulder too.

Rafe's eyes heated, and he ran the fingers of one hand from my mouth, over my chin and down my neck to the cleft between my breasts. "So soft," he murmured.

He paused and rubbed his knuckles across the top of my bra, just where the lace met the swell of my breasts. My nipples pebbled right through the thin fabric.

My turn.

In my hazy pleasure, I may have said that out loud. Rafe stilled and dropped his hand. I started to lift the bottom of his T-shirt but ran into trouble right away—he was too tall for me to pull it over his head. He got the idea quickly, though, and reached to the back of his neck to yank his T-shirt off.

I immediately pressed both palms flat to his ridged abs. Rafe took in a surprised breath, and his muscles tightened even further under my touch. I slid my hands slowly, oh so slowly, up over his warm furred chest, grazing his nipples on the way. Spreading my hands over his shoulders, I gripped his bunched biceps *hard* for a moment. Then wrapping my fingers around his head, I stretched to pull him down for another kiss.

About this time, Rafe lost patience. He groaned and picked me up by the waist to move me back flat onto the coffee bean bags. He crawled over me, propping himself up by his elbows, then grabbed my hands on either side of my head and slowly lowered his body to mine.

He used his strength to press against me, but not crush me. For just a moment, we stared into each other's eyes, and I swore he was restraining himself. I was too—even though I wanted to rise and rub my breasts against his hard chest, my core against his hardening length.

Why hold back? my devil whispered. *The fire coursing through our bodies might be smothered at any time. Who knows what the future holds?*

But we shouldn't go all the way in the café, my angel countered. *Think of the exposed flesh, think of the health codes. Maybe one more kiss before we call it a night?*

But I deserve this night, my devil claimed. *And so does Rafe.*

I surged up at the same moment that he must have reached his own decision to take what he wanted. Clutching our arms around each other, pressing our bodies closer, tangling our legs tighter, we melted into each other as we kissed.

It was that hot.

With the fever that gripped us, it took a while for the voices to penetrate.

Finally, we pulled apart and gazed at each other in horror. I was the first to get it.

"We forgot to lock the side door!"

Chapter 19

Rose

"Mateo was cool about the entire thing—which is more than I can say for Rafe!"

"Wait—did he get upset? You guys weren't doing anything wrong," Mica protested, laughing as she fended off Pirate's smouches. She knelt next to my big boy on the exam room floor, trying to listen to his heart.

"You were just test-driving the fling-thing in private," she added, "except for the whole windows-and-doors problem."

Trust my girl to put a positive spin on our kissing-interruptus adventure after the Howl-o-ween party.

As soon as we'd arrived that morning for Pirate's allergy shot, I'd jumped right in with my story. I was looking for a little sympathy because...what are girlfriends for?

Instead, I got a lot of laughter and even more encouragement because...what *are* friends for?

Luckily, we'd had enough warning before Mateo had switched on the brights. We'd slid off the bags and located our tossed T-shirts—plus a spare apron for me.

Still, we'd been caught in the act—what with my hurricane hair and Rafe's wild eyes. Even more telling, I'd backed into Rafe to block Mateo's view of certain hard facts and clutched the apron over my pebbly bits like a shy maiden.

Mateo had raised his eyebrows in mock shock. After winking, he'd turned off the lights and shut the door. We'd stood still and quiet—in the total dark—until Ana called that she'd found her backpack behind the counter. They'd left shortly after that.

I'd wanted to crawl under the pallet of coffee bags and never come out again.

"You know what Rafe did? He started to chuckle, not mad at all," I informed Mica. "He swung me off my feet and roared with laughter. With the way he was carrying on, I was worried the neighborhood dogs would start howling."

We'd gotten interrupted in the middle of making out like teenagers, and he was losing it.

"Good for him. So what *did* you do?" Mica asked.

"Well, I had no choice. I had to laugh too." I hadn't let go like that in a long time, and I suspected Rafe hadn't either.

"Good for you, Rose," she declared. "And even better, he didn't behave like your jerk of an ex."

Mica never minced words.

Yeah. My jerk of an ex-*fiancé* who was always embarrassed by any PDA—even, and maybe especially, my tendency to hand out hugs like chocolates.

So I shared the rest of the story with my girl. How we'd finally stopped laughing, and Rafe had turned me around to pull me close. How we'd kissed and nibbled each other's lips, yet only for a minute before heading back into the café to finish the cleaning job.

Later, after we'd crashed on that velvety-cushiony couch with pizza in hand and after we'd walked the dogs one last late-night time, we'd returned to our respective beds to crash again.

Hot play on delay, to be resumed at a later date.

"How are you doing?" Rafe asked.

Of course, it wasn't a loaded question. The thing was…I'd re-ignited my shyness after confessing to Mica earlier, so I blurted, "Do you mean have I recovered from last night? Or do you mean how are things going with planning for the meeting? Or do you mean are you hungry since cold pizza didn't make much of a breakfast this morning?"

There was silence on the other end, and I told myself to *stop* talking.

Rafe said, "Yes," and rumbled that deep masculine chuckle.

He'd let loose more in the past day than in all the days and weeks combined.

Before I could find my voice, Rafe took over and told me he was bringing lunch from the café. His treat, he insisted, even though I owned the café.

"I'm not taking 'no' for an answer, Rose."

We could eat, talk grocery store strategy and walk the dogs before needing to be back at the Chocolate Lab for the meeting. He reminded me that we had all day tomorrow during our beach trip to talk about *other things*—my emphasis, not his.

So this time, I was the one who uttered one word, "Yes."

"Dalmatian, *Dalmatian, Dalmatian!*" I muttered, each time getting a little louder. I was standing behind the service counter, staring into space and shoving truffle after chocolate truffle into my face.

I was supposed to be taste-testing the custom truffles to choose some for our holiday gift boxes. Instead, I was stress-consuming, my mind so not on the task at hand.

Rafe and Mateo were off to the next-to-last outdoor soccer match of the season, along with Mike to cheer them on. I was managing the café until we closed at eight and cleaned up by nine. I'd fed and watered the pups, and they were content to hang in my backyard until our last cruise around the neighborhood later tonight.

It was a slow Tuesday evening at the café, so I had a lot of time on my hands. To think and to worry—and to do what I do best when I was stressed. Eat sweet treats. No wonder my figure was getting a little curvier as of late.

I was *not* worrying about how the meeting had gone with Julie from PDX FOODS that afternoon. Turned out that the grocery group had been looking for a local resource to pilot self-service coffee bean displays in its Portland area stores.

Now it seemed the Chocolate Lab was getting what I'd wished for…and my stomach was churning at the thought. The truffles could've been contributing, but I suspected it was due to the shih tzu-load of work ahead.

We'd had to postpone the meeting for a few weeks, and Julie had been super understanding about the delay. Still, the first thing she'd said when we'd all sat down at the tasting table in the roastery?

"Let's get this dog show on the road!"

The "buy-local" grocery group loved everything about our Chocolate Lab Coffee brand. We were right in their dog, er, wheelhouse with our locally roasted coffee in coffee-mad Portland, dog-themed gear in dog-mad Portland, and custom chocolate rewards in chocolate-mad, well, anywhere.

They'd applauded our savvy proposal to provide the coffee bean bins and grinders, clean and restock the displays, and offer special promotions and sales. Yep, we'd do it all—all in exchange for exclusivity—meaning Chocolate Lab Coffee would be the "one and only" whole coffee bean display in each PDX FOODS store. We'd start out with a couple of pilots and expand to all their stores in the greater Portland area.

So why was I slugging down the chocolate truffles like they were shots of Irish whiskey?

I needed to pull this off to save the café—and I was on my own. Nobody knew how much I was counting on new roastery business. The café barely broke even in the best of months. It wasn't sustainable on its own.

I'd hidden this crisis from Mom in her last months, and I was sure as shih tzu *not* going to spill the beans now. I didn't want to chance anybody changing their plans on my account. Finn heading back to school, Pete truly retiring, Mike returning part-time only.... and Rafe leaving for his next gig. All going, going, *gone.*

No wonder my stomach—and now my head—were aching.

Suddenly, the double dark chocolate truffle was snatched from my right hand and replaced with...a variety pack of colored Post-it Notes? WTF (read: What the Fido)!

I looked up just as Rafe tossed me a pen *and* stuffed the stolen truffle through his lips. Evidently, the soccer match was over, and I hadn't heard him come back because I was too wrapped up in worrying.

Rafe closed his eyes, appearing in bliss for a moment as he chewed and swallowed the chocolate. I got distracted watching his mouth—*hmm...maybe we could do a truffle-tasting together*—and missed his first couple of words.

"Rose. You're gonna make yourself sick." Did he mean sucking up the chocolates or stewing over the coffee pilot...or both?

Rafe gently tapped my forehead and said, "Instead, why don't you transfer all those steps for the coffee deal from that busy brain of yours onto your Post-it Notes while I start closing the café? That way, we can get outta here early and go take the dogs for their walk."

I started to protest, and he interrupted me. "We've got a big day at the beach tomorrow—a well-deserved break for you—and I want all four of us to be fresh with a good night's sleep."

I raised my eyebrows, and he added, with a narrowed gaze, "In our own beds. This will all be here when we return on Thursday, and you can talk the next steps through with Mike, Pete, Mateo, Finn, your girls, me—whoever can help. You are not alone in this."

If only planning my personal life was so simple—one action step jotted on each Post-it Note, color-coded to show...what? Dreams, hopes, desires?

Nope. Not putting any of those in writing for anybody to read. Especially Rafe.

I barely understood them myself.

Chapter 20

Rafe

We'd be shaking the grit out of our clothes and shoes till kingdom come—and I didn't give one fuck.

The dogs' tennis balls and Frisbees, already caked with sand, were stuffed in one of my jacket pockets. The other one was reserved for the beach "finds" Rose kept handing to me—fragile seashells in iridescent colors, driftwood sticks worn smooth, and shiny, odd-shaped rocks. After I dusted each one off the best I could, I'd slipped it into the designated pocket.

"You've got a mission here, Rafe," she claimed, walking backward and pointing both index fingers at my chest.

"Should I choose to accept it," I stated.

"It's not possible to turn it down," she countered.

"Let me hear it before I decide," I warned.

"Your mission," she paused, "*if* you choose to accept it, is to keep each of my treasures safe and uncrushed until we get home."

Now, in all fairness, her pockets were smaller and crammed too, with her phone—she was snapping a ton of pics—a water bottle, leftover scones and loose dog biscuits. In those circumstances, the only thing a man could do was *accept the mission*.

I gave her a brisk nod. She grinned and flipped forward to continue her amble down the beach, dogs running circles around her. Me following.

Not long after that, Rose tugged off her sneakers and socks to dig her toes into the hard-packed sand at the shoreline. Dangling the sock-stuffed shoes from her fingertips, she waded into the shallow edge.

"Rafe, come on—you know you want to get your feet wet," she called. "Think of the little fishies tickling your toes!"

I was not a barefoot kind of guy—at least not outside.

"Aren't your feet freezing?" I called to her. *They must be turning blue by this time.*

"Sure, but it's worth every moment." She flung her arms wide and started jogging toward Haystack Rock, the piercing squawks of the seagulls filling the air as they scattered around her.

Princess and Pirate, fur ruffled up from rolling on their backs, raced after her like a pair of loons—the rarely seen beach loons. I followed.

So, yeah, gritty, cold sand was everywhere—and I didn't fucking care, since I got playful Rose, laughing Rose, carefree Rose.

I got Rose all to myself for a day.

Sure, the grocery store project would be waiting when we got back. Sure, the clock was ticking on our time together. Sure, we had things…personal things…we wanted to talk about.

But that was for tomorrow. Today, I got you all to myself.

"A dollar for your thoughts?"

I jumped and reached out for the sand dollar she offered me.

It was a perfect circle—a rarity when most were chipped or broken after being washed up on the rocky shore. A delicate, five-pointed star appeared engraved on its surface. I pulled off my knit beanie, inserted the shell carefully and put it in my treasure pocket for safekeeping.

Rose nodded and smiled up at me. "You looked lost in thought," she prodded gently. "Anything to share?"

"No," I said. "No, not really. Other than that I remember another place north of Cannon Beach I used to visit when I was training with Pete. A park with trails, beautiful views and secluded beaches...more isolated than here, with fewer people around and no houses overlooking us."

She nodded again and leaned close to whisper, "I like your thinking. How about we head there after lunch?"

This time, I nodded. And because her face was so close in that moment, I reached down with my right hand to brush back her wind-blown honey hair and pressed a kiss to her soft lips. When I leaned back, her eyes were still closed. She opened them slowly and teased, "Thanks, Rafe. I appreciate the pretty innocent PDA for such a public place."

I laughed and baited back, "Let's see what happens this afternoon."

We called Princess and Pirate so we could hook up their leashes—in vain, as it turned out. They were having such a good time with their other dog buddies that they decided to play "keep away." Only when we turned our backs and started to slog through the deep, dry sand toward the stairs up to town did they surrender and follow us. A treat or two got them closer where we could grab their collars and snap on the leashes.

Rose sat on a log to brush the sand from her feet and put on her shoes. The socks went into her pocket. Up the stairs we went and down the side street to my pickup. We offloaded our beach finds, Frisbees and tennis balls, then dried the dogs with old towels Rose'd brought. After they slurped their water bowls dry, we walked over to the main drag and down to the Driftwood.

There were two seats left around the firepit on their outside deck, and we snared 'em. A notice on the railing read *Licensed for 21 and over, except dogs*. Princess and Pirate settled under our feet, worn out and ready for naps. After ordering Dungeness Crab rolls, onion rings and beers, we settled down too.

When our lunch arrived, we fell on it like ravenous…dogs (sorry, Princess). The third time we tried to talk with our mouths full, we both laughed and finished up silently.

After I paid the bill—promising slash lying that Rose could get lunch next time—and after stopping at Bruce's for house-made taffy and chocolates—provisions, she called them—we drove north through Cannon Beach to the entrance of Ecola State Park. I paid the five bucks for the day-use permit, and we parked in the area closest to Indian Beach. We walked the dogs a short way down the trail so they could do their business and locked them back inside the pickup. There were tidepools to explore, plus we wanted a little… private time without chasing the pair of beach loons.

Less than an hour later, I had Rose right where I wanted her. Pressed close to me from shoulder to hip, arms encircling my waist, head tilted up at just the right angle.

We'd been kissing—deep, wet, open-mouthed kisses—for the last fifteen minutes, and neither of us were willing to come up for air. It'd been her idea. I'd unzipped my jacket so she could step close to me (*to get warm*, she'd said), and I'd wrapped it around us both. Leaving my arms free to reach up and weave my fingers through her thick honey hair. And I started kissing her as I'd wanted to do all day long.

Sure, first thing, we'd checked out the tidepools. I'd held Rose so she wouldn't tumble in trying to get the best shots of the starfish and anemones. Next, she'd caught pics of the coast looking south toward rock stacks and an abandoned lighthouse. Then, we'd found our own secret huddle of rocks at the foot of the looming cliff.

That briny smell coming off the cool breeze from the ocean was stronger here, too, away from the crowds. This stretch of the beach was almost deserted at this time of year, aside from a couple of surfers riding the rough waves.

Deserted, secluded, just our secret...all was fine with us.

Rose pulled her mouth back and peppered my jaw with short, sweet kisses. We took mutual breaths and leaned in to press our foreheads together for just a moment...and stepped back.

All good things must come to an end. At least, temporarily.

"Rafe," she said and stopped. She took in a full breath and started again. "Rafe, pull up a log. We need to talk."

Shit. The words no guy wants to hear.

But this was Rose. And there were things that needed to be said, things we needed to talk about, before this went any further. Above all else, Rose got to set the ground rules, the parameters, for whatever this *thing* was we had going on.

We found a driftwood log a bit back from the shoreline, a little sheltered from the now-brisk breeze. Sitting down side by side, we gazed out at the ocean. On our nightly dog walks, we'd found we could talk more freely when we were looking straight ahead. Figured Rose felt this way about whatever she wanted to say.

When she paused, I glanced down. She'd clenched her hands tightly together on her lap, the knuckles almost white. I pulled my gaze back up, and Rose began to talk.

Chapter 21

Rafe

"You know, you must know, that I'm attracted to you," she said quietly. "And I think you feel the same way."

I wanted to say *that's an understatement,* but I kept quiet and smiled.

"We've been doing a slow dance toward acting on that attraction for the last few weeks. I want to be with you, to...to...have sex with you, but I want to be wise about it. I want us to be clear up front that this is short-term—no expectations, no strings, no...feelings. Because you're not staying, you're leaving. Leaving before Christmas."

She swallowed and went on. "I also want to talk about protection and testing—how's that for being direct? It's just that, because of what happened with Finn's father, I like to be *very* cautious and *very* clear."

I wanted to know more, to know everything, but again I shut it. This was Rose's story to tell at her own pace.

She shifted a little closer, still staring out at the waves. "It's not that mysterious—you probably already figured out that Finn was born when I was pretty young...and that I was never married to his father. Same last name as my parents—not rocket science, right?"

She flicked me a sideways look, and I nodded.

"It's a pretty old story," she said quietly. "Naïve girl goes to college, meets boy and falls for him right away, falls *in love* with him. *And I was so sure he'd loved me.*"

Rose shifted a little away from me. I stayed put, even though I wanted to follow her.

"See, I was pretty sheltered growing up. It was my first semester at the University of Oregon, my first business course, my first attention from a handsome, older man—the TA for the class.

"My first secret—from my parents, my friends, even my new roomie. My first time."

I resisted the urge to put my arm around her, gripping the log harder instead, staring harder ahead.

"He'd used condoms, and then, at his urging, I'd sorted birth control from the campus health office. Whatever mix-up in timing or lack of effectiveness, I'd gotten pregnant. After I took the test— oh, I don't know, like five times—I called David and left a message for him to call me. No details, just call me ASAP."

Rose stopped and sucked in a big breath. "He must have sensed something because he ghosted me. He didn't call back, he blocked me on his phone, he never answered his door or my emails, and my letters were returned. My roommate, Lauren—you know her, my girl Lauren—found me sitting on my bed in our dorm room, in shock, crying. She took over, thank heavens.

"We called my parents—her translating, me sobbing—and then she drove me home. This was right before the holiday break, but I was in no shape to take my finals. I walked through the front door into Mom's arms, and Dad was right there holding us both. We cried and talked and cried some more…and decided that we were keeping the baby for our very own. I dropped out of school, moved back home…and Finn was born the following summer.

"Happiest day of my life, hands down. Best thing that's ever happened to me. No regrets. And aside from a few judgmental types, our family, our neighbors and my girls have stepped up to help raise Finn. *It takes a village and all that.*"

Rose rocked back and forth on the log. "Probably more than you wanted to know. Probably not too sexy. But I wanted you to know why I'm so cautious…and why I want to be clear about what we each expect."

I reached over and untangled her cold hands to hold them in mine, trying to rub some warmth into them. "There's more, isn't there?" I asked.

"Yes, a couple of things that you may be wondering about…or not. But here goes anyway. All designed to make my almost middle-aged-self more attractive to you."

If I hadn't been rubbing her hands, I would have grabbed her shoulders to give her a good shake for her silliness. Instead, I jammed close to her and kept at my rubbing.

"So why we didn't go after David for child support? During the months before Finn was born, we talked it out as a family and decided we needed the peace more than the aggravation.

"However, one thing I've never told anyone?" Here, Rose turned her head to look me in the eye. "Not my mom, not my dad, not Lauren or the rest of my girls, and, heaven forbid, not my son. When Finn was about two, I contacted David. I tracked him online and found he was finishing up his master's…still at Oregon. I used Mom's cell phone so he wouldn't recognize my number."

She hesitated. "I guess… I guess…I just wanted to give him another chance to get to know his son. Not renew our relationship, not get married, not ask for money or other support. To get to be in the life of his own son, this wonderful boy.

"So you can guess how that went. He said horrible things, vile things—he claimed he wasn't even sure Finn was his son. Implied I'd been a slut and had been sleeping around, when he knew, *knew*, that was *not* the case. I was so shocked, it took me a moment. I hung up on him and cried…for the last time."

At that, I dropped her hands and pulled her to me. I tucked her under my chin and hugged her as tightly as possible. *How could I not?*

After a couple of minutes, I asked casually, or so it seemed to me, "Where's this guy now?" The fucker.

Rose was onto me. She stirred and said, "Nuh-uh….that's sweet…I think. But nuh-uh. I don't know, and I don't want to find out. His name is *not* on Finn's birth certificate, and I've erased him from our lives.

"See, when Finn was old enough to start wondering why he didn't have a daddy like the other kids, why we all had the same last name, I kept my explanation simple…and honest. I told him his dad had decided he wasn't cut out to be a father and moved away before Finn was born. He accepted what I said without question—he already knew he was surrounded by love and by family.

"When Finn was older—high school age—I told him the whole story. Well, except for the phone call when he was two. Not for sympathy points, mind you. More so he could see the connection girls…and women…sometimes make between sex and feelings."

Rose stopped there, pulled her hands back, and moved out of my embrace down the log. The tide was coming in, and the waves were getting louder. I had to lean down to hear what she said.

"Wow," she breathed out. "How's that for oversharing?"

Before I could reassure her, she went on. "So I told you all that to tell you this. Please don't think I've been a hermit when it comes to sex. Sure, I didn't see men when Finn was young because I thought it would be confusing to him. But later, I did ease into dating…and some casual connections that involved sex—always at the man's place. Not lately, of course. However, I do have a good relationship, if you'd call it that, with Mister Vibrato."

Whaaat? Oh. I had to smile at that. And, luckily, Rose smiled right back before going on.

"Needless to say, but I'll say it anyway because I can't seem to stop talking, I'm cautious about using birth control now—the three-month shot— and getting tested periodically. Thank you, Rafe. Thanks for listening…and for holding me.

"Now, I'll shut up. It's your turn—not the oversharing bit— but your turn to talk about protection, testing, anything else you want to tell me. Or…you can tell me if you don't want to go forward after hearing all that."

I slid toward her and reclaimed her hands. I didn't let her pull back this time.

"First off," I said and dipped my head to look straight into her beautiful green eyes, "thank *you*, Rose, for trusting me—actually, *entrusting* me—with your story. I won't tell anyone. And you're right, I'm attracted, no, *pulled* to you. I want to be close to you in all the ways possible in this time we have together. In this time…with no expectations for afterward."

She closed her eyes briefly, opened them and nodded. Holding her hand, I told her my story…although I couldn't be as candid as she'd been. I stuck to my sexual history—she didn't need to know about my dark years in foster care or my criminal past. Yeah, yeah, it was a long time ago, before my military service. But parts of it were…bad.

Rose deserved somebody better than me for the long haul, somebody worthy of her love, worthy of her. So, no. No expectations on my part.

I told her that I always used condoms, even if the woman said she was using birth control. I'd gotten tested regularly during my army years…and since then. She seemed to understand that I was super cautious too, based on my mamma's experience and my unsettled life in and now out of the army.

She was right—I only trusted myself to make the decision on protection.

"Have you ever been married or in a serious relationship?" she asked.

I told her the sad truth. Well, I didn't say *sad* out loud.

I shared that all my connections with women—really, hookups—had been random and short-term. Probably related to why I hadn't moved on to that trust part of *not* using a condom.

Since retiring from the army, I'd been intent on operating in the moment, being responsible for nobody but myself, doing the roaming coffee roaster thing. Sometimes I'd meet women at the café or a local bar wherever I was working, and we'd get together on a casual basis.

"Oh. Kinda like us." Rose looked away and got real quiet.

I cupped her cheek gently and turned her face back to me. "No, not like us. No one's like you, Rose."

"But for the short-term…like we've agreed, right?" she pointed out. "No expectations, right?"

My lips tightened in a line, and I nodded slowly.

Rose fell asleep on the drive back from the beach, her head slumped against the passenger window, arms wrapped tight around her middle. Princess and Pirate were subdued, sensitive, as dogs often were, to the atmosphere around them.

When we got home, I was able to rouse Rose enough so she could walk into the house on her own—with my arm around her… for safety. I guided her to the couch so that I could go back out to get the dogs, both making a racket about being left behind. After wrangling them to the backyard to wash the sand off their paws and coats—and hoping Rose had a good vacuum to suck that shit up—I fed them their supper.

After coming in the back door—grr...she'd left it unlocked... again—I stopped in the utility room to unload my pockets of the dog toys and Rose's treasures and place them on top of the dryer.

Nothing crushed, thank fuck.

My souvenir was still nestled in my beanie. I stowed it back in my pocket for later.

I figured Rose would be awake by now so we could see about getting our supper. But she was still sleeping, curled up on her side, arms crossed and hugging her shoulders tight.

My woman—*I could say that to myself, right?*—was dog-tired. Beach walking will do that. Covering hard ground too.

I debated whether to rouse her again. It was mid-evening by this time, and she was opening the Chocolate Lab at six tomorrow morning.

Decision made, I walked around the house, locking doors, checking windows, turning off lights. The dogs followed my every step. I arrived back at the couch and squatted down beside Rose, gently brushing the hair out of her face.

"Time for bed." No answer.

"Rose, I want to carry you up to bed. Is that okay with you?"

That got a mumble...one I took to be in the affirmative.

I slipped my arms under her knees and shoulders and lifted her up, tilting her so her arms and head tucked close to my chest. Stepping around the couch, I headed up the stairs, Princess and Pirate dogging my heels. At the top, I made an educated guess and turned left down the hall into the biggest bedroom. The dogs pushed past me and settled on a huge bagel bed in the corner.

I laid Rose down on the side of the bed with the head-indent-ed pillow. I was able to pull off her jacket but figured she could sleep in her clothes—that was a step too far for me. She could also miss brushing her teeth for one night. I hated to leave her bare feet in those sandy sneakers though. Thankfully, I spied her slippers by the nightstand and bent down to pick them up.

That was when I saw the bat under her bed. *The. Fucking. Bat. Still there.*

Grabbing her slippers with one hand, I stood and pinched the bridge of my nose.

She's going to be so pissed at me.

Another decision made, I carefully eased off her shoes, catch-ing as much sand as possible, and replaced them with her slippers.

Maybe the sand all over her sheets will distract her—right?

Rose turned on her side, still not waking, and I pulled the covers up to tuck them securely around her neck.

I walked into the bathroom, easing the door shut, and turned on the light. It was pretty easy to knock off the sand into the waste-basket and put the shoes aside to be cleaned later.

I stood in front of the mirror for a moment, staring past her rows of Post-it Notes.

What are you doing, man?

I had no ready answer, so I brushed my teeth with a little sto-len toothpaste on my finger and took care of business.

Back in the bedroom, I set an alarm for five thirty and laid my phone on the nightstand. I shucked off everything except my T-shirt and boxer briefs and climbed under the covers. Pulling Rose's back flush to my chest, I wrapped one arm around her middle and bent the other to pillow her head.

I held my breath when she stirred. Then she settled, backing closer, and we fell asleep.

Chapter 22

Rose

I pushed back against a wall of warmth and hugged an arm to my chest. So toasty.

Pirate chuffed right in front of my face, and I slowly opened my eyes. As usual, my pup was sitting by my bedside, urging me to get up. This time, though, Princess was planted next to him, perked ears barely coming to his shoulder, peering at me too.

What the...fido?

I looked down at the fist and forearm I was gripping...yes... right between my breasts. Luckily, I was wearing my bulky sweater (weird), my tight jeans (weirder), and my fuzzy slippers (weirdest).

No wonder I was toasty. Although I think the arm tucked to my chest—thankfully also clothed with a T-shirt tight around the biceps and a sleeve of tattoos to the wrist—had something to do with that. Plus, I was resting my head on a bent elbow, and steady breaths heated the back of my neck. To say nothing of the hot hardness that dared to press against my *entire* backside.

So, again, no wonder I was "toasty." It was a miracle I wasn't going up in flames.

I jumped when a bugle playing…reveille?…sounded from the other side of the bed. Not my phone, because all my ringtones were Elvis songs.

Rafe jolted awake with a groan and pulled me even tighter to his chest before releasing me to turn off his phone's alarm.

He whispered, "Rose? Babe? Are you awake?"

I rolled onto my back and looked up at him, my face flushed from all the…clothing, all the…covers. Yeah, that was why.

I had questions, so many questions. But the first one was, "How long was I out?"

Rafe quirked his lips and did the math for me. "It's five thirty now, so that means you slept about fourteen hours straight, including the time in the pickup."

Fourteen hours. Fido. Fourteen hours. I haven't slept that long through the night since…well, since never.

I yelped and jumped out of the bed, pushing the dogs aside. Five thirty, and I needed to be at the Chocolate Lab at six o'clock to start getting ready to open at seven. And I was closing tonight too, since Mateo and Rafe were playing their final outdoor soccer match. Mateo had been kind enough to cover the entire day when we'd gone to the beach yesterday, so I was returning the favor.

"Rose, Rose, slow down." Rafe stood and started to herd Pirate and Princess out the bedroom door. I couldn't help but notice his snug briefs.

"Why don't you catch a shower and get dressed while I take care of the dogs? You'll have time for a little breakfast that way. Do you want coffee now or later at the café?"

I was finally catching up—and I had questions. What was Rafe doing in my bedroom, let alone in my bed? Why was he still here? Why hadn't he vanished in the night after what I'd shared— and overshared—yesterday?

I crossed to the door and grabbed the front of his T-shirt to tug his head down to my level.

"Now," I whispered, pressing a hard kiss on his lips. "Thank you."

And…what would he do if he found out the rest of my story? Yes, I had questions. But they'd have to wait for tonight.

After my short shower with a dollop of personal grooming, coffee—fake sweetener but real whip…I know, I know—and Rafe-scrambled eggs, quick but hot and protein-rich, I grabbed my laptop and walked down to open the Chocolate Lab.

Rafe had said he had some errands and would be there later to do roasts.

I was happy for the break from our close to twenty-four hours of togetherness. Even though I planned to use the time and space to think about those said twenty-four. Analyze each word, dissect each look, relive each touch.

Thankfully, multitasking was my superpower. I could think—and overthink—about my day with Rafe at the same time I refocused on the realities of keeping the Chocolate Lab alive. Not that I didn't trust Mateo to run the café's day-to-day operations—I did, with all my businesslike little heart.

No, it was the realities of keeping the café side of the Chocolate Lab in the black while speeding up the growth of the wholesale coffee bean side. If I didn't kick off the grocery store pilot, and soon, I'd be looking at closing the café next spring.

Maybe that was why a fling with Rafe would be so appealing—and so dangerous.

So dangerous because getting busy could distract me from the true business at hand. Yet so appealing because it would speak to my sensual nature—which seldom got the chance to play off-leash.

But so dangerous because it would offer me a taste of true intimacy, a flavor of a true relationship—complete with a guaranteed date of departure.

Could I do this without getting hurt?

Even more, should I feel guilty about not telling Rafe *all* my history with men? Sure, he'd heard about my bad judgment in trusting Finn's father, and he'd still been there this morning…in my bed.

It was different with Brent. I'd been older and should've been wiser. I'd let the smooth talker into our lives with his promises of love, a home of our own, security for the future.

Only, the dog butt had deserted me at the last moment. Literally, the last moment, at the church. No wonder his family hadn't flown out from New York.

The subtext in his text—yes, text—had shouted loud and clear. *Rose, I can't do this.* I made a decision without talking it through with you. *We're not right for each other.* It's you, not me. *We don't want the same things.* I don't want to be a stepdad to your son, or be a dad, ever. *Sorry. Send me all the bills.* As if it was the money that mattered.

I stilled in the back of the bakery case, clutching a scone a smidge too tightly. How would Rafe react if I told him about how I'd misjudged a guy *again*? Would he think I was looking for more sympathy points? Or worse, would he fear I was expecting *more* from him?

So many questions, so little time. That was where multitasking came in handy—doing my thinking about *personal* business while taking care of *business* business.

I sighed and finished stocking the rest of the bakery goods. At any moment, the kids on the morning shift would start swinging through the door. I faced a packed day and a bazillion-and-one Postits, ranging from getting ready for the Dogwood Treat-n-Treat Saturday to calling Kenzo for more chocolate truffles from his new shop to posting pics from our Howl-o-ween Pumpkin Carving Contest.

Oh, fido, that's right! I need to dump my Post-its on the grocery pilot into the project management software on my laptop.

I reached back in and grabbed a chocolate-chip scone to stuff in my face. *Who says stress-eating doesn't relieve stress?*

Later that night, at least two of my questions had been answered. To be fair, I had already known the answer to one of them.

I was jammed close to Rafe at the Hair of the Dog, helping the Dogwood soccer team celebrate winning its last outdoor match of the season. WAGs and friends—I was firmly in the "friend" category—had been texted to join the guys for beer and pizza after they'd changed out of their soccer gear. I'd had plenty of time to close up the Chocolate Lab, check the dogs at home and walk over. Jen and Katt were there, along with Jean-Luc, Liam, Mateo, Mike and the rest of the crowd.

So, when Liam asked Rafe if he was signing up for the Dogwood team's indoor session scheduled to start in mid-November, I wasn't caught off guard. Although I felt a little awkward for some reason, what with Rafe side-eyeing me and Jen throwing me a pitying look across the table.

"Sorry," Rafe said gruffly and stopped to clear his throat. "Sorry. I don't think it'd be fair to start the season when I couldn't finish it. I've got to leave for my new job in Boise by mid-December."

The entire table quieted down, much to my delight. Not.

Liam, of course, had to ask the question I could already answer on my own. "Oh. You're not staying on at the Chocolate Lab after Mike gets back?" He shot a glance at me before saying, "I thought you were expanding the coffee operations?"

It was a small neighborhood—word got around.

Luckily, Mateo dove in before it could get any *more* awkward and answered for me, "Yeah, things are in the works for growth. However, Rafe has a commitment he made to another coffee company even before he got here. Right, man?"

"Yeah, right," Rafe finally spoke up. "The owners are leaving on a trip to celebrate their fortieth wedding anniversary, and I'm filling in as the coffee roaster and operations manager for at least two months."

Thankfully, conversation resumed around the table. And I took a looong pull on my beer to celebrate that.

Rafe edged closer to me on the bench, if that were possible, and put his warm hand on my knee under the table. I shivered at his touch and got an answer to my second question of the night when he whispered in my ear, "Ready for me to walk you home?"

So we really *were* going to act on our attraction to each other. After yesterday—after sharing histories, setting expectations, sleeping-but-only-sleeping together. I supposed we weren't hiding anything from anybody here if we left together, because…all adults—right?

I just hoped that, this time, I could truly separate the physical from the emotional.

Chapter 23

Rose

"Wait!" I demanded.

"Wait?" Rafe groaned.

"Yes, wait! Look over there," I directed. "Don't you think we need a *little* more privacy?"

No, we weren't still at the Hair of the Dog. Nor were we sprinting down the sidewalk toward my house. We'd even made it past the front porch and into the entry hall before we dropped our jackets and started kissing.

No, now we were half-sitting, half-reclining on my velvety-cushiony couch—to be accurate, I was lying at one end with my head on a plush pillow, and Rafe was pressing his not-inconsiderable weight along my definitely flushed self—getting ready to reignite the kissing portion of the evening.

However, we had an audience. Two sets of amber eyes were gazing at us like we held all the answers to the universe—or more likely the keys to the treat safe.

Pirate and Princess had planted their fannies on the other side of the coffee table and were staring us down. No doubt, they expected their nightly walk and the accompanying array of treats.

Rafe looked over, and we groaned in unison—not the sexy kind, but the frustrated kind.

"Rose," he ordered, pulling off me and standing up, "go upstairs and wait for me on your bed. I'll take care of the dogs and stick them in my apartment for the evening. Do *not* take off any of your clothes," he directed. "I get to do that."

Bossy much? You'd think the guy had done this for a living. Oh, wait. He had.

I knew I didn't have much time, so I jumped off the couch and hustled up to my bedroom. I had a couple of things to do before Rafe returned.

Rafe thundered up the stairs and down the hall, stopping abruptly outside the door.

After lighting the candles, I hadn't been able to catch my breath. My first time in years, and my body had rebelled—face flushing, hands shaking, stomach flip-flopping,

In for a count of five, out for a count of five, in for a count of five...

This exercise had continued for a few minutes until Rafe arrived and got an eyeful of the room—and me.

I liked to prepare in advance—no surprise there! Thanks to all that thinking today, I'd stopped off at home before going to the pub in order to turn up the heat—in more ways than the obvious. Although, I *had* punched up the thermostat in the upstairs hall—it gets chilly in rainy Portland.

I'd gathered candles of all shapes and sizes to scatter around my bedroom. Next, I'd set up my laptop to play my favorite Elvis love songs.

Finally, I'd tugged off the clothes I'd worn all day at the café, along with my comfortable—yet beyond boring—white bra and granny panties. I'd saved just the thing for this occasion, courtesy of my girl Lauren's gift shopping spree. After tucking my curvy self into a black lace balconette bra and the matching cheeky panties, I'd thrown on a fresh T-shirt and jeans.

As a final touch before heading off to the pub, I'd left a pair of black pointed-toe stilettos (from the same spree) by the bed.

I'd figured I was ready for Rafe. And by ready, I meant *ready*.

However, nothing prepared me for the way Rafe looked—and looked at me—when he paused in the doorway to my bedroom.

I'd followed his commands to the letter. I'd gone upstairs— check. I was sitting on the end of my bed—check *check*. I didn't take off my T-shirt or jeans—check, check annnd *check*.

Could it be the fact that I'd exchanged my hot pink sneakers and socks for black five-inch-high stilettos? Or maybe it was the way I was lounging on the bed, leaning back on my elbows, crossing my legs and dangling one stiletto off one foot? Or even the shock of all those candles sizzling the room with their flames?

After all, Elvis was at his seductive best, belting out "Burning Love" in that deep, sultry voice.

Whatever the reason, when I looked at Rafe—arms gripping the doorframe overhead, triceps bulging, T-shirt stretched tight across his chest—and saw the way he was looking at me—eyes hooded over his cobalt stare, heavy brows furrowed in intensity—I questioned whether I was prepared for all the hotness that was him.

So...in for a count of five, out for a count of five, in for a count of five...

I almost stopped breathing when he rumbled, "I see you've been busy," and smiled a gorgeous, full-watt smile.

Instead, I managed to huff out, "You like?"

"I like," he returned and stalked over to stand in front of me.

Abruptly, Rafe reached behind his neck with his right hand and jerked his T-shirt over his head. He flung it toward the door, toed off his shoes and stepped even closer. Partly in defense and partly in awe, I sat up straight, uncrossed my legs, and found myself face-to-face with the man of my dreams. Literally, my dreams—at least recently.

However, "face-to-face" was not entirely accurate. More like face to…sculpted chest and ridged abs with a good view of the muscular vee disappearing down his low-riding, tight-fitting jeans. Yeah, that was more accurate.

I wanted to rub my hands all over his, well, everywhere, but I looked back up when Rafe said, "Here, let's lose this."

He tugged the hem of my T-shirt upward, his knuckles brushing my sides and lingering along my breasts. After a pause, he slid it off the rest of the way and tossed it over his shoulder. On the floor, in the dog bed, over the lampshade. I didn't know and didn't care—as long as it didn't set the place on fire.

I'd closed my eyes at some point. When I opened them, Rafe was leaning over me, thick-lashed eyes glowing in the candlelight. Like they were lit from within. I was close to panting. His chest was flexing with his breaths.

"May I kiss you all over now?" Rafe asked.

I nodded and licked my lips. He glanced down and flashed that blue stare back up to my eyes.

He crowded closer between my legs and trailed his fingertips up my sides again and over the demi-cups of my bra to brush the swells of my breasts. His hands flattened for a moment, palms rubbing my stiff peaks. Suddenly, without any warning, he gripped my shoulders, bent his dark head, and swiped his tongue across first one nipple barely covered by lace and then the other.

I gasped at the same time a hot pulse burst from my breasts to my core.

Rafe pulled his head back and gave a hoarse hum of satisfaction. He slid his hands up my throat to cup my jaw as he leaned

142

down again to lick and kiss between my breasts, that soft hollow between my collarbones and the side of my throat. Without stopping, Rafe wove his fingers through my hair, angled his head and took my mouth in a deep, hot kiss.

I, of course, obliged by tangling my tongue with his.

After a few beats, Rafe broke off our kiss. We stared into each other's eyes, breathing roughly, for a count of ten or maybe a thousand. Moving his hands under my arms and shifting me further onto the bed, he pressed me gently down on my back. He stood and looked down at my feet, now dangling off the bed, still wearing the stilettos.

Rafe contemplated them, seemingly deep in thought, and said, "Oh, these heels are coming off too…and then going right back on. I'm gonna make you come while you're wearing them."

With that, he pulled my stilettos off, one in each hand, and dropped them at the foot of the bed. Next thing I knew, he was leaning over me again, this time to unbutton, unzip and yank off my jeans—all in one motion. Somehow leaving on my damp panties, now riding higher on my cheeks, exposing virtually everything to his view. So I got a little nervous. I closed my knees and started to scoot backward on the bed.

Rafe gripped my knees, pulled them apart and growled, "Stop."

I froze and then flushed. He reached down, snagged my stilettos and gently replaced them on my feet.

Like I was a sexy Cinderella.

Rafe crawled up over my body and lowered himself on his elbows to bury his face in my neck. Inhaling deeply, he muttered *something* about my sweet scent. I was trembling so hard, it affected my hearing. He took my mouth again for a luscious kiss before reaching to lift my left breast out of its lace cup. He thumbed my beaded nub twice and bent down to lick and suck it. He treated my right breast the same, so that both were wet and aching.

I arched my back as Rafe continued his journey downward, stopping to nuzzle my belly and circle his tongue in my belly button. When he reached the top lace edge of my cheeky panties, he sat back on his knees and placed a hot hand on each of my thighs. Spreading them wider, holding them firmly apart. He leaned in and planted wet kisses on the insides of my thighs...so close. He sat back again, unzipped his jeans and pulled out his hard length. No briefs—he'd gone commando.

By this time, I was rolling through shudders and gripping the sheets on either side of my body. An earthy mix of sea salt, musk, sweat and—I don't know, lust?—filled the air.

Rafe stroked his length *hard* while staring at my core.

"Rose," he let out, like it pained him.

"Right here, Rafe," I managed to groan.

"Rose, unless you want me to destroy those pretty panties, push them to one side so I can get at you."

I stopped my frantic sheet-grabbing action and reached over to hold my panties to one side. He made an inarticulate sound and kept pulling on his cock, looking his fill.

After a few seconds, he dipped down to run the flat of his tongue all the way up my seam. He thrust his tongue into my core, alternating with sucking my clit. His pulsing rhythm had me tossing my head back and forth, eyes closed.

I'd let go of my panties by that time. Rafe had curled one or three fingers into my core, reaching deep, finding that particularly sensitive spot. I closed my thighs around his head, felt his stubble rubbing me raw—beard burn for real this time—and shot off like a rocket.

In the midst of my bliss, with all that warmth gushing out of me, Rafe ramped up his licking and sucking and kissing to keep up.

Finally, finally, I could catch my breath. Yes, I was still hot and flushed all over, but at least my heartbeats were slowing down to what passed for normal. When I parted my eyes just the tiniest sliver, Rafe was sitting back on his knees again, swiping the back of one hand across his lips. He met my hazy gaze and gave me the most delectable closed-mouth smile ever.

Did he need to know that was my first all-natural, all-man-induced orgasm in, like, forever? Oh no, there were some things that made me feel too vulnerable to share.

But was I going to return the favor? *Oh, yes.* Especially when his hard, velvety length looked so...*appetizing.*

I think I surprised Rafe when I suddenly pulled my legs in, turned to my side and pushed myself up on my knees to face him. Stilettos still fitted to my feet.

I gripped his shoulders to steady myself and announced, "Turnabout's fair play."

Chapter 24

Rafe

I looked down and searched those gorgeous green eyes that I swore had been glazed over with satisfaction a moment ago. Like in my imagination, or my dreams.

Did Rose somehow think *I* had not been *just as satisfied* when she'd come all over my fingers and face?

Sure, I needed to go take care of myself, and I'd do it in the shower in a few minutes. But first, I needed to nip this line of thinking right in the bud.

So I shook my head and said, "No. No, I'm good. This time was about you. Making you feel good. I'll have *my* turn the next time—and there *will* be a next time. Now let me…" and I trailed off.

I was going to say, "Let me get a warm washcloth to clean you up." But Rose was shaking her finger back and forth in front of my face.

"Not so fast, Rafe. You may want to wait until another time. But what about me? What if I don't want to wait? You know I'm impatient. What if I don't want to wait to make *you* feel good?"

I opened my mouth and closed it again. I had nothing.

Of course, in the time it took for me to figure that out, Rose grabbed my arm and forcibly swung me around to topple me onto my back. Yes, I could've resisted—twice her size, combat training and all that—but why?

She climbed off the bed for a quick minute to lose both her bra and her panties. She was back up in no time and straddling my thighs—still wearing those fucking heels. I thought she was going to wrap those plush lips around my cock—and believe me, that would have made me feel *real* good. I was close to erupting at that point, despite my earlier claims I could wait. Especially since I had a front-row view of her beautiful, tear-shaped breasts. But Rose was full of surprises.

Instead, she leaned over me to rub both palms up my chest and down over my biceps and forearms—again and again. Her tight tips brushed all the way up my groin to my chest each time. Her tongue popped out to lap at my nipples and my neck on the way by.

I may have groaned once or twice.

She leaned back and yanked my jeans further down my hips. She rebalanced on her knees and swayed way over to grab a foil packet from her nightstand. In one swift motion, she brought it to her mouth and ripped the top off with her teeth.

Fuck. My woman was prepared. I'd stuffed a few of those in my jeans pocket when I took the dogs back to my apartment—I'd even made a special trip outside the neighborhood to buy new ones today. Suddenly, I'd gotten an attack of the "shys"—fucking new for me. Didn't want to seem overly confident we'd go all the way tonight.

Nothing shy about Rose.

She pulled out the condom and used one hand to stroke, stroke, stroke my arousal upward. I swallowed hard when she swooped in to lick a drop of precum off the tip. She pinched the end of the condom, snugged it into place and carefully smoothed it all the way down. After smiling and muttering, "I guessed right," she rose on her knees above me.

By this time, I was the one grabbing the sheets on either side of me—rather than going with my first urge—grabbing her hips and driving her down swift and hard. Rose needed to be the one in charge, the one setting the pace. And she needed to come *again* before it was my turn.

Regardless of what she thought was fair play.

Rose steadied herself with one hand on my abs and notched me in place. She lowered herself, one tormenting inch at a time, until she was fully seated. She whimpered at that point, and I groaned in response.

We rested together like that for a minute or ten while she adjusted to me, and I absorbed everything that was hot and tight and wet about her.

I found my words.

"Rose. Babe. I could stay like this forever. But so-help-me-god, if you don't start movin' soon, I'm gonna take matters into my own hands."

At that, Rose opened her eyes and speared me with their green power.

"I got this, sweetheart," she declared. She braced her hands on my hips and rose on her knees, releasing me almost the entire way. I started to protest, and she ground back down, fast and hard.

She did that again and again, and the friction was fucking incredible. I shut it and went along for the ride, although I couldn't resist reaching up to palm her breasts. My grunts mixed with her moans. Her breathing went ragged. I knew she was there when she shouted, "Rafe!" and came down hard to stay as she throbbed around me.

I was thinking *my turn now*. Or maybe I wasn't thinking at all. Maybe I just lost my mind.

I reared up, still deep in Rose, and wrapped my arms around her shoulders and hips. I rolled us over so I was on the top and she was on the bottom. She cried out, and I covered her mouth with my own, twisting her tongue with mine.

She shuddered and kissed me back. Thank fuck—I didn't want to stop. But I would have.

I couldn't hold back any longer and started to move, thrusting in, pulling out. Rose squeezed her knees on either side of me and lifted her hips to meet mine, setting a hard-to-break rhythm. We locked eyes and wouldn't, couldn't look away. Until, finally, I jammed mine shut when liquid fire surged through me—and I buried myself in her heat.

I finished with a *roar* and collapsed. For a minute. Then I realized what I'd done.

"Oh, shit. Sorry, sorry. I must be crushing you."

I started to shift up and pull out...and she tugged me back down.

"Don't move," she said. "I'm savoring the moment."

I stopped and raised an eyebrow.

Rose looked up at me with hazy, hooded eyes, before going on, "Yeah, like a creamy piece of dark chocolate. You know what I mean. Savoring."

I smiled and sank back into her, resting some of my bulk on her and most of it on my forearms. We stayed that way for a time, a good long time, until I rolled us over on our sides. Still facing each other, still connected. Still *home*.

Later, much later, after Rose had dozed off, I got out of bed. I soaked a washcloth in warm water and liquid soap for the gentle cleanup and secured the covers around her to keep her warm. After hurrying downstairs to get the dogs from my place, we three together did our nightly perimeter check of the entire house—lights, doors, windows—the usual drill. No alarm system yet, but that was coming. The two trotted into the bedroom, noses held high at all the unfamiliar smells, and settled into Pirate's bed with no fuss.

I slipped under the covers to gather a sleeping Rose into my arms…and nudged something…spiky…with my feet. She was still wearing the fucking (great) high heels. I debated whether to leave them on but decided to dive down and pull the things off. Figured my feet would keep hers warm…since I always ran hot.

Rose stayed asleep through all this, and I soon followed her.

Chapter 25

Rose

I'd been distracted this past week-and-a-half. And by *distracted* I meant sidetracked from my usual customary and regimented life by this non-relationship *thing* I had going with Rafe.

A *thing* that involved not only body-and-mind-blowing sex but also the *little things* I didn't know I'd been missing in my daily life.

Like starting the morning with a hot breakfast and a hotter kiss. Like hearing Rafe let loose and laugh like crazy when Pirate and Princess got the zoomies. Like handing out Halloween candy with Rafe agreeing—albeit grudgingly—to wear the angel halo headband while I stuck on the devil's horns.

Like each of us claiming an end of the couch to sit and read—not talk, not kiss—just read (well, maybe a kiss here or there). Like taking the dogs out for that last walk before bedtime…and talking away as we headed to the park—or maybe I was doing the talking and Rafe was doing the listening.

Yeah, little things like that.

Yet still, I never expected that Jen and Mateo would take advantage of my distractedness to start the ball rolling on security systems for both the café and my house.

I should have suspected something this morning when I'd ducked under my bed to retrieve my stilettos—and discovered Dad's bat was missing.

Was their partner-in-crime sharing my bed?

Sure, I'd been dragging my feet on getting a professional alarm system for the Chocolate Lab. Right after the break-in, I'd met with a couple of security companies Jen had recommended from her contacts in the real estate community. She knew people who knew people since she staged homes for sale.

Since then, I hadn't had the bandwidth to compare options and make a decision. More to the point, I hadn't wanted to fork out the money, given all my other struggles to keep the café going.

So that little project had been put on the back burner.

Or so I'd thought, until today, when I came in lugging café supplies to find Mateo standing with the rep from one of the companies. The guy had a clipboard with an order form and was making notes like mad. They both turned when I fast-walked over, big smiles on their faces. Jen saw *my* face and jumped up from one of the tables to join us.

Before I could say anything, she headed me off with, "Rose, I'm so glad you're here. We Protect You has offered you a huge discount for installing security systems in both the Chocolate Lab and your home—it's their two-for-one, end-of-the-year special. And a discounted monthly monitoring fee is part of the package deal!"

Mateo put in, "I know you'll like this too—I threw in coffee service at our special friends-and-family rate for their call center. Right, Bert?"

Jen hurtled right on. "They even have an opening in their schedule in a week and can install everything in one day. Right, Bert?"

Mateo didn't lose a beat. "We've worked up the specs for here, and Jen is meeting Bert at your place this afternoon for the same thing. We wanted to save you the time and trouble."

Jen wound up the pitch. "They've promised to have a contract ready for your review in a couple of days. Right, Bert?"

Of course, Bert, being no dummy, was nodding like a bobble-head doll. He also knew when to make an exit and quickly said his goodbyes.

I soon realized we were going to have this "discussion" in front of several attentive parties with their ears pricked up—and those were just our regular customers, let alone their doggos. Feeling all those ears and eyes on us, we headed back to the meeting room for some privacy. To give them credit, the pair had their arguments ready.

Mateo went first. "Rose, you know it's wise to protect all this café and roastery equipment from vandalism. And now you're going to have this huge coffee bean inventory on hand with the contract for the grocery stores. It makes good business sense."

He added, looking all hurt with those puppy-dog eyes, "I thought you gave me the responsibility to make these decisions when you made me café manager."

Jen stuck her oar in. "Girl, I get worried about you living alone in that big ole house. Burglaries and home invasions always ramp up this time of year."

Then they hit me with the double—actually this time, triple—whammy.

Jen took the lead again by saying firmly, "Finn is expecting you to have the alarms in place by the time he comes home for Thanksgiving. Your mom and dad would always put your safety first over finances. And you can't count on Rafe living nearby after he leaves in December. Let us help you get this done!"

I opened my stubborn mouth to argue and…shut it. It seemed that the stress of the last several months was messing with my brain. I clearly, *clearly* remember Mom getting on my case about trying to do everything myself.

Needing help is not a weakness, sweetie. Giving people a chance to help is a sure sign of strength. Just say "thank you."

For Jen and Mateo, even though they'd ganged up on me, I added huge hugs to my thank yous. Afterward, I crossed the hall to the roastery to confront their accomplice.

I leaned against the locked roastery door, arms crossed, waiting for Rafe to finish the loud roasting cycle. His back was to me, and he had no idea I was there. After he dumped the hot coffee beans into the cooling tray, he started to turn around—and that's when I caught him by surprise.

But Rafe being Rafe, he didn't jump or jerk or portray shock like any other normal human being. *Huh. Probably all that army training.* Instead, he stopped, raised an eyebrow and got a big grin on his too-tough-but-handsome face.

Until I said, "You know, there's usually a punishment for theft."

His grin dropped like a lead balloon, his entire face pulled into a frown, and I swore he turned white under all that stubble.

Did he think I was serious? Did he feel guilty? Did he think I was mad at him? Whatever was going on, I needed to set him straight.

In my haste to get to him, I stumbled. Luckily, he unfroze in time and caught me in his arms. I looked up into his stricken face and gently pressed my hands to his cheeks.

"It's okay, Rafe. Really it is. I'm not upset at you for stealing my dad's bat from underneath the bed." I'd started babbling and couldn't stop. "I forgot I put it back there. You've moved in, at least for now, and I won't need it. At least for now."

Rafe narrowed his eyes at that, and I went to town. "No, no, what I mean is that I won't need the bat at all, thanks to the new alarm systems. And I know you had a hand in working with Jen and Mateo to get that all going. And to strong-arm, er, negotiate such a good price. I'm grateful, and…and…"

Rafe pushed his fingers against my lips and said, "Rose. Stop talking."

I did, but only for a moment. I had a diabolical idea. "My idea of punishment is actually something pretty sweet."

He leaned down to kiss me hard before saying, "Go on, talk."

I had to laugh, like he was going to ever stop me. I wrapped my arms around his neck and pulled his head back down to me.

After giving him a peck on the lips, I started, "I know you generally don't eat pastries or cakes or candy or pie or sweets of any kind." The man either didn't like the sugary side of life or had freakishly strong willpower.

"Therefore," I paused to swipe the tip of my tongue across his lips, "your punishment for grand theft bat will be…"

I went in for a full-contact, tongue-twisting kiss before continuing. Or trying to continue, because Rafe was getting the idea and starting to "help." When I wrenched myself away, we were both a little breathless.

"…will be to undergo a chocolate-truffle-tasting challenge, all in service of our holiday gift tins."

Rafe angled back down and grumbled against my lips, "Where and when do I need to report for this so-called punishment?"

I was able to gasp out, "Next Tuesday, right here in the roastery, after we close and lock ourselves in," before he invaded my mouth.

I happily stopped talking and settled in to enjoy our non-verbal communication.

Chapter 26

Rafe

Fuck. I was a paranoid fucker. If I kept reacting the way I did, I was going to screw up this time with Rose. I was already lying to her by not sharing my entire story.

Omitting certain facts is a lie by any other name—right?

It was late Sunday morning, and I was over at Pete's, replacing the shocks on his old beater. For a guy who'd always prided himself on owning the most up-to-date roasting equipment, he sure had a thing for junk cars.

The problem was he was getting too old and too arthritic to get down on the creeper and slide under the chassis. Of course, Pete would never admit to that, and I'd never say it to his face. However, he knew I knew cars and liked to keep my hand in, so to speak. When he had something tricky to fix (read: hard to get to), he'd call me. I'd come with my tools and stay afterward for a beer and a talk.

And did I ever need to talk this shit out.

Pete was the only one in Portland—well, anywhere—who knew everything about me. The good. The bad. And the criminally ugly. Although even I wasn't dumb enough to think I'd be held liable twenty-five years later for boosting cars as a juvie. That statute of limitations had long run out.

I needed to get Pete's advice on whether to tell Rose everything. Every *fucking* thing, including the real reason I started the enlistment process the week after I turned eighteen.

Rose was trusting me—*me*—with her beautiful body, her feelings, her hopes, her secrets, herself. And I didn't deserve her trust. I wasn't *worthy* of her trust.

I needed Pete to give it to me straight, to confirm what I already felt in my gut. He'd known Rose since she was young, knew everything she'd gone through. He'd do the right thing and tell me to be on my way before I broke her heart. And mine.

Job done, I rolled out from under the car in time to see Pete walk down the driveway, Princess trotting alongside. He lifted one hand to show two long-necked beer bottles dangling between his knuckles and motioned to his front porch. I stood, wiped my hands on a rag, snagged one of the bottles and followed them to settle with a groan on the padded porch swing. Another reason I didn't flick Pete any shit about getting older—I had my share of aches and pains from the life I'd led.

Princess stretched out in front of me and heaved a sigh. I started to take a strong pull from the icy bottle when Pete said, "Okay, son. What's got your boxers in a bunch?"

I choked and reared back from my bottle.

Fuck, was it that obvious I had something on my mind? Probably. Usually, I had no trouble talking with Pete about anything—I guessed my grunts and one-word answers and tight expression had given me away. I wouldn't want him to think I was mad at him for the world. And I *was* here to get his thoughts about what, if anything, to tell Rose.

I didn't know where to begin.

Pete solved that problem for me in short order. "Is this about Rose? You and Rose?"

I eyed him for a moment while I finally took a swallow of my beer. "How did you know that?"

"I hear things," he shared. "I see things. And I know you."

I raised my eyebrows. *Ahhh…right, Liliana.*

"So tell me," he continued, "when are you coming back from Boise?"

Pete was always one for cutting to the chase.

"Nah…I wasn't planning on it. Just got a call from that guy in northern California for a gig after Boise. Maybe you'll have a line on some other jobs coming up."

Pete frowned. "But I thought all that was before Rose…before you two got close. Isn't she worth coming back for?"

"Since you know me and my history so well, do you think that's a good idea?" I asked.

"What the hell are you talking about? Your military record?"

We were getting circular with all the questions, and I was frustrated. I jumped up, setting the swing in motion and startling my pup. I paced the porch in front of Pete, getting all worked up.

"Yes. No. I couldn't keep my kids safe in the sandbox. No matter what I tried."

"Bullshit," Pete interrupted. "You can't put that on your shoulders. You know as well as I do that half the deaths over there were due to IEDs."

Still, you can't help but feel responsible when it's your kids, your unit.

I shook it off. "But, no. I'm talking about before. With the gang in Oakland."

"That's water under the bridge," he protested. "That's when you were a teenager. That's not you today. Rose must know that."

"I haven't told her anything about that part of my life…yet."

"What! Any of it?"

"Well, yeah, the earlier part. We talked about my mamma, her death, my time in foster care...." I trailed off. *Well, not the dark times, but she didn't need to know that shit.*

"Rafe, tell her the rest. I know Rose, I knew her folks. Good people. I was around helping her dad start the roastery when she dropped out of school to come home and have Finn. Rose isn't going to get all judgmental on your ass and think you're a bad guy."

I was still pacing back and forth, feeling my heart thumping harder and harder. *I'm too young for a heart attack, right?*

"That's the whole point, Pete. She *should* see me as the bad guy. If it were just about stealing cars, that'd be one thing. Bad enough, jail time if I'd been caught, but not hurting anybody."

I shook my head and slumped back down on the porch swing.

"How could she ever trust me again?" I whispered. "How would she feel about me if she knew I'd almost beat somebody to death?"

There was the heart of the matter.

It didn't matter that my brothers and I had been in danger. It didn't matter that the guy who'd surprised us when we were boosting his Chevy had popped his knife. What mattered was that I'd fucked him up when he'd attacked us, and I hadn't even called the medics.

For me, that was the tipping point. The shame if Mamma had been alive. I got out of there by enlisting in the service. Outta the gang, outta Oakland, outta that life.

I hadn't told Pete this shameful thing right away, either. No, it had taken a couple of years, some real-life war stories over beers and the realization that Pete was going to be the closest thing to a father before I opened up to him. I was still amazed he'd accepted me "as is."

But it was different with Rose. Rose deserved a better man than me. I wasn't worthy of her. And I damned sure didn't want to be responsible for her just so I could fall down on the job again.

Pete knew it too, but he also believed in redemption. In forgiveness. In the power of love to solve everything. That was the way he was built.

So he wasn't going to tell me what I needed to hear. That I could have this short time with Rose, safeguard her as best I could. That then I needed to get the hell gone so she could find a good man, a better man, for the long term.

Though the thought of Rose with another man made my gut wrench. *Get a fucking grip, man—it's gonna happen.*

"Rafe. Son," Pete said quietly. "Don't make any decisions about Rose without Rose. I bet you're not alone in this…this…whatever you call this thing you've got going on with her. So talk to Rose and trust *her* to do the right thing."

I nodded my head slowly. He was right. I *should* talk to her, *should* tell her how I feel. *But I had to be honest with myself—could I do that when I was so afraid?*

Pete, smart guy that he was, got off the heavy-heavy. "Stay for lunch? Got the fixings for sandwiches if you're interested."

"Sure," I agreed. I knew the old man was lonely, so I'd stay, and we'd talk some more about…other things.

Chapter 27

Rose

"Hang on a moment, Lauren." I laid my phone on the dryer and reached down to snag a crumpled, blue-colored square from the wastebasket. When I straightened it out, the words "clean up flower beds for winter" emerged, in my handwriting.

I glanced over to the mirror above the laundry sink. Blank spaces stuck out like sore thumbs among the orderly columns of Post-its. Columns usually stacked full with my Post-its for yard and house maintenance tasks.

What the fido?

It was Tuesday morning, and I was catching up with my girl before running out to do some errands and head to the café. Lauren's disembodied voice echoed in the utility room, asking questions like *What's going on?* and *Are you okay?*

I snatched up the phone and informed her, "We're moving this convo to the backyard. I gotta check something out."

Pirate and Princess raced up to me when I stepped out onto the back patio. They were sure it was walk time, treat time or chase-the-ball time. I dispensed some ear and chest rubs, and they allowed me to push past them to look around the yard.

"That—that—that sneak." I gasped. "He's got some nerve."

I swung around and…yep, further evidence of cunning. The storm windows were installed on all the windows on the back of the house, which led me to think….

"Rose Eleanor Connolly, if you don't tell me what's going on right now, I'm hanging up and calling the police," my friend shouted in my ear.

"I knew it was a mistake giving Rafe a key to the house."

"Why? What's he done? Do we need to get up there now?"

Lauren and Finn were driving up from California together early the week of Thanksgiving. Two weeks were too long for us to go without dissecting our lives in the most normal of times—and with all we had going on, this was anything but. We'd been talking for a few minutes when I'd noticed the Post-it in the trash.

"No, girl, it's fine. I'm fine," I reassured her. "Rafe stole some of the Post-its from my household to-do list and…did them. That's all."

Silence filled the moment. Lauren being Lauren, it didn't last long.

"You mean you're all twerked out of shape because Rafe, this muscly hot guy you've been sharing your bed with, did something nice for you? Without you asking?"

Huh. When you put it like that…

"Okay, okay, you've got a point there, judge," I admitted. "I guess I'm more annoyed at myself for not noticing. Rafe must think I'm a real dope for not thanking him by now."

"From what you've told me, he doesn't seem like the type of guy looking for thanks. Or expecting something in return."

"Yeah, that's true. I trust him to *not* have an ulterior motive."

Lauren remembered the dark days after David ghosted me when some college "friends" had come right out and said that I'd slept with him in exchange for good grades. And post-Brent, I'd agonized over the idea that he'd just wanted to get in my pants.

"You have a lot on your plate right now, Rose," she noted gently. "And this is your first holiday season without your mom."

I parked my heinie on top of the picnic table and set the phone beside me. It was sprinkling, and I could see Pirate and Princess chasing each other around the yard. It looked like both would be due for their favorite thing—towel rubdowns—before I took off.

Lauren waited patiently on the other end of the line while I sorted my thoughts.

Mom loved everything about this time of year. Throwing our Family-and-Friendsgiving party. Dressing up Pirate for the Turkey Dog Jog. Decorating the café and our house until there was hardly a square inch left bare. Baking and gifting a crazy array of holiday cookies and Swedish breads. Leading Karaoke and Karoling at the Chocolate Lab, even though she couldn't carry a note.

I had a choice here. I could either sink into my sadness—and drag Finn, Mateo, my girls and maybe Rafe down with me—or count on my friends and family to lift me up and help me make it through this holiday season.

Lauren cleared her throat, reminding me she was still there. At the same time, the dogs ran up to me and shook themselves head to tail, spraying raindrops all over.

I yelped and came back to earth. Picking up our convo where we'd left off—knowing my girl would understand even though it'd been a good five minutes—I said, "Yes, I've got a lot going on, and yes, I'm missing Mom more than ever. But I know I'm doggone lucky too."

"How so?"

"Because I'm *not* alone in dealing with my life," I pointed out. "In fact, I'm probably one of the most 'un-alone' people you know."

Although I had to ask myself, can you still feel lonely even if you're never alone?

Lauren started laughing. She got it. I had friends and family and honorary family and faithful dogs and a cat or two coming out of my wazoo. Even a sweet, if overprotective and definitely temporary, gorgeous guy.

"And once you get yourself and my baby boy up here, I'll be even less alone."

Now she was snorting. Probably because my *baby boy* was eighteen, six-foot-one and 187 pounds. I chose this moment to continue, "Speaking of Rafe…"

She snorted harder and louder, if that were possible.

I managed to talk over her. "How is that little Sherlock Holmes project coming along?"

Since Lauren lived in Sonoma Valley, at least for now, and did marketing slash market research for a living, she was perfectly positioned for a little detective work. Perfect too, because…bestie.

She stopped laughing. "I should have something by Thanksgiving. I used some online search tools to find people with the Amato name in both Oakland and San Francisco. Good news? There are a couple dozen men, along with phone numbers and addresses. Sorta bad news? No info on their ages. Another way to narrow down the list is to search Facebook or Insta, but I'm not sure older men do social media much.

"Oh, and I was also able to locate the death certificate for his mom, which, unfortunately, didn't have any info on her family." Lauren paused. "Are you *sure* you don't want to let Rafe know what we're doing and see if he remembers his uncle's name?"

"I'm sure," I claimed with more confidence than I felt. "Please, please, keep on researching, and we'll figure out what to do when you come up."

Rafe might get mad at me for sticking my nose into his personal life. I'd already violated his trust by sharing some details with

Lauren. Maybe it was the loss of my own mom that prompted all this…intrusion.

But it was a risk I was willing to take. Was it wrong that I wanted to give Rafe something *tangible*, something he'd never pursue on his own?

Anyway, that was the way I justified what we were doing. I could live with his anger…especially since I wouldn't actually be *living* with it, once he left.

"I'll do my best, girlfriend—don't you worry," Lauren assured me. "One last thing. Sleeping arrangements."

Shih tzu. In my weekly call with Finn, I'd forgotten to mention that Rafe had virtually (and by virtually, I meant literally) moved in with me. Or maybe that was a fib that I'd forgotten.

I'd been stalling for time, deciding what to do. Now I realized it was a no-brainer. I needed to be "Mom-with-a-capital-M" for my son this holiday season. I had faith in Rafe that he would understand.

And there was a little part of me—not a kind part, but a pragmatic part—that needed to separate people who were staying in my life from people who were leaving.

"Yes, right, okay. Sleeping arrangements. You're going to have my old bedroom, and Finn will keep his own room this time around." In the past, we'd shifted Finn to the couch in the basement family room so Lauren or other guests could use his bedroom.

"I'm going to ask Rafe to move back to the apartment, at least while Finn's home. And we'll take a little break from nocturnal activities for the duration."

Lauren snickered. "Your kiddo's pretty smart. I think he'll pick up on the fact that you two have grown…closer."

"Hmm…maybe. We're not much for PDA, and we're trying to hold the smoldering looks to a minimum."

She snorted one last time and said, "All righty, girl. Mother knows best."

"Kiss Baby for me!" With that, we ended our call with promises to talk next week. I let the dogs in for their rubdowns and headed out for my errands.

My first stop was Johanssen's Meat Market, where I placed an order for a twenty-five-pound turkey *and* a seven-pound bone-in ham. We were expecting a crowd for our annual Family-and-Friendsgiving dinner. And that wasn't even counting those who were non-meat-or-poultry eaters in our group.

I was also dropping off a stack of registration forms and checks for the Turkey Dog Jog. Ever since third-generation Erik Johanssen had started making turkey dogs nearly twenty years ago, his family had been holding the charity event the Saturday after Thanksgiving in Dogwood Park.

We were one of the early sponsors, and the Chocolate Lab was also a place where people could turn in their forms and fees. Sure, folks could now register and pay online, but many of our customers were older and preferred to do things "the old-fashioned way" as Miss Ada liked to say.

The Turkey Dog Jog had never been publicized outside our neighborhood—no need since there were more than enough entrants and sponsors from canine-crazy Dogwood to make the event a success.

Finn was enthusiastic about doing the honors with Pirate this year. He'd probably dress up the big galoot in some sort of fun and funny costume like Mom used to do. Up to Finn to engineer that when he got home.

Hmm. Wonder if Rafe would like to enter Princess in the Turkey Dog Jog too? Or would she be nervous around all the other dogs? Maybe Finn and Rafe could walk Pirate and Princess together, since the two seemed to be joined at the hip these days. I'd be busy helping out at the check-in table, but Rafe would see other people he knew there too. He wasn't shy…at all.

I'd talk with him about the idea tomorrow. I had plans for tonight.

Involving my last stop at Chocolat Je t'aime.

Chapter 28

Rose

I almost changed my mind about punishing Rafe with a chocolate-truffle-tasting challenge after all his help at the house.

Almost.

This year, we were introducing the Chocolate Lab gift tins and trying a new cross-marketing scheme—offering chocolate truffles from Kenzo's new shop along with other gear, coffee and goodies from the café.

Sure, I could've asked Jen or Mica or Liliana or Katt or even Mateo to taste-test the samples. But what was the fun in that?

Instead, I'd devised a *blind* chocolate-truffle-tasting challenge for Rafe, based on the blind wine-tasting events Jean-Luc held every once in a while at his shop.

One time, my girls and I had gotten oh-so-toasted when we'd demanded multiple "tastes" of each wine—disguised in brown paper bags—so we could figure out which wine matched which description on the scorecard. *Was that the first time that Lauren met Jean-Luc? Have to ask her when she gets here for Thanksgiving...*

Anyway. Was I hoping to get Rafe drunk on chocolate? Shake him out of his seriousness? Get him to reveal his secrets under the influence? Maybe. Sometimes he seemed too guarded for his own good, even with me.

Or maybe I wanted to live out some more fantasies before he left next month. Guys could have fantasies too, right?

Now I stood in the middle of the roastery floor, hands on hips, surveying my handiwork. I'd chased all the kids out after closing so I could clean up—and set up—on my own.

Nine chocolate truffles paraded around the revolving oak cupping table, each covered by an anonymous white box with a number on the top and a label hidden on the bottom.

A blindfold—aka Chocolate Lab dog scarf—sat rolled up on the table, since I couldn't rely on Rafe to keep his eyes shut. A raspberry filling here, slivers of candied ginger there, a coconut coating everywhere would be dead giveaways.

A score card listing each chocolate truffle by its fancy name and description rested on my stool. Once Rafe used his magic tasting skills to tease out the ingredients (because roasters cupped—that is, taste-tested—new coffees all the time), I'd write its number next to the closest matching description.

Shot glasses of water and espresso ambled through the middle of the round table, ready to serve as palate-cleansers between truffle bites. Yes, I did consider the cumulative effects of sugar and caffeine, but the whole...experience was going to be a guaranteed rush anyway.

Last but not least, two lamps from home shed a soft glow, balanced by shadows in the corners of the windowless room. Off with the glaring overhead lights, on with the intimate vibe. Well, as much as I could get in this space with the ginormous roaster looming and burlappy bean bags huddling on nearby pallets.

Once Rafe arrived, I'd lock and set the alarms for the three outside doors. I'd also lock the roastery door to the hall—and check it twice. I was taking no chances with intruders of any sort this time around.

"What's all this?"

I jumped a mile. *Stealthy, thy name is Rafe.*

Whipping around, I found him leaning against the hallway doorframe. He raised one eyebrow and moved into the room, looking around. I was speechless for once, and Rafe took advantage by walking right into my personal space.

He buried one hand in my hair and grasped my shoulder with the other, pulling me to him for a kiss. And not just a haven't-seen-you-since-I-fed-and-walked-the-dogs peck on the lips. No, this was an in-your-mouth-and-planning-to-stay-a-while kiss, complete with tongue lashings.

Needless to say, I remained speechless...and a little breathless.

Rafe finally leaned back. I followed his lips before I knew what I was doing and gradually opened my eyes.

He smiled down at me, and I allowed myself a moment to feast on all that was Rafe. His short hair sparkling from the rain, his thick brows slanting over those intense cobalt eyes, his dark end-of-day stubble covering his strong jaw, just a hint of that rough scar showing through.

My face, my shoulders, my entire body relaxed under his warm gaze.

We stood there for I didn't know how long. Coming out of my haze, I shook myself. I grabbed his hand and led him over to the cupping table.

"This, Rafe, is your official blind chocolate-truffle-tasting challenge."

I rotated the tabletop so that the chocolate truffle in the box labeled "#1" faced him.

"Sit. Stay. And no peeking. I'll be right back after I lock and alarm the outer doors."

I waited a moment for his response—a grin this time *and* a chin lift—before I left to take care of the café doors. When I returned, I locked the hallway door—*another knowing grin*—and the outside roastery door.

Rafe was sitting on the stool where I'd left him, legs braced on the floor. I got distracted for a moment remembering those long muscular jean-less legs tangled around mine this morning. When my eyes rose to meet his and he smirked, my face got all hot. Probably hot pink to match the pink dog collar in the Chocolate Lab logo.

Guess I have to show him who's boss...at least in this little blind chocolate-truffle-tasting scenario.

I strolled up behind him and reached over to snag the blindfold from the table. My chest may have pressed against his back in the process, and that may have been why he stilled. He stayed that way...still, that is...while I tied the rolled-up scarf around his eyes.

"Rose. Babe," Rafe growled. "I don't like to be kept in the dark."

Oh, so serious, for the man of few words. And why did those few words cause another hot flush...elsewhere?

"Rafe," I whispered close to his right ear. "This chocolate-truffle-tasting punishment is all in good fun. You'll describe each truffle, based on *only* your talented coffee-tasting tongue, not your eyesight. I'll match your words to one of the truffle descriptions on my scorecard. At the end, we'll see how many you got right."

"Will there be a reward for the most right guesses?" Ahhh... now he was catching on...to the point of the challenge. Other than helping me narrow my choices of truffles for our gift tins.

"You'll have to wait and see." Literally. Wait and see what I was wearing under my usual T-shirt and jeans.

"I'm game," he grunted out.

Oops, did I say that last part out loud?

171

All righty then. I picked up the scorecard and settled my heinie on the stool next to Rafe. I opened the first little white box…and saw the not-so-little chocolate truffle inside. *Dalmatian. I was going to need a knife to cut this hulk in half.*

"Rafe, hang tight for a minute. I have to go get a knife from the kitchen."

"Nope."

"Nope?"

"Nope. You don't need to go anywhere."

"This thing is huge." I paused and waited for the "that's what she said" moment. Not forthcoming, so I guessed Sergeant Amato had missed out on *The Office* overseas.

Instead, he said, "I have a knife you can use. If you can pull it out of its sheath. Unfold it carefully. Watch it because it's honed sharp. And sterilize it afterward."

How could I turn down that gracious offer? From a man of apparently many words, at least when it came to my safety.

I slid from my stool and crowded between his legs. He held still, again, while I dragged the knife out of the leather holder on his belt and unfolded it. Rafe was right—it had a keen edge and looked ready for business. I was surprised he was letting me use it for something as…as…*frivolous* as our tasting game.

I turned around to the table and startled a little when he wrapped his arms loosely around my waist. *To steady me—right?* Pinching chocolate truffle number one out of its box, I sat it down on the bare wood. Ever so slowly and, yes, carefully, I cut that big boy in half. I laid the knife down with the blade pointed away from me and spun back to face Rafe, truffle bite in hand.

"Open your mouth," I commanded. Before I could push the chocolatey goodness through his lips, he reached up and circled my wrist.

"Wait."

"Why?"

"Part of tasting is smelling." He inhaled deeply, his chest expanding to meet mine. When he breathed out, I leaned in to catch his warmth on my lips.

He opened up, and I placed the truffle half on his tongue. He chewed for a few seconds, swallowed and swiped his tongue around his lips to get any stray bits.

"Are you ready?" Rafe asked.

"For what?" I mumbled, a tad...hazy at this point.

"For me to tell you what's in this truffle thing," he grumped out.

"Oh. Yeah." I had to get with the program here. "You sound pretty confident. Go for it."

I leaned over and grabbed the scorecard and pen from my stool while Rafe started to describe what he'd tasted.

"Besides the dark chocolate, I picked up notes of something floral. It's spicy too—I think there's cardamom. Maybe a dash of cayenne. I also got some coconut—not the actual stuff, but like extract or oil."

He paused, rubbing his lips together. "Good thing it's rolled in cocoa powder. Offsets all that sweetness."

It was a match, almost word for word, with the description of the Lavender De-luscious Truffle. But I couldn't let his tasting talent go to his head.

"Not bad for your first challenge, Master Roaster. Let's see how you do on a new one."

Rafe muttered something about a "tough audience" while I marked "#1" in the blank beside that truffle's name.

"Before we move on, would you like a shot of espresso or some water to clear your palate?"

"The espresso...no, wait! Only if you didn't put a fuck-ton of sugar in it—or any, for that matter."

"Wow, suspicious much?"

"Well, what do you expect? I can't see a damn thing, and I didn't pull the shots myself."

Ooh, somebody was getting testy.

"No worries," I reassured him in an overly sweet tone of voice. "See for yourself...well, if you could see."

I handed Rafe one of the espresso shot glasses. While he downed that, I shoved the other truffle half into my mouth, chewed (de-luscious!) and chugged my shot. Could anyone say sugar *and* caffeine high?

We put the blind tasting routine on repeat three more times... with one variation for the last one.

Rather than placing the truffle bit on Rafe's tongue by hand, I positioned it on *my* tongue and made the transfer.

He grunted in surprise but recovered and attempted a full-on French kiss. I turned my cheek just as fast—although he left a smear of chocolate there—and pulled back to demand a description.

He grumbled a bit but moved on from there. His talented tongue was on a roll, teasing out ingredients that matched the written descriptions.

When I tried to turn back to the table to cut up the rest of the truffles—four down, five to go—I couldn't.

Was it my imagination, or were Rafe's thighs caging my hips more tightly? It was getting humid in here too. Maybe I'd forgotten to turn down the heat when I locked the doors?

Or was it the sugar-caffeine-Rafe rush getting me all hot... and bothered?

I didn't get answers to my questions because Rafe ripped the blindfold off his eyes, grabbed my hips and lifted me onto the table. All in one movement, I swore—although I may have been a little distracted while yelping my fool head off.

He nudged my knees apart so he could stand between them. Leaning to my left side, he swept the truffle boxes and shot glasses away to make room on the table...for me. I didn't know what happened to his knife, but the shot glasses? Good thing those sturdy little guys would bounce, not break.

"Rose. Lift your arms," Rafe demanded, all brisk and abrupt.

I was in an obeying mood—or maybe I was getting hotter by the second. The moment I raised my arms, he whipped my T-shirt off and threw it toward the roaster.

Rafe followed this with a "lie back" command, but before I could move, he pressed me gently down, using one hand between my breasts. The other hand cushioned the back of my head. Once I was lying flat, he stood up straight again and made short work of my shoes and socks. When it came to my jeans and my new hot pink cheekies, he yanked them both off in one go.

By this time, I was staring up at the high roastery ceiling and surrendering...to an attack of the giggles. I couldn't help it.

Maybe I was light-headed or...or...lighthearted, for once in recent memory.

Evidently, I didn't put out enough serious vibes for Rafe.

"I'll give you something to laugh about," he growled. He reached to grab both my arms and pulled them together over my head. The next thing I knew, he wrapped the scarf around my wrists and tied it in a tight, but not painfully tight, knot. Hooking his hands under my knees, he lifted them up so my heels sat on the edge of the table.

Yeah, I felt a little exposed, even though I was still wearing my balconette bra—new and lacy and hot pink because, you know, matching.

Not afraid, though—I trusted Rafe. *And* I trusted myself that I'd locked all the doors.

"Turnabout's fair play. Although this isn't a *chocolate-truffle-tasting* challenge. This is a *frozen-Rose-tasting* challenge, and I'm the sole judge."

I stopped giggling and started shivering. I didn't think it was from the sugar-caffeine double-whammy.

"Hmm. Where's my knife?" He was talking more to himself than me. "I need to remove that last layer."

Uh...what? No, no, wait a minute. I raised my head and peered down my body at Rafe. He'd retrieved his big ole *sharp* knife from somewhere and was eyeing my bra. Or maybe my breasts, I wasn't sure. Even from this angle, I could see *my* sharp points sticking up and over the balcony.

"Stop!" I whisper-shouted.

"Stop?" he groaned. "You want me to stop now?"

"Yes!"

He started to back away.

"No!" I said, a little panicky. "Well, I mean 'yes'—please stop."

He raised an eyebrow. "Which is it, Rose?"

"You can unhook my bra in the front. No need to cut it off."

He put the knife back on the table and reached over with both hands to undo the clasp between my breasts. He spread the halves back so I was fully revealed, and he leaned down to give each breast peak a quick lick. Warmth gushed, and I rubbed my thighs together.

Rafe stopped and raised his head.

"Rose, be still. Your challenge is to remain frozen," he cautioned.

Ha. Easier...challenged than done.

Rafe disappeared from view. *What is he doing down there?* While I was oh-so-tempted to lift my head and look, I knew better and stayed still.

I even closed my eyes and tried to slow my breathing so I wasn't panting.

That helped when he waved something under my nose—chocolate with a hint of ginger?—and settled it in the hollow below my throat. He repeated this scent-and-settle routine five more times, and—I admitted—I was back to panting at the end.

Mostly because of where the different truffle bits arrived. Besides the hollow between my collarbones, one balanced on each nipple, one cushioned in my belly button, and one nestled in each crease where my thighs met my groin.

How long can I keep up this whole frozen thing? Who's going to melt first—the chocolate or me?

I had my answer when Rafe's mouth landed on my throat. Sucking up the truffle, chewing and licking, seemingly all at the same time. I opened my eyes and looked down, afraid to move my head. He met my glance and smiled like the devil he was—chocolate coating his lips and, no doubt, smearing my neck.

He moved to my breasts, lapping up the chocolate bit from each tip in turn. When he paused to suck and nibble and bite each one again, I started to moan and shift my thighs together. He immediately stopped and stared me down—hard to do when I was already lying down flat, but he managed.

I froze…on the outside at least. Inside, hot pulses shot from my breasts to my core. Rafe whirled his tongue around my belly button to scoop up the truffle there. Before moving on, he drew in a big breath. Did he detect the chocolate or my arousal—or both, in a succulent mixture?

I had no answer since I was out of my mind by this time, thrashing my head back and forth. He sucked up the remaining truffles, nipping my thighs in the process, and settled between my legs.

"Rose. Babe. Rose." Rafe called my name a few times before it penetrated…my moans were so loud. To be fair, he was hoarse and groaning and hard to understand.

"Rose, I'm going to get you all messy and dirty with chocolate, but I need to taste you right now. Okay?"

The last was barked out more like a command than a question, but I understood what he wanted. I lifted my head and nodded once.

That was all he needed. He buried his face between my thighs and licked into my core, tasting chocolate, no doubt, and me. I came with a scream...unfrozen at last.

We were gonna need to sterilize the cupping table first thing tomorrow.

Chapter 29

Rafe

It was Monday morning of Thanksgiving week, and I was totally fucked up.

I stood in Rose's bathroom shoving my shaving gear, toothbrush and paste, deodorant and other stuff into my Dopp kit. I'd been using her shampoo in the shower—something that smelled like roses, believe it or not. Kinda girly, but why dupe when you didn't need to? I aimed to get her a replacement bottle today and go back to my old generic brand.

I was lying. Lying to myself, worst of all.

I was going to buy two bottles of the flower-scented shampoo, one to give to Rose and one to use in the bathroom back at the garage apartment. It'd be a reminder of the best shower sex in my life—well, the only shower sex, if I was honest with myself.

Rose had asked me to move back into the apartment before Finn and Lauren arrived this evening. They were expected in time for dinner. Finn was staying in his childhood bedroom and Lauren in Rose's old room.

I got it. I did. And respected it. From Rose's viewpoint, she wasn't throwing any new stuff Finn's way right on the heels of his first semester at college and the first Thanksgiving without his grandmother. She was a good mamma, the best.

Didn't mean I wasn't feeling the loss though. Hard.

Usually I kept that shit under check. I stuffed any feelings away and moved on—literally. I couldn't afford them if I were traveling light.

This time, not so much.

It wasn't only the daily, sometimes twice daily, lovemaking I'd miss. Although that was fucking spectacular. We'd christened the shower after the chocolate-tasting mess, and it'd become one of our favorite spots.

My lathered-up hands running all over her curves, inside and out. Kneeling in front of her, the water pounding on my back.

No, I'd also miss living with Rose. This was the first time *ever* I'd lived with a woman, *any* woman, my woman. That meant, while we occupied the same airspace, I claimed responsibility for her well-being—whether she liked it or not.

Yeah, I'd avoided looking out for others since getting out of the army—caring for Princess was about the best I could manage. Now I was getting all bent out of shape because I was headed back to that solo existence sooner than scheduled.

Go figure.

Of course, Rose had fought me tooth and nail on assuming too many duties. It had been a matter of "she said, he said."

She'd said *I don't need your help, I can do it on my own.* I'd said *Tough shit, if I'm living here, I'm doing my share to make your life easier.*

I'd fixed her a hot breakfast every day because she tried to run out the door on a cup of coffee. I'd filled the grocery cart with healthy shit that she generally avoided in favor of ice cream. I'd dealt with household chores so she could crash after her busy days.

The thing I'd miss the most from living together? Drifting off to sleep curled around her and waking up still wrapped around her, shielding her.

Well, yeah, I'd also miss the talking—another first for me. Or, more, I'd miss listening to Rose talk.

Sure, I'd done *some* sharing. Rose had coaxed me for my story in her gentle yet relentless way. I'd edited or skimmed over the details, leaving out the bleak parts of my foster experiences and the sad parts of losing brothers in the sandbox wars.

When she'd squeezed my hand while we walked the dogs or buried her face in my neck while we sat on the couch, I'd suspected she'd read between the lines.

What I hadn't shared yet—what Pete had urged me to tell Rose—was the rest of my story. I was running out of time, and I hadn't gotten to the parts I feared most.

Rocky had called over the weekend and said he wanted me earlier than planned. That meant leaving the roastery...and leaving Rose...by the beginning of the first week in December. I'd told Rose right away—it was only fair. Her face had dropped before she thanked me for letting her know. I hadn't said anything about returning or about us, other than I'd roast as much coffee as I could before I left.

So I was both fucked up *and* a coward.

I *knew* I was a fucking coward the moment I considered writing the shameful parts of my past on those sticky note things she plastered everywhere. Before I could grab the pad and add some to the bathroom mirror, I pushed back from the sink.

Man up, soldier. Trust Rose with your entire story. She'll understand why you're not good enough for her and why you have to leave.

I nodded at my reflection and walked out of the bathroom. *Decision made.* I wouldn't put it off any longer. Well, any longer than one more week. I'd have "the talk" with Rose after the Thanksgiving weekend.

"What's up, manito?"

I heaved the big-ass turkey into the space I'd made in the Chocolate Lab's refrigerator and turned around to face Mateo. I'd already found a place for the smoked ham on a lower shelf. Bottles of white wine were chilling in another part of the fridge, and red wine sat on the adjacent counter.

The wines for Thanksgiving were courtesy of Jean-Luc, no surprise. The turkey and ham were my contribution to the cause…and a surprise for Rose. I'd volunteered to pick up the preordered meats from the butcher shop today to free up their coolers for other orders.

Actually, I'd volun*told* Rose I'd do pickup duty for a couple of reasons. The brakes had been feeling mushy on her POS car—an easy fix, but it would need to wait until next week. I also wanted to avoid a debate about who was paying for this part of the Thanksgiving dinner.

"Hey, brother, nothing much. Just storing the bulky things here rather than in Rose's fridge at home. She said she'd retrieve the turkey early Thursday morning when she has her mamma's stuffing ready."

"Yeah, you haven't lived until you've had Mrs. Connolly's cornbread and sausage stuffing. Well, I guess it's Rose's recipe now—right?" Mateo raised an eyebrow. "You better get ready, man."

"Ready? Ready for what?" I'd only had turkey day dinner in the mess hall before, my life lacking big family holiday gatherings.

"For the crowd at Rose's for Thanksgiving. Upward of twenty-five people—and that's not counting the dogs. Everybody brings something. They add leaves to the dining table so they can keep adults and kiddos together. We've been coming for years, even before Papá died. They take everyone in—family, friends, orphans who don't have family around. That's how Jean-Luc got invited the first time. I heard Pete's coming this year too."

That's right. Pete had mentioned that his daughter and grand-kids were going to the in-laws, and he didn't want to drive back and forth to Seattle. He'd see them all here for Christmas.

"Thanks for the heads-up. Rose gave me setup duty for the night before, and now I know what that means. She also said Finn's in charge of peeling and mashing the potatoes. Sounds like KP duty to me."

We smirked at each, remembering our early days of KP in the army.

"Do you want to hit Hair of the Dog tonight with Jean-Luc and me?" I asked. "We're heading there about seven-thirty for some pizza and beers."

"What? You're not staying around to have dinner with Rose and her boy?"

"Nope. That's a family reunion. I'm not part of that."

I must have sounded a little abrupt. Mateo narrowed his eyes at me.

"Oh. Sorry. I thought that since you've been staying with Rose—"

I cut him off. "We've been keeping that on the down low, at least from Finn. He still believes I'm living in the garage apartment. In fact, I moved back there this morning."

If Mateo picked up anything from my borderline rudeness, he was decent enough not to say so. "No worries—I can keep a secret. And yeah, I'll join you guys around nine. Gotta close up here tonight since Rose will be spending time with Finn and Lauren. Save some pizza for me."

I gave a chin lift and walked down the hallway to start the afternoon's roasting.

On cue, all three of us pushed back from our table. The top was littered with pizza scraps and empties.

"I'm out," said Mateo. "I gotta get up early to open the café."

Jean-Luc nodded. "Me too. Seems like tout le monde decided to pick up wine orders for Thanksgiving a day early."

"Yeah," I added. "I've got a full day of roasting ahead." *And I'm gonna take both dogs out for their last walk of the day.*

I didn't say that part out loud. Neither of the guys knew that Rose and I had been walking Princess and Pirate together most every evening for the last two months. It wasn't a secret so much—doing it more for Rose's safety than anything else. But still...our private thing.

Tonight I was taking the dogs out by myself. Rose had called earlier to say Finn and Lauren had arrived and to ask—again—if I'd like to join them for dinner. Again, I'd said no, probably too forcefully. *Didn't feel entitled to be part of the homecoming celebration.*

She'd said she wanted to take her girl out for drinks afterward to catch up, and Finn was meeting old high school friends somewhere. To not sound like a total sad sack asshole, I'd offered to take the dogs for their late-night walk.

Outside the pub, Mateo headed one way toward his place, Jean-Luc and I the other way. Jean-Luc lived over his wine shop for now and said he'd be looking for a house in the neighborhood when he got around to it.

I thought he was going to ask about Lauren again, but instead he said, "What's up, Rafe?"

He was my age, maybe a little younger, and wary of me until we'd gotten to know each other better. I didn't share a lot and neither did he—we were guys, we didn't spill our guts—but I sensed he had trouble in his history too.

When I hesitated, he repeated the question with a different spin, "Are you returning to la belle Rose after your time in Boise?"

Fuck. Not the roastery, but Rose. Was I that obvious?

"I found out I have to leave early—beginning of next week. We haven't talked beyond that."

"Time is running out, n'est-ce pas?"

"Yeah. But she hasn't invited me to stay. And I haven't offered." I paused. "Rose deserves better than me."

Jean-Luc shook his head. "You're an idiot."

I grunted. *No argument there.*

After leaving Jean-Luc at his place, I walked slowly to Rose's house. The air was crisp, no rain in sight, and a crescent moon was pinned high in the sky. As I moved down the driveway, the dogs were raising a racket—snuffling, barking and scratching at the backyard gate.

"Everybody calm down. It's just me, guys…no Rose tonight."

I flipped the latch and crowded through the mob scene to grab their leashes from the back porch. We geared up and headed out, the pups pulling me down the street toward the park. We made our rounds and a pit stop or two before going back to Rose's house.

I don't know who was more surprised—Princess or Pirate— when I opened the front door and disarmed the alarm. You could see their doggy minds going a mile a minute. *Where's Mom? Wasn't the Boy here? Don't I get a treat now? Why am I still on the leash?* This last one from Princess.

It had come to this. I was narrating the dogs' thoughts.

I handed out treats and made sure Pirate had a full water bowl. I rearmed the system on my way out, dragging Princess all the way. Her royal highness was not amused.

Later, much later, I was lying in bed, arms crossed under my head, staring at the ceiling. When Princess whimpered, I looked down at her on the rug beside the bed. She was lying on her belly, front legs shoved out straight, muzzle resting between her paws. She was staring too—at the cardboard, life-size, stuck-in-time Elvis in the corner.

Great. Now I was going to have "Are You Lonesome Tonight?" stuck on repeat in my mind.

Chapter 30

Rose

"I found him, Rose! I found him!" Lauren blurted out as we walked into Fay's. My heart started beating faster, and my belly clenched. Finally. Our first chance to talk without little ears—well, not so little these days—listening in.

"Up high!" Lauren wiggled her hip onto the stool at our bar table and pushed her hand toward me head height, fingers spread wide. I obliged, knowing what was coming next in her version of a high-five.

"Down low!" She giggled, lowering her hand and turning it palm up. When I made a move to slap my hand on hers, she pulled away at the last moment.

"Too slow, Joe!"

"You're a dork, a complete dork," I informed her, hugging the fido out of her. "I've missed you like crazy."

"Yeah, the phone calls don't cut it, do they?" Lauren patted my cheek with her impossibly long and polished fingernails and smiled into my eyes. One high heel hung off her foot as she swung her crossed leg back and forth. The same shoes from the drive up—my feet would've been aching, but she wore heels every minute of every day.

"Nope. We need in-your-face time." I smiled back.

An old joke with my first, best and only roomie. My found sister. My ride-or-die.

Literally.

She'd stuck by me and shouted down the mean girls when nobody believed me. She'd bundled me and future-Finn into her car and got us back home to my parents.

Now it was *my* turn to have *her* back. Lauren could count on me for any help—legal, illegal or just liquid—in escaping her control-freak-smothering-soon-to-be-ex.

And help in winning the custody battle. *Her heartbreak would…well, break my heart if she had to leave her Baby behind.*

"Hey, before we get started, I've got a new one." We had a running contest for the most creative and obscure insults. Extra points for incorporating canine references.

"Great! Lay it on me," Lauren said, raising an expectant eyebrow.

"*Dogbolt*. It's old English, kinda like Oliver, for a wretched, contemptible fellow—definitely like Oliver."

She giggled again. I loved it when I could make her laugh these days.

Vera ambled up to take our order. We decided on Manhattans—no surprise there. She headed back to the bar, and we got down to business.

"So, Rafe's uncle. Spill," I urged.

Of course, Lauren had to drag out the suspense.

"You remember I was trying to narrow down that list of Amato men in the Bay area by searching Facebook and Instagram—right?"

"Yes, yes, yes." There was no hurrying her at this point. I didn't know why I was even trying.

"Epic failure, as we expected." She started laughing, although I didn't see the humor. "The only guys I found with the surname of Amato looked like they were in their twenties. Not nearly old enough to be Rafe's uncle."

I frowned. "Well, then. Doggone it. So much for my idea…."

"Until…." Lauren grinned big time.

"Until?"

"Until I got smart. Lucky, really. I saw a post from one of the guys, with a 'like' and a comment from a woman…"

She paused. Aaand I was having second thoughts about her moving up here.

"…by the name of Angelina."

Lauren must have seen something on my face because she reached over and grabbed my hand.

"Oh, girl, it gets better."

My face scrunched up. I pressed my knuckles below my eyes to blot the sudden tears. Of course, our drinks arrived at that critical moment. I stared down at my lap while Vera unloaded her tray. We murmured our thanks, and she left.

When I looked up, Lauren had pulled out her phone and sat it face down between us.

"First, Rose," she said, raising her Manhattan, "a toast to the good luck we both deserve."

We clinked our glasses and tossed off healthy doses. Then she flipped over her phone and tapped her way to a screen.

"I linked to her page, and our girl Angelina seems to post her entire life on Instagram. Including these pics from a recent birthday party for her dad." Lauren pushed her phone over in front of me.

I was looking at Rafe. Rafe, ten or fifteen years older. But Rafe.

Yeah, his uncle had longer hair, more pounds, deeper wrinkles on his smiling face. Even so, the strong family resemblance was there. Angelina's brother and another younger guy, all crowded close for a group photo, had it too. The Amato men "look."

My tears escaped, sliding down my face. Lauren reached around me and hugged me tight.

"When are you going to tell him, Rose?" she said softly.

"I'm not," I breathed out. "At least, not right away."

"Okaaay.... Help me understand here. You've found Rafe's lost family—his uncle, his cousins, maybe more relatives. You don't want to pass on the good news to him?"

I swallowed around the big lump in my throat. "He doesn't know we've been searching, right?"

"Right. You wanted to keep it secret in case nothing panned out."

"There's another reason. He's so...private, so...reserved in many ways."

"Reserved? Really? That's not what you said when we talked earlier." Lauren gave me an exaggerated wink.

"Oh, snap!" Now it was my turn to laugh. "That's not what I meant, and you know it. In fact, what's the opposite of reserved? Friendly, outgoing, forthcoming? Yeah, that's Rafe when we're to-gether *together*."

We grinned at each other for a moment and took swigs of our drinks.

"No, what I mean is that I've had to coax him to talk about his past. Well, to talk period. He's shared some things, but I feel he's holding stuff back. I realize a lot of veterans don't like to talk about their experiences. My intuition tells me there's more to it than that."

I paused and winced. "I'm afraid he might get upset or even mad that I've looked into his background without asking him first."

"Is that gonna hold you back?"

"You know what? Nope. I refuse to be a scaredy dog." I sat up straighter on my stool and wiped my eyes. "If this search for his mom's family results in something good for Rafe, I'm gonna do it."

"You go, girl," Lauren cheered and raised her glass to me.

"So here's the thing. I want to reach out to the family *first*, before I tell Rafe."

"Why's that?"

"I need to take the hit if his uncle doesn't want to acknowledge him, or if there are some bad feelings in the family." I shook my head. "I don't want Rafe hurt."

"Makes sense. How can I help?"

"Let's start with Angelina. Since we still don't know her dad's name, maybe she'd be willing to introduce us. What do you think about DMing her? Could you help me compose the message?"

"Of course! Let's get going on a draft right away." She pulled her phone back and opened up her notes app. "When do you want to send it?"

Vera delivered another round of drinks to our table, along with a basket of Fay's spicy tater tots and dipping sauce. We needed something to soak up the Manhattans. Lauren must have given the high sign to Kurt behind the bar while I'd been gaping at the photos.

"I'm thinking I'd like to contact Angelina after Thanksgiving—maybe even Monday or Tuesday. People are usually super busy with family things the entire long weekend—look at us."

Yep, we had turkey day prep Wednesday, the big day itself, a meeting to plan the grocery store pilot on Friday, the Turkey Dog Jog the next day, and the Finn-and-Lauren-leaving-and-me-crying-all-day on Sunday. Busy, busy, busy this year—the one benefit being there wasn't much time to be sad about Mom…and the other people I'm losing.

"Except…" I sighed. "Except the problem is…I might not hear back before Rafe leaves."

"Wait…he's still leaving?" Lauren asked, her eyes widening in shock.

"Uh-huh. He's had this commitment in Boise like…forever. What's changed is that he got a call yesterday that they want him sooner. Like early next week. The owners decided to visit their children before they leave on their trip and wanted to get Rafe over there ahead of schedule."

"Oh, damn, Rose. That's coming right up. Have you guys talked about what happens after that job is over? About him coming back here?"

"Coming back to the roastery...or coming back to me?"

"To you, girl." Lauren rolled her eyes.

That's the question. Does Rafe have staying power, or will he leave and not return, like the others?

"Nope, we haven't talked yet," I admitted. "Guess I'm afraid of what he'll say. Maybe it's all in my mind—this closeness between us. Maybe it's just pure physical chemistry, nothing more."

You know better, girl. He wouldn't be doing all these things for you, he wouldn't be saying words of more than two syllables to you if he doesn't care. Would he?

"Anyway, Rafe hasn't asked, and I haven't invited...so far."

"Time's a-wasting, Rose," she cautioned. "I get it's hard for you to trust, but you gotta put yourself out there. He's not a mind-reader."

I sighed and finished off my drink. *No argument there.*

His toothbrush and toothpaste were nowhere to be seen—ditto for his shaving gear and nail clippers. His toiletry bag had disappeared from under the sink too. The dresser drawer I'd cleared out for him was barren—I'd checked there first thing.

Even the shrinking supply of condoms on the bedside table had vanished. Although by mutual agreement—and, yes, trust—we'd dispensed with those barriers a while back.

I peeked into the shower. Hmmm...nothing different here.

Wait. Is that a brand-new bottle? Could've sworn we had at least half of one left.

Oh. I squeezed my eyes shut. *Rafe's strong fingers massaging the shampoo from my head down through my hair, me returning the favor on his silky short cut. Kneeling in front of him, water buffeting my back.*

I turned to stare at myself in the mirror, rubbing one hand back and forth, back and forth, across my lips. What a crybaby—shaky, head-achy and holding back tears.

Well, that was partly from those three Manhattans on little food. But mainly the teary state swelled up when I'd come home to find Rafe gone. I didn't know why I was getting so worked up. I'd told him to move out, after all.

Shuffling into the bedroom, I stood by his side of the bed. Pirate chose that time to grumble again, turning around twice in the bed he usually shared with Princess before settling down with a huff. He was sulking because I'd yelled at him to stop scratching at the closed bedroom door.

I grabbed Rafe's pillow and buried my face in it. Inhaling deeply, I got all those notes of roasted coffee, dark chocolate, even roses—*roses?...strange*—that seemed to cling to him. After a minute or three of indulgence, I crawled into his spot and pulled up the covers.

It was some time before I could sleep.

Chapter 31

Rafe

I rubbed the palm of my hand on my chest, right in the middle where it suddenly felt tight. *When did she put that there? Right in the open, where anybody and everybody could see.*

"Hey, is that new? Nice shot." Pete had come up behind me, and I hadn't even noticed. "You kids look like you were having a fun time."

I nodded slowly. *Yeah, that was a good moment. A good day.*

We'd snapped the leashes on the dogs after their run in the surf. Rose had handed her phone to some lady walking by and asked her to take a pic. Us and the pups and Haystack Rock in the background. Rose was laughing and looking at the camera. I was looking at her.

Sometime since then, she'd printed the photo, stuck it in a frame, and set it here among the other family stuff in her living room.

I turned and met Pete's eyes. Lucky for me, he smiled and didn't say anything more.

Earlier, I'd taken on setup responsibilities. Rose had said they were expecting an even bigger crowd this year.

Your mission, she'd informed me, *should you decide to accept it,* she'd followed this with a wink, *is to find enough chairs for every person to sit at the same table. By any means necessary.*

194

I'd almost saluted her, but held off in favor of a return wink. She'd burst into giggles. *Yeah, the element of surprise—gotta love it.*

While they were busy in the kitchen, I'd brought up the extra leaves and card tables from the basement. By the time I'd finished, the dining "table" extended from the dining room through the arches into the living room. Chairs had been a challenge, but I'd hunted up enough from around the place. Rose had snorted when she saw my finds.

Nevertheless, it'd all worked. Barely.

Now I was parked in a corner of the living room, beer in hand. Pete swung around to my side and stood there shoulder to shoulder. People continued to pour in through the front door.

"Good place to stay out of the way, eh?" he commented, taking a long swallow from his bottle.

"Mm-hmm," I agreed. Rose was commanding the kitchen quarters where the chow line would be set up on the counters. The turkey was halfway to being done. Jennifer was setting the table with Mateo's little sister's help. The television was blasting from across the front hall—sounded like a game was on from all the cheers and boos. *And some barks?*

"Nuh-uh! Stay!" I said this loudly and sharply to Princess and Pirate. They'd jumped up from my feet when Cab lumbered through the front door. Jean-Luc followed close behind, hefting a box of wine bottles.

"Hi, guys," he called out. "Pete—Dr. Mica's out at the curb with her papa. Looks like she could use some help."

We both moved forward, but Pete handed me his beer. "Familiar face and all that, Rafe. Can you stick this in the fridge for me?"

"Sure, you betcha. If I can find room."

He laughed and headed out the front door.

Eyeing Princess and Pirate, I muttered "stay" again. Cab plodded over, weaving around the dining table and dodging other furniture. *Agile for a big-ass lug. Annnd…let the butt-sniffing begin.*

Jean-Luc and I made our way toward the kitchen and paused in the opening from the dining room. *Chaos? Or a normal Thanksgiving?* We looked at each other and shook our heads. *Who were we to know or judge?*

Rose spotted us and waved from her post in front of the stove, where she was stirring something in a big saucepan. She wore a Chocolate Lab apron over a short jean skirt, her hair was bunched on top of her head with strands falling everywhere, and there was a smear of, yeah, that looked like gravy, on her cheek. She looked flushed, hot and stressed—and I wanted to kiss the ever-lovin' fuck out of her.

A little hard to do when the kitchen was crammed with people.

Finn stood by Rose at the stove, mashing potatoes in a big pot and adding hot milk and stuff as he went. Mateo and his mom were piling apple empanadas on a platter to join the pumpkin pies others had brought. Jennifer's twins were putting rolls in a basket. Miss Ada was brushing a glaze on the ham in front of the convection oven. Some women I didn't know were arranging foil-covered dishes on corkboards on the chow line.

Everybody and their mother was here. Plus a few dogs—Miss Ada's dachshunds were begging for ham scraps, and a corgi was sticking close to the girls.

"Jean-Luc, there you are. Oh, that must be heavy!" Rose indicated a cleared space on the counter with her elbow. "Thank you so much! Can you and Lauren open a few bottles and space them out down the middle of the table, please?"

Lauren was coming out of the pantry carrying a full tray of wine glasses and startled when she heard her name. Jean-Luc quickly put his box down and covered her hands on each side of the tray to steady things. She froze, he froze—although the back of his neck turned red—and everyone went quiet. After a beat, Jean-Luc stepped away, and Lauren continued into the dining room. The chatter resumed.

On my way to the fridge to stow the beers, I bumped him with my shoulder. He ignored me and moved over to the counter to start opening wines. Lauren joined him a moment later.

Are Rose and I that obvious? I shook my head and turned from the fridge…to come face-to-face with the lady in question.

"Come with me. I need your help reaching something." Rose hooked her right arm in mine and dragged me half backward over to—and into—the pantry. She switched on the light and closed the door.

I must have been slow on the uptake—*on half a bottle of beer?*—because the next thing I knew she reached up to wrap her arms around my neck and hug the soft length of her body against mine.

I went hard in response. Not suitable for the PG audience outside the pantry door, but I'd deal with that later.

"Rafe, I've missed you," she whispered before pulling my head down for a wet deep kiss.

She tugged back when I wanted to keep going.

"It's been too long! How long has it been? Why can't I remember? I know it's been too long."

Three nights and almost four days since we've been alone together. But who's counting?

Rose frowned, and I wanted to smooth out those furrows between her eyes.

"And it's all my fault," she mumbled. "I should have never asked you to leave."

Shadows under her eyes. Obvious, even in the dim light of the overhead bulb. Like when I first arrived, and she was sad about her mamma.

Shit. She was having trouble sleeping too.

"It's…it's…too overwhelming right now," Rose said, her throat clogged with tears. "Staging the perfect Thanksgiving like Mom and Dad used to do. Protecting Finn from change like he was a little boy. Wishing Mom were here when she'll never be again. Trying to save the Chocolate Lab by myself."

She stopped abruptly. *What? What the fuck is she talking about? Save the—*

She started again and caught my attention. "And you…you leaving in a week. It's too much."

I pulled her close again and wrapped my arms tightly around her. She resisted for a moment and then relaxed against me. I laid my cheek on her hair and breathed her in. Roses combined with the scents of roasting turkey and spicy pumpkin pie. It worked for me.

"I've got you. Don't you worry—you're safe. Let's concentrate on today. You've got a house full of people who love you and who are thankful to be here, spending this time together."

Rose sighed and nodded against my chest. We stayed close a moment more, and I said, "We still have one problem."

"What's that?" she asked, angling back to look up at me.

"How am I gonna walk out there like this?"

She looked down to see my ever-present desire for her on full view. I'd worn a black button-up and jeans for the occasion today, rather than my customary T-shirt and flannel overshirt.

"Oh, that's no problem. That's what aprons are for."

She grabbed a spare Chocolate Lab apron off a hook and handed it to me. For our cover story, I reached up to get a huge platter off the top shelf of the pantry, and we strolled out into the kitchen.

After Mateo, Katt and some of the kids took the dogs out back to do their business, after Finn carved the turkey with Pete's help, after plates were piled high on the chow line, we sat down to dinner. A seat for everyone at the same table, even if a couple were upturned planters. Someone thought to bring a high chair for their toddler.

Turned out—unlike the army where everyone fell on their food like ravenous dogs and unlike my few foster families who made even meager attempts at holidays—Rose's home had an important tradition.

It happened before anybody picked up a fork. The oldest and youngest guests got things rolling with a blessing. This year, Miss Ada and Liam's little girl, a real cutie—couldn't be more than four or five—did the honors.

Meggie climbed on the old lady's lap and snuggled under her chin. Miss Ada started off, and Meggie repeated each line. Both voices were soft, and the little girl stumbled over a few words. No matter. The rest of us were quiet, even the toddler in his highchair and the dogs under our feet.

Dear earth who gives to us this food,
Dear sun who makes it ripe and good,
For the meal we are about to eat,
For those past and present whose efforts made it possible,
For family and friends who share this bounty today,
We are thankful.

Maybe we were supposed to say "amen" or something at the end. Instead, we applauded. Meggie got shy and hid her face while Miss Ada smiled around the table. Liam reclaimed his daughter, and we all dug in.

After a few bites, I lowered my head, trying to catch Rose's eyes across the table. There'd been wet streaks down her cheeks during the blessing, and she'd squeezed Finn's hand so hard her knuckles had turned white. She was still quiet, pushing food around on her plate and sipping from her wineglass. Her neighbors were busy talking around her, letting her be for now.

I didn't want to yell over the hubbub to get her attention, so I stretched out my leg past Princess to nudge her in the ankle.

Except I got Pirate instead, who yelped and surged up. Only to bump his damned domed head on the underside of the table and rattle the plates and glasses in front of Rose and Finn. Princess reacted and did the same on my side. Nothing fell over, but not for lack of trying on both their parts.

We stuck our hands under the table to grab their collars and shouted at the same time, "Calm down, you big babies! You're fine."

The table erupted. "Did somebody drop their plate?" "Oooh… watch the wine bottle…it's tipsy!" "Are you guys okay?" "Mom?" And barking, lotsa barking.

Rose met my eyes, shook her head and started laughing.

I laughed back. *There she is.*

After everyone settled down and finished their dinner, after big plates were exchanged for small plates with both pie *and* empanadas for some of us, after leftovers were shared out, most people started heading out the door.

Rose and Finn stood in the front entry hall, giving and getting hugs. Never saw a group exercise so much physical contact, outside of my fighting days. I almost escaped, standing on the edge of things.

"Young man, I need your help getting home." Miss Ada clutched my arm and thrust leashes into my free hand. She kept her giant handbag, jammed with plastic containers, hooked on her elbow. Must've weighed a ton, the way she was listing to one side.

"Yes, ma'am, of course. Why don't you let me carry your bag too." Not making it a question, I slipped the bulky damned thing from her elbow to mine.

Miss Ada hugged my arm again, and I muttered, "quiet, you two" to her bickering dogs. We walked out the door, down the porch steps and up the block toward her house.

When I returned, I found Rose in the middle of the kitchen, directing cleanup traffic. A big crew had stayed behind—besides Finn and Lauren, there were Mateo, Jean-Luc, Pete, Katt and even a couple of Finn's buddies.

So…enough of this shit.

I marched over to Rose and interrupted her mid-order, "You and I are gonna take the dogs out for their walk. Grab your jacket—it's cool out but not raining."

She opened her mouth…and closed it when I reached around her to loosen the strings, pull the apron over her head and toss it on the counter.

I turned to Finn and said, "Leave the roasting pan for me to scrub out when we get back. I can take the trash bags over to the café's dumpster too."

He smiled. *The boy had Rose's sweet smile.* "Nah, we got this, man. Right, guys?" Everyone else closed their mouths, smiled and nodded too.

"Goodnight, Mom. Great Thanksgiving—Grandma would've been proud." Finn hugged his mamma and pushed her out of the kitchen.

She grabbed her jacket while I got Princess and Pirate. We walked out into the cool starry night, not saying much. Going toward the park, we held hands. The dogs tugged on their leashes, tracking scents on either side of us.

Chapter 32

Rose

"Oh, dalmatian. This would work a lot better if you weren't so big."

I turned my back to Rafe and managed to get a face full of water and bang my funny bone at the same time. *Youch...tingling and burning alllll the way down to my fingertips.*

"Babe, stay still for a minute," he gritted out.

"Are you okay?" I asked over my shoulder. I *had* swung around quickly...maybe I'd clocked him with my other elbow?

"Uh-huh. Stop wiggling around."

I was trying to tilt my head back under the shower so Rafe could rinse out the shampoo. We were in a rush this morning because I had to return to the house before the others got up. I needed to change clothes, eat something and check in with the café before heading to the park.

Of course, after my spur-of-the-moment sleepover at his apartment, we'd overslept.

Rafe stilled me with a touch to my neck. He wove his long fingers into my thick hair close to the scalp and gently, oh-so-gently, started to massage my head under the steady spray. Slowly, he drew his fingers out through my hair, rinsing and detangling as he went.

202

Ahhh…bliss. I closed my eyes and sank back into him.

Oh. The penny finally dropped. Things were not only hot and steamy in the crowded shower stall, but hard.

"That's *it*, babe," Rafe grumbled. His huge hands dropped and grabbed my hips, a little less gently this time. In one move, he shifted me to the back wall and turned me to face him. His broad back blocked the spray, and he leaned over to kiss me.

Or at least started to.

I reached up and spread my fingers on his lips.

"Wait."

"Wait? Why?"

"We don't have tiiiime." Yes, that was a whine, and I wasn't a whiner—normally. Except we were running out of time.

Rafe had the answer though.

"Fuck time." He bit my fingers, and when I snatched them back to shake the sting out, he was on me again.

This time, he nipped and licked along my neck before moving to my mouth. He slid one palm behind my head so I wouldn't bang it on the shower wall and used the other to pull my hip closer. My already tight nipples stiffened further against his chest.

He paused, hovering over my mouth. Hot breath on my open lips. Part robust coffee, part dark chocolate, all Rafe.

"Rose. Are you okay with this?"

At some point, I'd squeezed my eyes shut. The shower continued to beat down on us, although Rafe was getting the brunt.

I nodded, but before he could take my mouth, I surged up and took his. I curled the fingers of one hand into his clipped hair and pushed my tongue past his lips. He groaned and pressed my head even closer, sucking my tongue at a furious rate.

Hot pulses shot from my breasts to my core, and I flushed even hotter than the water. Wet outside and in. Reaching down, I gripped his swollen length and started stroking. I did my best, even though we were crammed closer than ever.

After a minute or ten, Rafe pulled back and shoved one hand between us to stop my up-and-down, up-and-down.

"Not yet, not yet."

He slipped his hand further down to plunge fingers into my readiness. His thumb rubbed my achiness there. I groaned when he pulled out... *noooooo, don't go.*

"Hang on to me," he grunted.

My hands flew to his biceps, barely getting a grip on those bulky muscles before Rafe lifted and held me against the slippery wall. He nudged my legs apart and notched at my entrance.

When he paused again, half-lidded eyes staring at where we were joined, my patience ran out. I wrapped my legs around him and started to grind down.

"Now, Rafe," I insisted.

One thrust, and he sheathed himself completely. He hit that deep spot that put those hot pulses into overdrive—and stayed still as I tried to catch my breath. I needed all of that short span of time to get used to his sheer size.

We fell into a frantic rhythm, in and out, in and out, until I shattered. I throbbed around him, and he followed a moment later. Moaning together, sharing the scorching rush.

Yeah, it was tighter quarters than our shower back at the house, but we'd made it work.

Chapter 33

Rose

I was leaning over the end of the table to grab another stack of race bibs when Princess stuck her muzzle in my face and gave me a big smouch.

I dragged the back of my hand across my lips and kissed her head in return.

"You made it, baby girl!" She and I communed for a moment while I gave her some belly rubs.

Rafe stood grinning down at me. He was dressed for the chilly-yet-not-rainy weather in a tight T-shirt revealed by an open-necked Henley covered by an unbuttoned flannel shirt. I knew what was hidden under all those layers. I didn't trust myself to know what was buried in his heart…I'd gotten that wrong before.

I grinned back though, because I was too chicken-shih tzu to ask him *or* to reveal what was hidden in *my* heart. We were running out of time, and not just for the event.

The Turkey Dog Jog was due to start in a half hour, and I was staffing the registration table along with Lauren. We were checking in people who'd already submitted their forms and fees as well as collecting said forms and fees from last-minute newbies like Rafe.

"So Finn got to you, eh?" He'd been reluctant to join in the fun since he was busy roasting up a storm before he left next week. But I'd sicced my son on him—that boy is hard to resist.

I slapped a registration form on the table with one of Mica's vet clinic pens. "That'll be thirty bucks, please."

Rafe pulled out his wallet and handed me three tens. Once he finished the form, I passed him a race bib and recorded the number and other info on my sheet.

"That goes on your chest," I informed him, circling my finger over my front to demonstrate. "Not on your back or on Princess."

He flicked a glance down at my long-sleeved Turkey Dog Jog T-shirt and back up again. His eyes heated, and so did my face.

Easy to read your mind. And that's a big "nope." No time to get all hot and bothered. I've got a dog jog to run.

"Want to know how this works, seeing how this is your first time?"

His lips quirked to one side, and he nodded as I stood.

I pointed to the starting line where a banner stretched overhead on two poles: *19th Annual Johanssen's Turkey Dog Jog* in huge bold letters.

"At ten o'clock sharp, Erik will stand to the side and wave a Chocolate Lab dog bandanna above his head to signal the start. One year, he stood on a ladder in the middle—nearly got knocked over. Another year, we tried a whistle for the start—dog howling and baby crying ensued."

"Yeah, I can imagine." Rafe and Princess exchanged a look.

"Everyone takes off to walk or jog on the path outlined by orange cones. Luckily, Dogwood Park is pretty level. Some folks push their dogs or kids in strollers. We've even had participants in wheelchairs and mobility scooters. In fact, there's Calvin now."

I waved at one of our neighbors who was sitting nearby on his custom scooter and talking to Jen. His ancient peke snuggled on his lap, already fast asleep.

"How long is the course?"

"It's based on a 2K running path around the park—not too long. That's less than one-and-a-quarter miles."

He raised an eyebrow at me. Oh yeah, right. Army. He knew kilometers.

"Katt's set up a photo booth in that tent over there. Choices of two or three standing frames with *Turkey Dog Jog* painted in fancy letters across the bottom. She'll put the photos online this coming week, and people can buy print or digital versions. Super generous—donating all her time, materials and sales."

Miss Ada wandered by, and Rafe barked out a laugh. "Are those hot dog buns on top of her girls?"

"You bet. Costumes are definitely a 'thing' today. That's part of the reason for pictures, you know—recording the moment for posterity."

"Don't some of the dogs break ranks on the course?" He side-eyed a pair of passing Jack Russells as he asked. "Start barking or get combative?"

"Oh, sure, sometimes. But we count on their people to know their dogs and judge if this is the right place for them. Although, I shouldn't talk." I scrunched up my face before going on.

"One of our earlier Labs—Bonny Lass—got a case of the zoomies. She tugged her leash out of Mom's hand and ran around like a loonball in the middle of the course. Mom tried to be embarrassed, but she was laughing so hard, I don't think she succeeded."

I pointed to another tent where a big sign proclaimed *THE DOGTOR IS IN.*

"If any dog does need first aid—like for a cut or a sliver in the paw—Dr. Mica is set up over there. If it's more serious, she'll get them into her clinic, refer them back to their own vet or even call the animal hospital."

Rafe swung back to me and pushed out, "Well, BZ, Rose, BZ."

"Yuh-huh…." I squinted up at him. "We've all been busy with this event."

"Nope," he corrected. "BZ is short for Bravo-Zulu. Army-speak for 'well done.' So…BZ."

"Ah. Okay. Thanks." I rubbed the toe of my sneaker in the grass. "Me and an army of other helpers."

"Yeah, but you were the general," he stated.

I stepped closer and looked up to meet his warm, cobalt-blue gaze.

"Hey, Rafe, how's it going? All packed for Boise?" Lauren piped up from beside me. We both jerked back.

She'd finished checking in Jean-Luc and Cab and was now eavesdropping. I frowned at her, and she widened her eyes at me. *What a troublemaker. She knows I'm trying to work up my courage for a talk once Thanksgiving was over.*

Finn saved the moment by walking up to hand Rafe a tiara headband, trimmed to an inch of its life with pink feathers and sparkly rhinestones.

"For Princess?" Rafe asked, eyebrows pulled together.

"No, for you," my smart-aleck son answered. He waited a beat and said, "Of *course* it's for Her Highness. See—Pirate's got his own headgear."

Finn had engineered a pirate's tricorn headband from one of his old Halloween costumes, complete with a skull and crossbones in the center and a tiny parrot plushie attached to the side. The creation hung lopsided off Pirate's head as he nuzzled his girlfriend's ears. *Hmmm...how long is that hat gonna hang in there?*

Finn must've had the same doubts. He clapped a hand on Rafe's shoulder and said, "Let's get over to the starting line, man. We'll hit Katt's tent afterward if things are still...intact."

Princess graciously accepted her tiara from Rafe, and the four of them moved toward the starting area.

As soon as they were out of hearing, I turned to Lauren and started with "Why are you—" when Kenzo rushed up to the table with his sweet pittie mix, Nama, in his arms. Besides donating gift certificates for his chocolate shop to the treat bags sitting behind our table, he'd entered his girl in the dog jog.

"She threw up over there,"—he motioned with his head—"and tried to eat it!"

"Oh, poor baby!" we cried in unison.

"It's probably just the excitement of so many dogs around, but I want to get her checked out. I need to clean up after her first though."

He was torn. Touching to see the panic on the face of the big guy for the little pup in her bedraggled tulle tutu. We'd both been there with our own pups, so we got it.

"You're in luck—we've got a veterinarian here today for that very purpose." I nodded toward Mica's tent. "Don't worry—we're experienced dog moms. We'll clean things up in a jiff."

Kenzo nodded his thanks and headed off. We grabbed plastic bags and paper towels from our supply box and found the pile of throw up. I was about to get back to Lauren's blatant prodding when there was a burst of barking and cheering and, yes, some howling too.

The Turkey Dog Jog was underway.

It was hard to hold my tears back, and we were only halfway through the evening.

The Chocolate Lab always stayed open late Thanksgiving Saturday, what with all the families in town for the holiday and the holdovers from the Turkey Dog Jog. Adam was seated at his keyboard taking requests, with Elvis songs still a fave. Finn, Lauren and a couple of our kids were on hand to run orders out to the tables. Mateo and I kept busy pulling coffee drinks and prepping food.

Rafe was in the back, packing coffee beans he'd roasted this afternoon.

Crowds and noise aren't my thing, he'd reminded me, returning to the roastery after a quick sandwich for dinner. Although he *had* weathered the packed dog jog just fine and even stayed behind to help dismantle the tables and tents for return to the rental place. Pete had wandered back there to help after he'd walked Liliana and Ana in.

Finally, I was taking a breather behind the counter. Big mistake...because I was losing it.

Up until then, I'd been in motion *every* moment of the holiday week. I'd planned it that way—no gaps permitted.

When I wasn't catching up with Finn, I was drinking and scheming with Lauren. When I wasn't buried in stuffing prep for Thanksgiving, I was assigning dinner duties left and right. When I wasn't working at the café, I was huddling with our team for the grocery store pilot.

Overseeing the dog jog had filled any spare moments. And organizing our traditional post-turkey music night—that'd served as the last distraction. Or was it the last straw?

Even during my limited time with Rafe—because we couldn't seem to stay away or sleep away from each other—I'd been bent on squeezing every feeling, physical or otherwise, out of each moment.

Yeah, I'd gotten through my first Thanksgiving without Mom—thanks in part because we'd celebrated her memory everywhere. Now I was a mess, facing tomorrow, the next day, the next week…alone.

Finn was going back to college, my bestie was departing to wind up her divorce, and now Rafe was leaving early on Tuesday. Why, oh, why—when I was hoping for a few more days to delay talking to him? An early snowstorm was hurtling down the Gorge midweek.

I swallowed hard and dropped my head back, blinking fast to absorb the tattletale tears. *Cannot, should not, will not, do this here.*

"Ah, Rose." Lauren grasped my hands on the counter, her voice full of sympathy. That was enough for the tears to slide out when I brought my head back up.

I was losing it when I most needed to get it together to talk to Rafe on Monday. To screw up my courage, put on my big-girl cheekies and tell him how I felt.

Tell him what fears I'd kept to myself, what dreams I'd hid from him.

Ask him to come back. Come back to Portland, to Dogwood, to the Chocolate Lab.

Come back to me.

"You don't need to be scared," Lauren whispered, stretching closer to talk over the deafening sounds of "Burning Love" coming from the corner.

"You haven't seen the way he looks at you on the QT."

"And how's that?" I whispered back, grabbing a paper napkin to blot my cheeks.

"His eyelids go to half-mast, he tilts his head back like he's going to stare you down, but instead he stares *at* you," she shared. "Like he can't get enough, like he can't turn away, like he's watching to jump between you and a speeding car."

I laughed and shook my head. "Okay, enough. You had me going there for a minute."

"No, I'm serious. In other guys, I'd cry *stalker*. In Rafe, I shout *smitten*."

"That's you exercising your marketing-guru superpower," I protested. "You read consumers' minds for a living. After my false starts..."

"In the far past, girlfriend!" she interrupted me.

"Still. After my *heartbreaking* false starts," I hissed, "I don't trust my own judgment when it comes to guys and what they want."

"Girl, since you're not a mind-reader, there's only one way to find out. Why don't you ask the man himself?"

"Because I'm afraid of his response."

Lauren drew back and cupped my cheek across the counter, wiping away a last tear with her thumb. We stood there until the song finished.

Chapter 34

Rafe

It was late Sunday afternoon, and Rose was shutting me down.

Last night, Pete had read me the riot act. Pacing back and forth in the roastery, he sounded like my old sarge trying to drill some sense into the eighteen-year-old me. Trouble was, I was the forty-one-year-old me and still as stubborn as hell.

I could tell my friend was frustrated by what he saw as my inaction. Here it was, two days until I left for Boise, and I was still holding back on telling Rose my history. Telling her why I wasn't right for her.

Although Pete saw it differently. Giving her a choice, he called it.

I'd had my reasons for waiting until after the long weekend. But now I wasn't so sure. I wasn't sure *any* time was going to be a good time to say what I had to say.

And Rose was shutting me out. After the music had ended, I'd locked up the roastery and walked up front to take her home. She'd stayed behind the counter, arms wrapped around her middle, eyes red and wet. Lauren and Finn were out on the floor, cleaning up.

Rafe, she'd said, hardly looking at me, *I need to go back and sleep in the house tonight.* By "going back to the house," she'd meant sleeping by herself.

I have to get up early to open the café because I'm giving Mateo the day off. She'd cleared her throat. *Then I need to get home to eat a last breakfast with Finn and Lauren and pack their lunch for the road. I want to say my goodbyes before I*—her words, not mine—*start bawling. After that, I need to finish out the afternoon here.*

I'd stood on the other side of the counter, nodding dumbly. Mumbling something about taking the dogs out for their last walk, I'd gotten out of there.

I would've been glad to hold her for the bawling part, but I got it. Not family, not a boyfriend, not a friend—not expected or entitled to be on the scene.

Well, *maybe* a friend with benefits. But I'd never had that type of *friend* before, and besides, I hated the term. Too detached, too cold, too casual.

It didn't describe who she was to me. Why my eyes found her in any room. Why my gut ached when we were apart too long. Why my heart beat all over the place when I heard her sudden laugh. Why I couldn't wait to lay hands on her skin each day.

The fucked up part? Maybe what we had was all in my head. Worse, I had shit skills for figuring out what was in Rose's head.

The zinger from Pete last night? *Son, you should just ask her.*

I was better at using my talents for something concrete—if you could call solving anything mechanical a "talent." I had her POS jacked up in her driveway and was lying under her back axle. I was intent on replacing her brake pads this afternoon because I couldn't leave town knowing the state they were in.

And no. I didn't ask permission beforehand.

The dogs started snuffling and ruffing and whimpering.

"Princess! Pirate! Quiet the fuck down, you two!" I shouted. *Bet they can't hear me with all the racket they're making.*

"It's not supper time yet. And, no, I'm not letting you out—you'll squeeze under the car and lick my face again. I'll take you for a walk in fifteen minutes."

The gate rattled, and I turned my head. *Are those fuzz butts trying to get out?*

Guess not, unless they're wearing hot pink sneakers and crazy dog socks.

"Rafe…" Giggles, gasps, snorts. Kinda delicate-like, but still… snorts.

She started again, "Rafe, are you trying to reason with…" Her rich laugh busted out. "Do you expect the dogs to tell time?"

I slid out from under the vehicle and scrambled to my feet. Rose stood on the other side of the car, grinning at me. Her honey hair was bunched up in its usual messy knot. Dark smudges ran rampant under her red-rimmed eyes. A food-stained Chocolate Lab apron, sporting a torn pocket, hung off her neck.

She was beautiful, and she was too far away.

I rounded the rear end in three strides. Grabbing her up, I proceeded to…hug the hell out of her. Wrapping her as close as I dared, I buried my face in her hair.

Rose let out a high squeak that set the dogs off again. Pressing her cheek against my chest, she slipped her arms around to hug me tight in return. We stayed that way until the barking got too loud and Pirate was throwing himself against the gate.

We untangled, pulling ourselves apart slowly. I couldn't resist reaching out again to cup her cheek and rub my thumb across her full bottom lip. Back and forth. Back and forth.

Meanwhile, the dogs were relentless.

Rose broke the spell this time. She nipped and sucked my thumb in quick succession. Before I could do anything about it—like grab her again—she danced away and headed over to the gate.

She glanced over her shoulder and said, "C'mon, let's feed these loonballs their dinner and take them for a walk down to the park. I need some air, and you can tell me what you've been doing to my poor car."

She was talking to me again, and on a relatively safe subject. It was another chance to avoid the unavoidable. Or at least postpone it.

How could I say no?

"Sure." I grunted. "It's getting dark soon anyway. Let me get your car off the jack, and I'll be right in to help you with the dogs."

We sat kitty-corner at the butcher block island, my knees bumping into hers when I tried to stretch my legs out. She was chowing down the ham-and-cheese-scramble I'd fixed when I'd found out she hadn't eaten a thing today...not the breakfast she'd made for Finn and Lauren, not lunch at the Chocolate Lab while she was working, nothing.

Four-shot mochas didn't count, but nice try on her part.

"Mmm...yum." Rose closed her eyes and moaned as she shoveled the food in. "Rafe, where did you learn to cook like this?"

"That's not cooking," I scoffed. "That's a fry-up, what I do when I'm camping. Usually, I throw in some mushrooms and onions, but we, er, you were all out."

"Well, whatever *you* call it, *I* call it *delicious*." She smiled up at me, gesturing with her fork. Her eyes were a brighter green, her cheeks rosy rather than pale, her dimples peeking out.

"Thank you for taking care of me."

The moment those words were out of her mouth, she froze and stared down at her plate. Frowning, she continued eating—quiet now, subdued even, shrinking somehow.

I hated to see that.

Earlier, Rose had shared what she thought about me taking care of her.

Rafe, I appreciate it, I do. I'd sensed a *but* coming when she'd pulled her hand out of mine to tug Pirate away from something suspicious...and hadn't reached for me again.

We'd been walking the dogs around the park while I explained why it was urgent to put new brake pads on her junker.

Rose, I couldn't waste any time. With thin pads, the brake fluid can leak out real fast—even while you're driving. And your brakes would fail—no warning.

If I'd sounded a little over-the-top about her safety, I guessed I was. She neglected things or put herself at risk, and soon...I wasn't going to be there to safeguard her.

Then she'd hit me right between the eyes. *Rafe, it's not your job to do all these things for me. I'm not your responsibility.*

True. I didn't want to be responsible for anybody ever again. But fuck me, that'd hurt.

It hadn't gotten any better.

Sometimes I wonder if you think of me as a list of chores. Chores to take care of and check off before you go on to your next thing. Before you leave... She'd kinda trailed off there.

I must've made some sort of protest because she'd picked up again.

Don't get me wrong. We've had something...intense going on here. She'd waved her free hand back and forth between us. *You're a good man with a good heart. I just think whatever we have is marked with a sell-by date.*

She'd stopped and pulled up her hood against the rain. *I'm sorry, Rafe. I'm exhausted from this week, and I'm not making any sense. Plus, I'm so hungry I could probably eat Pirate's weight in kibble. Let's go home.*

So I'd taken her back to her house and fixed her breakfast for dinner.

Now I stood and carried our empty plates over to the sink. Princess and Pirate dogged my heels, hoping for scraps, but there was nothing left.

I returned to the island and took both of Rose's hands in mine. I drew her to her feet and started walking backward, out of the kitchen, through the dining room to the base of the stairs.

"I'll deal with the dogs and clean up later. Tomorrow, there are things I need to tell you. Tonight...tonight is for us alone. Will you come upstairs with me?"

She held my gaze and nodded slowly. Then she took me by the hand and led the way up to the bedroom.

Chapter 35

Rose

I've got to catch him before he leaves. I've got to let him know.

I sit up in bed and grab my phone to text him. Where's his message thread? I don't even see him in my contacts. Ah...maybe he's still packing—that'll be faster. I run out of the bedroom, down the stairs and out the front door. Barefoot, but I don't care.

When I get to the apartment, I try the door, but it's locked. I pound away, calling his name. No answer, no barking, nothing.

Oh. The roastery. He's there doing the extra roasts before he takes off. I can still catch him. I run down the sidewalk, slipping and stumbling in the rain, but I don't care. I push open the side door and rush in, skidding to a halt in the middle of the room.

There he is. I start to talk, to tell him...and Mateo turns around. Rosita, he says, you missed him—he's already left. And I just called the police—somebody broke in last night and vandalized the place.

He steps aside to show the battered roaster, looking like a crowbar had been used to beat it to pieces.

I'm shivering, and I can't get any words out. I sink to my knees, hang my head.

Not again.

Lauren's ringtone jarred me awake. I lay on my back, arms and legs tangled up in the sheet. I was panting, my throat dry and scratchy. Salty tears ran from my eyes down my cheeks to land on my lips.

No sleep T-shirt, panties or socks—only the cool, brutal rub of the sheets. I ached between my thighs and tasted bitter dark chocolate on my tongue.

Had any of it been real?

My phone stopped ringing, and a moment later, a *ding* sounded. I pulled my arms loose and scrubbed my face dry with a corner of the sheet. I expected Pirate to start complaining about his breakfast…or lack thereof…but he and Princess were nowhere to be seen.

I swung my legs around to sit up, swaying a bit. It was getting light outside. How long *had* I slept in? Thankfully, I didn't have to go in until one o'clock to relieve Mateo.

When my phone dinged again, I grabbed it from the nightstand. Rather than pick up the messages, I called my bestie directly.

"Lauren…" I swallowed and tried again. "I had the most dog-*awful* dream. It seemed so real."

There was silence for a beat. "Well, hello to you too, girlfriend."

"Oh, sorry, sorry, sorry! I got your message last night and haven't had a chance to call," I rattled on. "Finn texted that he was back safe and sound at school too. Thanks again for driving him. How's Baby? Was she happy to see her mom?"

"Yes, she slept cuddled on my chest all last night. I missed her so much!"

"I'm happy you got home in time to pick her up—and that dogbolt didn't try to keep her." I started to shiver for real this time and dragged the sheet back around my shoulders. "So…that was you? You left me three messages?"

"Yes, those were all me—I kept thinking of one more thing. But first, tell me all about your dream. Or was it a nightmare?"

"Definitely a nightmare. I was lucky I wasn't sleepwalking too."

"Why was that?"

"Somehow I ended up sleeping naked last night. My neighbors and the café customers would've gotten a real show."

"Ah…panties-optional attire. I need deets! Tell me all about your nightmare…and about your night with Rafe."

It was a relief to talk about my dream out loud. Made it less real, less scary, less a repeat of the past. Lauren even got me laughing about how, in real life, Pirate would've been racing behind me, barking his fool head off, begging for his breakfast.

When it came to Rafe, I shared the flavor, not the details, of our time last night.

"It was different," I whispered. "He was different."

"How so?" she asked softly.

"Rafe was quiet last night, not talking at all. I know that doesn't seem unusual, but when we're together…like that…he's not shy about talking. Asks me what I want, tells me what he wants, growls hot and dirty the entire time."

I shifted on the bed, tugging the sheet tighter. "Last night, he was…I don't know…intense. Everything he did was serious, deliberate. How he stared into my eyes, how he stroked me all over, how he kissed me. I barely had room to breathe when he held me so close between times."

"Between times? There was more than one time?" Lauren was diverted for a moment.

"Yes. With Rafe, there's always more than one," I shared, then plowed on. "For all the thrills we've had giving in to our physical attraction, this felt more like lovemaking. It also felt like the last time, like goodbye. Am I reading too much into last night?"

"Rose, you won't know until you've talked to him." My bestie set me straight. "And this is the day to do it. In fact, it's the *last* day.

Get Rafe alone. Tell him what's in your heart. Ask him what's in *his* heart. You're brave, I know that for a fact. You've got this."

"Lauren, you're right. I've got this." I climbed out of the bed and headed to the bathroom. "And he *did* say over dinner that he had things to tell me today. We need to find a time before he leaves for Boise early tomorrow."

"You go, girl! Call me later with the upshot."

"Anything else before I go?"

"Yes, send that message pronto."

"Yeah…no turning back now."

"You're doing a good thing."

"Okay, okay. Kisses for Baby."

"Ear rubs for your pup."

An exchange of *bye-bye-bye,* and we were out.

Before I had a chance to change my mind, I opened Insta to message Angelina:

> Trying to locate the brother of Angelina Amato on behalf of her son. They lived in the Oakland/SF area 35-40 yrs ago. Your father & brothers (?) look like her son. Not a solicitation for money or request to meet. Looking for family history or pics to pass on to my friend. Thx for replying! Rose Connolly

I included my phone and links to our website and social media pages. Fingers and paws crossed that Lauren's word magic would work its magic.

Next up, I found "Red Hot Roaster" in my contacts. Still there, nightmares to the contrary.

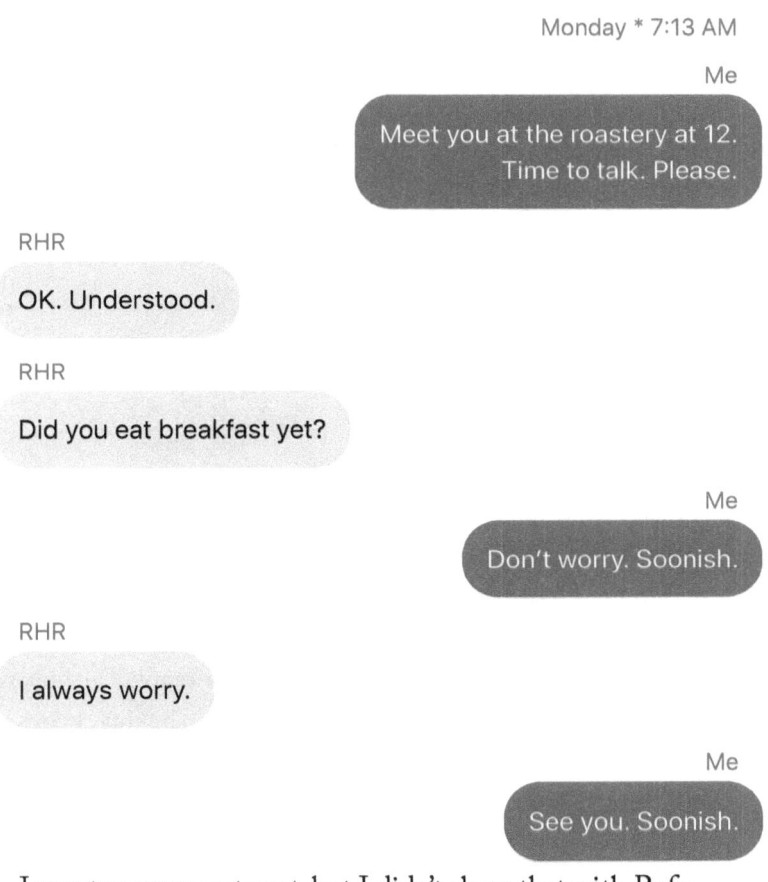

Monday * 7:13 AM

Me

Meet you at the roastery at 12.
Time to talk. Please.

RHR

OK. Understood.

RHR

Did you eat breakfast yet?

Me

Don't worry. Soonish.

RHR

I always worry.

Me

See you. Soonish.

I was too nervous to eat, but I didn't share that with Rafe.

Chapter 36

Rose

I slipped in the side door of the roastery, locking it behind me. Rafe stared, blank-faced, from his post by the roaster while I walked across to the hallway door and locked that one too.

Turning, I leaned back and took a big breath. I was trying to be calm, cool and collected…and failing miserably. My heart was thumping, my throat was dry, and my legs were shaking. I considered fanning my face but kept my hand glued to my side.

I'd called this meeting, even practiced my opening lines in the bathroom mirror. Yet here I was…stuck. The woman who could—and did—chat nonstop to anyone about anything at any time was stuck when it came to the most important conversation of her life.

It isn't like I'm going to let loose with the L word, right?

Rafe crossed his arms, biceps bulging under his tight black T-shirt. His face gave nothing away. If anything, he looked more guarded than ever. His sculpted lips pressed in a flat line. His cobalt eyes glinted under his hooded gaze. His dark brows clenched in a frown.

The only movement? His jaw flexing like he was grinding his teeth.

Gone was my intense, passionate, lingering lover of last night. *Did I dream the entire thing?*

When I finally got the courage to open my mouth, Rafe unfolded his arms and pushed one hand toward me.

"Wait," he said gruffly. "This is gonna be hard enough without us facing off across the room."

I sucked in a breath and solved my heart-thumping problem right then and there. Because my heart stopped. Well, almost. A sluggish beat later, my throat clogged up, and tears pricked the corners of my eyes.

I had to admit it, I was a crier. Happy or sad moments—when Finn was born, losing Dad so suddenly, saying goodbye to Mom. Touching moments on social media—soldiers seeing families after a long time, rescue pets realizing they're going to their forever homes, new dads cuddling their babies. Also, when I was tired or scared or laughing out of control. And sometimes, I cried walking around in the rain, when I could let it all out.

However, this was a first for frustrated...no...was that *angry* crying?

I needed to get a grip. I needed to get control of myself if I had any hope of telling Rafe what was in my heart—and finding out what was in his. I blinked my tears back—fast.

"You're right," I agreed. "I locked the doors so we wouldn't be interrupted...or so one of us couldn't escape."

Rafe said zip, zilch, nada. *So much for humor to lighten the situation.*

"Let's sit at the cupping table. Side by side-ish. It's kinda neutral territory—right?"

Okay. I was rethinking the whole "roastery meet-up" thing right now. What with our history in this place—the rough feel of the burlap bean bags on my rear, the smooth coolness of the round oak table on my back.

Rafe seemed unaffected by these memories as he took a seat—two stools around from mine—at the table. Still, he wasn't *categor-*

ically opposite from my seat—he was just *barely* out of reach. Thank heavens for small favors.

I clasped my hands and held on for dear life, my knuckles whitening. *Why is this so hard? It's not like you're telling the guy you love him...yet.*

Taking a big breath, I raised my head and met him stare for stare. "I'll go first. I know we started out with the idea of acting on our attraction for each other—nothing more."

I swallowed and gripped my hands even harder. "Now I've come to realize I *do* want to see if there *is* something *more*. Something more between us than the obvious physical push-pull."

Rafe shifted like he was going to interrupt. This time, I held up *my* hand in the universal "stop" motion.

"Let me get through this. Please."

He stilled, and I went on. "This fall, only two months really, was not enough to find out what we could have together. And I've been a mess, what with Mom's loss, Finn off to college and all my worries about the café going under."

"What? Wait...that last part—" he tried to cut in, but I headed him off.

"I'd like more time to get to know you, and for you to get to know me." I was speeding up, getting to my big finish...aaand Rafe was shaking his head.

"So here's what I want to ask you. Could you, *would* you, come back to Portland after your Boise job ends?"

He was still shaking his head. I rushed on, "*Not* to pick up where we left off. *Not* for you to live in my apartment...or stay in my house. *Not* even for you to keep working at the Chocolate Lab if you don't want to. I'm sure Pete could connect you with another roastery nearby."

My rehearsed pitch was going faster and faster. "Come back to give us more time together under what passes for normal. To give us a chance to explore where any feelings might lead us."

I stopped abruptly, tears threatening once more. *At least he'd heard me out. Although the whole head-shaking thing was the shih tzu.*

Looking away from me, Rafe crossed his arms again. He grumbled, "Rose…"

Of course, the hall door chose that time to rattle.

Mateo muttered, "Why is this locked?" Louder, "Hey, Rafe, have you seen Rose?"

We both shouted, "Not now!"

Mateo stopped trying the door handle and, to his credit, didn't say a word more. His footsteps got fainter as he headed back down the hall.

Rafe picked up where he'd left off. "Rose, I'm not sure I'm the right man for a woman like you. I'm not the kind of man you think I am."

"Oh. Okay." My stomach sank. "This is the 'it's not you, it's me' speech."

"Uh-uh. I mean my early years were fucking sketchy. Not sure I'm a good fit for you for the long haul."

"Why? Help me understand." It was supposed to be his turn, but I couldn't help myself. "Is it because your mom wasn't married? Because you were in foster care? Because you didn't have money?"

He nailed me with a glare. "Nope. Different reasons. I fell in with the wrong crowd in Oakland, a youth gang. Bad people, Rose. Trust me—nobody I'd want you around."

"That's like…what? Twenty, twenty-five years ago?" I protested. "You were Finn's age, even younger—right? That's not who you are now."

"You don't know that. I was outta control, had a hard time keeping my temper. I was good with my fists, fighting other gangs, fighting underground for cash. I lived for the thrill of illegal racing, boosting cars for chop shops. I never got caught, never got sent to juvie."

"What made you stop? Going into the army?"

"I beat the shit out of some low-life who surprised me and my crew on a boost," Rafe gritted out. "He tried to knife one of the younger kids, and I got in the way—that's where I got this thing." He rubbed the scar along his jawline for a moment.

"We fought, and I damn near ended him. One of my boys pulled me off, and we got outta there."

I kept quiet and still, for once.

I hadn't seen this…this confession coming. What did I feel about it? I needed time to think. Could I get my head around the… the…violence? So foreign to me. But this was Rafe.

"I almost killed the guy," he stated again flatly. "Sure, I was protecting my crew. But I knew, I *knew* that wasn't what my mamma would've wanted for me. It felt like I'd failed her. Again.

"I'd hung in there until graduation—my latest foster mom had made sure in order to get her last dime—and I'd just turned eighteen. I met with a recruiter right away and started the enlistment process."

Rafe slammed both hands down on the table and pushed himself up. "Look, Rose. You deserve a better man, a man who can protect you, who won't let you down. I'm not that man."

I stumbled to my feet to face him. "So that's it? This is the first I've heard about your time before the army, and you've already made up your mind? Without talking to me, without asking me?"

He stepped back, and I followed, jabbing two fingers in the center of his chest.

"It looks like you don't trust me to make the right decision— to let you go—so you made the decision for me. You had to do it because my judgment was so…so…crap before."

Angry tears welled out and down my cheeks. I wiped my face with my fingers and paced away. And swung around. *Oh, no, it can't be.*

"Or…or…worse yet, you don't have enough faith in me to figure this out together. Yes, part of me is shocked about your past. No, I've never been around fighting or gangs or stealing or…or…bloodshed before. But I've had my share of bad times in my own past, what with David abandoning me and Brent leaving me at the altar."

He surged forward again, clenching his fists. "Brent? Who the fuck is Brent? What did he do to you?"

Trying to control my crying, I bit the last part out, "Yeah, we're quite the pair. I didn't trust you enough to tell you about Brent because I was afraid you'd see me as a fool. Again. And you didn't trust me enough to share your past because you were afraid I wouldn't make the right decision and let you go."

Rafe grimaced and started to reach for me. I batted his hands away and dodged around him to the side door.

"I'm going back home to wash up before my shift. I don't want to see you out in the café, and I don't want to see you in the house before you leave tomorrow morning." I tried to suck it up. "Give Princess a hug from me." I choked on a sob and ran out the door.

Chapter 37

Rose

The deep baritone asked if I was lonesome tonight, jolting me awake. When I tried to grab my phone to slide the alarm off, it fell on the floor. And kept on with the musical stab to my heart.

"Somebody make it stop." I groaned, flopping on my back. When no help was forthcoming, I guessed that somebody was going to be me.

Despite feeling like I'd buried my head in a bucket of sand—grit scratching my throat, nose and eyes—I managed to lean over and snare my phone. Squinting at the screen, I finally managed to slide off the alarm. Finally, peaceful silence.

That was when something large and heavy plunked down on my bent knees—luckily, on the outside of the covers. I looked over my shoulder, and there was a big ole dog's head. Pirate had started sleeping on my bed when Mom had died and Finn had left for school. He'd stopped with the advent of Rafe, and now...he was back.

I reached over and rubbed his nearest ear, murmuring "what a good boy you are" for his comfort and mine.

Yesterday came back in a rush.

I made it from the roastery to my house without seeing anybody on the way. Seeing *was stretching it—my eyesight was so blurred I didn't think I'd recognize my own dog. After scrubbing my face—and scrapping the whole makeup thing—I got back to the café in record time.*

I fast-walked through the front door to the prep kitchen, nodding to the thankfully few customers along the way. Mateo took one look at me and asked if I wanted to be there.

"I'm hiding out either here or at Fay's," I informed him. "And it's too early to start drinking."

He frowned but didn't argue with me. Instead, he hung up his apron, hugged me and said he'd be back at eight to do the closing. No debate. His parting shot: "Call your girls, Rosita—now."

That was a big nope—I'd cry again, and then where would we be? I turned off my phone and dove into making sandwiches and salads and soups—letting my kids run the front of the house. The only break I took was in the late afternoon when I ran home to feed Pirate and let him out back to do his business. Princess was nowhere to be seen, and Rafe's pickup was gone.

I made it until six-fifteen when I shut myself in the meeting room, turned on my phone and returned one of Lauren's umpteenth messages. I saw missed calls from Mica and Jen too.

Mateo had been busy.

My bestie listened while I cried, told her the whole sad story— word for word—and cried again.

She paused to make sure I'd finished and said, "Rose, I love you. I know this is so hard for you, and I'm sorry I can't be there—yet—to help."

I sucked in a big breath and settled down. "Oh, girl, it helps to talk it out. I knew better than to expect this could work with Rafe. If I'm disappointed, it's my own fault."

Lauren hummed for a moment—in agreement or disagreement, I couldn't tell.

"Enough conversation for now—time for a little more action. Your relief's coming in early..."

"Oh, you mean, Mateo, your new BFF?"

"Yeah, that's the guy. And Jen is picking you up at seven sharp to take you to Fay's to meet up with Mica. Don't worry, because I know you will—Mica got a neighbor to stay with her dad. You three are going to close the place down. Jen will see you home and get you settled for the night."

"But...but...but..."

"No buts about it. That's what's going to happen," she declared. "You are not alone."

"I do feel surrounded, but—"

She cut me off. "No buts."

"But in a good way," I assured her. "The only thing better would be if you were here. Soon, girl, soon. Kisses for Baby, and keep one for yourself."

"Hugs for you—and one for your pup."

After closing—bar closing, that is—and a few Manhattans, a force-fed burger and another sobbing jag (luckily, Fay's wasn't crowded on a Monday night)—Jen brought me back to an empty house. Well, empty except for one faithful dog.

This morning—despite a fitful night's sleep and a sluggish head—I was determined to get on with my life.

Or at least, get up and go open the café.

"One baby step at a time—right, Pi-Pi?"

He yawned, not impressed with my enthusiasm, and jumped off the bed.

I made a quick stop in the bathroom—where I was glad to see Rafe's stuff was gone—and hustled downstairs. While his nibs was out back doing his business, I scooped kibble into his bowl (no matching Princess bowl...sad to see) and topped off his water.

"Ah...coffee...breakfast of champions. Care for a cup?" I offered as I put the kettle on and readied the French press. It was all I could stomach this morning.

Pirate ignored me to start sniffing and pawing at the base of the island.

"What are you digging up there? I can't imagine there're any leftovers from last week."

He snorted and came up with a crumpled Post-it in his mouth.

"Drop it, Pirate," I said sternly, pointing to the ground. "Drop it."

This command had the usual not-dropping-it effect. I moved to Plan B and gently pried open his mouth to retrieve the prize. I put the pink square on the island to smooth it out and saw a bunch of other Post-its floating around the surface.

Doggone things never stuck to butcher block.

A keychain with a U.S. Army emblem weighed down one of the notes.

Ah, yes, I didn't even think to ask for those back…keys to the apartment, the front and back doors, the garden shed, the roastery, the café, the car…my life.

The kettle whistled, and I poured the water into the press. While waiting on the timer, I arranged the Post-its jotted in Rafe's bold hand in their likely order:

> **I'm SORRY I hurt you**

> **I DO trust you to make good choices**

> **Let me go, choose a BETTER man**

> **I'll text when I get there, I PROMISE**

> **Eat a REAL breakfast**

SET your house alarms

Say BYE to Pirate from Princess

"Uh-uh, Pirate. Nope. Too much for even *my* wooden heart right now." Snagging a roll from the utility drawer, I duct-taped those puppies to the countertop. "Later. I'll think about those later."

Ping. I plunged the plunger and filled my mug. Time to get dressed and get my day started.

Chapter 38

Rafe

The only trouble with the six-hour-and-some drive to Boise—longer, if you threw in pit stops for me and Princess?

A shitload of time to think.

It didn't help that we'd taken off in the dead of night. No heavy traffic or icy conditions or high winds occupied my attention. At that time of night, only a few long-haul truckers hauled ass on the interstate—trying, like me, to beat the early storm predicted for the Gorge.

Nope, that chance of snow hadn't held me back from leaving—no bad weather for soldiers, only bad gear.

I'd stowed tire chains, a semi-full container of gas, a cooler of food and water, and emergency supplies in the cargo box. I'd crammed my waterproof duffel full of clothes, kit, books and personal stuff. That duffel, plus an extra parka, snow pants, and boots, crowded the cab, along with a rain poncho for the pup.

I'd kept busy packing to leave—anything to distract myself from what I was leaving behind.

Because I was a coward. Yeah, I'd been scared shitless I'd do the wrong thing and run back to Rose. I'd demand that she forget about my past. I'd order her to let me fix her problems. I'd tell her my mission was to fight her battles.

I'd make her tell me all her secrets. How is the café in trouble? Who the hell is Brent? Why does she want to see if we could have...more?

"Well, I don't need to worry about any of that, do I, Princess?" I grunted. "I slammed that door shut for once-and-fucking-all."

Nothing sounded from my traveling companion—not a yip. I risked a look over my shoulder and found her curled up tight with her back to me. I could read her mood as easy as the highway signs. She was disgusted with me for bundling her off with no chance to say her goodbyes.

More likely, I was disgusted with myself for the way I'd left it with Rose. Now that I was on the road to Boise, I had plenty of time and miles to think. Nothing would distract me from putting the past two days on a continuous loop.

The last lame-ass notes I'd left for Rose.

I wasn't going without saying goodbye...and without saying sorry, either. Of course, I couldn't leave it at that and had to add a bunch of other bullshit. How was she gonna take care of herself when I was gone?

The last time I'd seen her in the roastery.

The muted light in her green eyes gutted me. Tears streamed down her pale-as-snow cheeks, and her normally lush lips clenched over her teeth. Her thick honey hair stood out in all directions, pulled by her furious fingers.

The last words she'd said to me.

"I don't want to see you in the café...I don't want to see you in the house." I don't want to see you...don't want to see you...don't want you.

The last time she'd touched me.

She poked me in the chest with two fingers, and I fell back like it was a punch. Yeah, she punched above her weight and knocked me out with her anger, with her disappointment in me.

The last time I fucked...*no, that wasn't right.*

I bit through my lower lip and hit the dash again and again. A coppery taste smeared my tongue. Princess yelped, jumped up and stuck her muzzle on my shoulder.

"It's okay, baby girl, it's okay," I soothed her…and me, tucking her head into my neck and rubbing her ear.

The last time I *made love* to Rose.

Her startled protest "you'll hurt yourself" when I banded my arms around her thighs and waist, lifted her and jogged up the stairs. Whimpers from the dogs when I kicked the door shut in their faces. How hard I was—and how soft she was—as she slid down my front to the floor.

Kicking off shoes and stripping off clothes in record time. The rosy flush all over her chest that she tried to hide with her hands. Her burst of laughter as she bounced where I threw her on the bed.

The way she squeezed her eyes shut when I told her, "I want to look my fill." The way they flared open as I crawled over her—"I'm going to kiss you everywhere."

Sucking her tongue for the flavor of her coffee and chocolate of the day. Biting the tender skin in the crook of her neck, lapping the sting away. Her moans shifting higher as I kept nipping and licking my way down. Pressing my tongue against her tight buds to swirl and scrape each in turn.

Nuzzling her soft belly before kneeling between her legs. Rising to stroke my shaft, balls to head, one, two, three times. Palming her thighs and pushing them apart to stare into her lush, swollen folds.

My name on her lips "Rafe, Rafe, Rafe" as I buried my tongue in her wet core. Her honey-flower taste when she came all over my face. Her head straining back as she shouted and shook all over. Sitting back on my heels and spreading more of her sweetness into my mouth.

Her eyes widening when I surged up. "Rose. Babe. Gotta be inside you. Now. Yes?" Her panting "Yes, yes" before I lifted her by the waist and thrust up. Fully seated on the first go, fully sheathed in her scorching core.

The fierceness of her nails as she clawed my shoulders and hung on. The clench of her knees on my hips when I lowered her to the bed. My gritted out "Wait, not yet" as I pushed up on my elbows to prolong the moment.

Our eyes locking again, as I pulled out, plunged in, at a furious pace. Her shuddering as her sweet-scented juices coated me again.

My answering last plunge, staying deep, my soul shooting into her. Her core fisting me to the very end, taking everything from me.

I veered back into my lane, heart beating double time like the wipers on high. Still standing behind me, Princess slammed into my seat. Her pile of blankets muffled her yelp and—hopefully—softened her fall.

Fuck. Talk about distractions.

"Sorry, Princess, sorry—you okay?" The cold nose on the back of my neck signaled proof of life, although I expected a full-on sulk at our upcoming stop.

We dipped south at Boardman, going away from the Gorge toward Pendleton. Just off I-84, I stopped at the travel plaza to fill up the tank and grab a hot meal. Baby girl got part of my sandwich as an apology. Then we chained up in the parking area—better chance of snow passing through the Wallowas.

Back in the pickup, I checked for any texts or voicemails. Nothing. No surprise—it was barely five-thirty. And who was going to contact me anyway?

Princess resettled on her blankets with a sigh—it sounded like someone let the air out of a tire. We hit the highway again with three, four hours to Boise—and no distractions from looping back to thoughts of Rose.

Starting with the last time I made love to her. *Only last night?*

Her startled protest "you'll hurt yourself" when I banded my arms around her thighs and waist, lifted her and jogged up the stairs. Whimpers from the dogs when I kicked the door shut in their faces. How hard I was—and how soft she was—as she slid down my front to the floor...

Chapter 39

Rose

"Nope, I haven't heard anything from her yet—or her dad." I grunted as I hefted the grocery sacks onto the counter. My phone, with Lauren on speaker, sat near Rafe's Post-its where I'd left them this morning.

Duct-taped to the butcher block and going nowhere.

When she'd called, I'd just walked through the front door. I'd dropped the sacks on the floor to answer—and to fend off Pirate. The alarm system had come in a distant third.

Now the persistent beeping was driving me crazy—and it wasn't a far trip.

"Hang on, Lauren—I've gotta disarm the alarm before they call."

Luckily, in recognition of the leaping-for-joy-knocking-you-over greeting expected from an excitable Lab, I'd programmed my new system with 250 seconds—the max—to cancel the alarm. Well, *re*programmed, that is, after the default thirty seconds proved a no-go when the monitoring center had called five times in as many days.

"I'm back," I announced. "Let me start getting things into the fridge and freezer while we talk."

"All righty," she agreed and paused as I rummaged around in the sacks. "How are you feeling?"

"About like you'd expect," I shared. "My head aches, my eyes are gritty, and my throat is still craggy. I couldn't stomach anything but coffee so far today, but that's got to change. That's why I stopped and got some food for the rest of the week."

"Geez, Rose. You could've called on Jen or Mica to help out."

"I know, I know. They were great last night at keeping me distracted. But I need to let them get back to their families. Hey, at least I managed to hold it together at the café this morning. The kids were pretty gentle with me—you know how they pick up on stuff. Or maybe Mateo said something. Anyway. Only one or two of the regulars asked when Rafe was coming back."

"Oh, girl. What'd you say?"

"You know me—I had it planned out. Said he was already contracted elsewhere for roasting jobs the next several months. And that we'd all miss him."

"So you didn't see him before he left? You guys didn't talk again?"

Wait. What the fido? Two unopened pints of Tillamook Chocolate Peanut Butter had been stuffed in the door rack of the freezer. I thought Finn had eaten us out of ice cream house and home when he was here.

Now I was trying to find room for my perishables down below—and not seeing a square inch of space.

"Rose? Rose? Are you there?"

"Lauren, can you wait another sec? I gotta go check something." I slammed the fridge door closed and dashed over to the pantry. When I slid in and switched on the light, I froze. More shelves jammed full of evidence that Rafe had struck again.

I returned to the island and grabbed my phone. "Hang up, Lauren. I'm calling back for a video chat."

"Rose, are you okay? Do you need help? Are you in danger?"

"Yeah, I'm in danger—of losing my mind. I'm okay, but I want you to hang up. I need to show you what Rafe left...when he left."

It didn't take long, and we were back on our call. Video this time, switched to the back camera.

"Why are you showing me the inside of your refrigerator?"

"Notice anything different?"

"Well, yeah. It looks like the produce, dairy and meat sections hooked up for a threesome and moved into your fridge with their love children."

I stopped panning and started giggling. Which turned into coughing and hacking, thanks to my hoarse throat.

Lauren talked over me, not concerned at all. "Quit waving the damn phone around. You said you went grocery shopping so…?"

I recovered enough to lift my phone and show her the two obviously still-full grocery sacks sitting by my fridge. Circling the island, I stepped back into the pantry to train the camera on the shelves. Chock-a-block with canned goods, cereal, bags of pasta, boxes of rice, flour, sugar, raw veggies—you name it, it was there. In multiples. It looked like I was all set to survive a once-in-a-century-snow-ice-sleet-hail-storm the likes of which Portland had never seen. Maybe throw in an earthquake for good measure.

"Oh," my never-at-a-loss-for-words bestie breathed out.

"Yeah," was my equally brilliant response.

"A little over-the-top, even for Rafe."

"Ya think? And that's not all."

I motored out to the island and held my phone over the row of Post-its. Starting at the left, I moved slowly along, giving Lauren plenty of time to read each. Her "oh" was followed by a series of gasps.

"But wait. There's more." I switched to the front camera and gave her "big eyes" before I thumbed the text icon to whisper, *"Just got in. Easy drive, no snow. Straight to roastery to meet owners. Sending house address later. Princess pissed at me. Set alarm? Eat breakfast?"*

"Wow. That's a book for him. How did you respond? Or did you?"

"I was overwhelmed by all the Post-it action," I said.

"Understandably," she assured me.

I went on, "He must've texted *right* when he got to Boise this morning to let me know they were safe—as promised. Which meant they left in the middle of the night."

"Rose, you *did* get back to him, didn't you?"

"Yes, about an hour later. Short and not as sweet."

"Uh-oh."

"In my defense, I was still sorting out his Post-its, and I hadn't seen his grocery shopping spree yet," I wailed.

"What. Did. You. Text?" My girl wasn't letting me off the hook.

"*Thanks for letting me know. Pirate pining. Yes. No.*"

She winced. "Harsh, Rose, harsh."

"Lauren, I don't know how to feel!" I almost, but not quite, shouted at my bestie. "When we met up yesterday, I laid it on the line. He cut me off—shut me down. I cried, got mad, cried some more. I said awful things to him, hurtful things."

She made some comforting noises, but I steamed ahead. "Then I come home to find everything that Rafe's bought for me. And that's after everything he's *done* for me in the past couple of months. When he *knows* I detest needing help or trusting anyone for help."

"Does he know?"

"What do you mean?"

"Did you tell Rafe *why* you're afraid to count on anyone for help?"

"I'm not afraid of anything!" I protested. "I've got it all under control."

"Sure, girl, sure," she said soothingly. "But did you ever think that *Rafe* might be the one who needs to be needed?"

Ooh…with his past, with his growing up. Maybe I need to get over myself.

I squeezed my eyes shut and pinched the bridge of my nose. One tear worked its way down my cheek before I brushed it off with my fingers.

"Rose, I'm sorry, I didn't mean—"

I interrupted her. "It's okay, Lauren. There's just too much right now—I can't process it all. You know what I'm going to do?"

"What's that?" my patient friend asked.

"I'm going to cram my groceries in the fridge, take Pi-Pi for a walk and lock us in for the evening," I informed her. "After wrapping up in my old flannel robe, I'm going to self-medicate with a pint of chocolate peanut butter and binge on Elvis movies. Hopefully, I'll be tired enough to fall asleep."

"Or crash from all that sugar," she said helpfully.

"Hey," I protested. "I figure the protein in the peanut butter cancels the carbs in the ice cream."

Lauren snorted. "Girl, the only thing healthy about you is your imagination."

We ended our call in the usual way—*a kiss for Baby, an ear rub for your pup*—and I proceeded to hunt down space in the fridge and pantry for all my stuff.

When I said, "Pirate, let's go for a walk," he nearly ran me down getting to the front door. I followed at a more leisurely pace, passing by the bookcases in the living room.

"Dusty, dusty," I muttered to myself, sliding my fingers along a shelf. I hadn't dusted recently, even for Thanksgiving. I stopped where there was a long gap between two framed pictures.

Huh. Did one of them fall? I glanced at my feet. Nothing. Shoved behind the other photos? I did a quick survey. No.

The penny dropped. *While Rafe left a lot of things for me, he left with something for himself.*

Chapter 40

Rafe

Me

Just got in. Easy drive, no snow. Straight to roastery to meet owners. Sending house address later. Princess pissed at me. Set alarm? Eat breakfast?

Tuesday * 11:47 a.m.

Rose

Thanks for letting me know. Pirate pining. Yes. No.

Dammit, babe. Not the only one.

Wednesday * 6:20 a.m.

Me

Bean Love Café & Roastery: 308 W. Overland Rd, Boise, ID 83709. House (housesitting for owners): 50122 Hill Rd, Boise, ID 83703. Eat or you'll get sick.

Wednesday * 7:04 a.m.

Rose

Ate pint PB Choc Chip last night—does that count? IDK, felt sick after.

Rose

Seriously, thx for providing ALL the food. Even healthy bits. Will eat better.

Rose

I promise.

Wednesday * 7:12 a.m.

Me

Hold you to yr word, Rose. Got to go check my roast. Later?

Wednesday * 7:14 a.m.

Rose

Bye for now, Rafe. A kiss for Princess.

Bye, babe…for now.

"Hold your fucking horses, Princess." I had her leash and a bag of groceries in one hand and was digging for my keys with the other. She was throwing herself against the door.

Baby girl was hungry for her dinner. My fault—I'd forgotten to take her kibble and treats with me this morning in the rush. Yeah, the café had a few dog biscuits for customers, and I'd snared a couple to tide her over.

She'd declined, thank you very much. They were apparently not up to her royal standards—or the Chocolate Lab standards, anyway.

Finally, I got the door unlocked and made it through the laundry room into the kitchen. Dropping the groceries on the counter, I unleashed Princess and grabbed her food dish.

"There you go, baby girl." Princess hoovered her meal in fifteen seconds flat and settled back on her haunches for her after-dinner mint, er, treat. Not too spoiled.

She headed out of the kitchen, nose to the ground, sniffing like crazy. She performed the same routine as the last two nights, searching all over this big-ass house—this floor, upstairs and basement—for Pirate…and Rose.

I'd tried telling her it was useless—no need to lie and say they lived here. She hadn't believed me and kept going. So tonight, I let her be and unpacked my groceries. Madge and Rocky had left me a few staples, but I wanted to bring in my own easy-to-fix go-tos—eggs, potatoes, bacon, bread, sandwich meat, shit like that.

After a quick breakfast for dinner (*what did Rose eat tonight?*), I let Princess out in the backyard. Good thing it was fenced because Hill Road was way too fucking busy for any walk, especially at night, and there were no nearby streets. This weekend in daylight hours, I'd scout out a park or a neighborhood or somewhere for her walks.

Standing on the patio, I opened my phone. It'd been *pinging* off and on for the past few hours. The first *ping*, I'd checked right away to see if it was Rose. Nope. Rocky had sent one last heads-up on the quirkiness of their roaster. After that, I'd restrained myself and let the *pings* go for a while. *Who'd be texting me anyway?*

Ah. Pete had left me a voicemail. And Mateo and Finn had texted me earlier. Still no Rose. *Why would she, you shithead, after the way you insulted her?*

Thursday * 4:34 p.m.

Mateo

> Hey, manito, R said you got there ok. Mama worried becuz of drinking & no sleep—saw me come in late from the pub. Know you feel you made the right D. None of my biz, but your woman has sad eyes.

Thursday * 6:32 p.m.

Me

> Yeah, shitty time all around. But right D. Tango Mike for that nite, pass on to J-L too. Will you & your mamma keep an eye on R? Worried abt eating. Will be back in touch.

Thursday * 5:14 p.m.

Finn

> WTF? Mom txted ur not coming back. Said she was okish. Don't believe her. Shook.

Needed an interpreter to keep up with this kid.

Thursday * 5:19 p.m.

Finn

BTW Pics from Turkey Dog Jog attached. FYI Posted on CLC Web, Insta & FB.

I had forgotten all about Katt's photo tent. First pic, Princess and me—her showing off her loopy grin, me sporting her feathered pink tiara and a frown. Next pic, Pirate and Finn—both smiling, teeth on full display, the pirate tricorn-and-parrot headband now shifted to Finn's head. Last one, Rose standing between Finn and me—the dogs sitting in front of us, both hats on Rose's head now, sticking out at side angles, our arms around her, all laughing at the camera.

Well, almost all. I was looking down at Rose.

Thursday * 6:48 p.m.

Me

Thx for the pics. Thx for posting them for all to see. Not.

Me

Your mamma is the best. I'm not. Better that she find a better man.

Me

Glad to have met you. You're lucky to have each other. Watch out for your mamma.

"Hello? Hello? Rafe, is that you?" Pete shouted. It was phone calls for Pete since the idea of texting was foreign to him. That being said, his grandkids might succeed in getting him on board.

"Yeah, Pete, it's me. Is this an okay time to talk? Not interrupting your dinner?"

"Nope, this is fine," he assured me. "Rose said you got there safely, didn't run into any snow or ice."

I took a big breath, closing my eyes for a moment. It sounded like Rose had no problem telling people I'd taken off in the middle of the night. I wondered if she'd shared anything else.

"Sorry I didn't call you when I got here. Kinda hit the ground running."

"No worries." He paused. "How're you doing, son?"

What the fuck could I say? That I was lonesome for Rose, and it'd only been—what, three days? That I missed her hot touch, but I missed her nonstop sassing more? That I was crazy with worry that she was safe alone in that big house?

That I was barely stopping myself from jumping in my pickup and storming back to Portland?

I could be honest with Pete though. He wouldn't judge me.

"I'm fucked up," I grunted. "But at least I didn't fuck up by caving and saying I'd be back."

He sighed, but didn't say anything.

Time to move on. "Appreciate you pitching in to help Rose while she's searching for a new roaster. Especially with the holidays, the grocery store, the hospital kiosk and all."

"Anything for our girl," Pete pledged. "Mike's been helping too—just can't do much with his leg taking so long to heal. His doc told him he'll have to quit after the first of the year."

"That's cutting it pretty close to the launch," I said before I could catch myself.

"I'm sure we'll find somebody by then. But no worries," he added. "Rose has asked me to train her in coffee roasting so she can take over the job. That woman will do anything to save the Chocolate Lab."

Shit, now I know what she meant. Why hadn't she told me she was that close to the line?

"So, sure thing, I'll put some feelers out for your next gigs after Boise," Pete offered, the sly dog. "It's the busy time so we may not hear until after the holidays. But somebody will need you somewhere."

I rubbed that achy spot in the middle of my chest, hard. Hoping to make it go away.

We said our *goodbyes*, and I whistled for Princess to come inside.

Thursday * 9:52 p.m.

Me

Goodnight, Rose. Sleep tight.

Chapter 41

Rose

"Pete! What do you mean you're not going to train me?" I pulled the phone away from my ear and frowned at the screen. *Yep, still connected.*

"You heard me, Rosie," he said sternly. "If you keep trying to juggle all those coffee mugs at once, they'll just come crashing down on your head. I'm giving you some tough love here."

"But who's going to fill in at such short notice? I can't ask you and Mike to stay through the winter to get the grocery pilot off the ground."

The pilot I'm relying on to save the café.

"Don't worry—I've put the word out in my network. And, hey, I'm not too old to—"

"Oh, Pete, I don't think that—"

He repeated himself, steamrolling right over me. "—I'm not too old to keep the roastery going in the meantime. You do *not* need to add 'coffee roaster' to your already-packed resume. Let your friends help you."

"Well, at least let me pay you—"

"Sure—free lattes for life."

"But you already…" I dwindled off. *Oh. The coffee bean finally drops.*

"You're a sweetheart, Pete. Thank you."

"Anything for you, Rosie."

We parted ways so I could pick up another call from Miss Ada—her fourth so far—to confirm her time for pictures with Santa Paws. I expected to hear from her at least twice more before the day was out.

"Yes, I've got you down for tomorrow, Saturday, at one-thirty. Remember to come to the side door a few minutes early," I reminded her. "If it's raining, you all can stand under the covered decks. Ana will be there dressed as an elf—you can't miss her."

"And Katt promises to have the copies ready by late next week?" she asked in her quavery voice. "I've got my cards ready to go, only waiting for the photos."

"Yes, indeed. We'll call you when they're here for you to pick up."

Her gentle "thanks, dearie, Merry Christmas, dearie" lingered in my ears after we hung up.

I resisted looking at Rafe's texts for the umpteenth time and called Katt instead. She picked up on the second ring.

"Girl, you are booked solid," I informed her. "Oh, wait. I think I left you fifteen minutes for a snack-and-wee break each afternoon."

Her signature raspy laugh came through the line. "Good thing this is only for the weekend. Now all we have to do is get the dogs and cats to behave—and maybe some of their people."

Katt was no doubt thinking of last year when we first offered "Pet Photos with Santa Paws" for the Dogwood Shop Local Days. She'd been on her own, with no help wrangling people and pets in and out of our meeting room—aka the Santa Paws photo booth. Archie, a handsome boxer, had escaped from his dad and chased his poodle girlfriend Colette through the café.

We got smart this year, and Katt had enlisted Ana as her Elf Helper with the promise of a handcrafted sparkly green costume. Joe, a retired firefighter with a full head and fluffy beard of snowy white, again volunteered his time for Santa Paws. Katt donated her skills, too, keeping the fees for printing the photos affordable for all.

Before leaving the meeting room, I rested my eyes for a moment. They still ached—less from crying, more from sleepless nights. I couldn't just lie there for hours on end, so I'd wander downstairs. Pirate would grumble but jump down and follow me. We'd snuggle on the couch, and I'd binge on Elvis movies, PB chocolate chip... and memories.

Rafe wasn't helping. Or maybe he thought he was by not ghosting me—by not deserting me entirely. I broke down and opened my phone to stare at his texts.

After the first couple of wordy ones, they'd boiled down to more Rafe-like messages:

Thursday * 8:52 p.m.

RHR

Goodnight, Rose. Sleep tight.

Friday * 6:24 a.m.

RHR

Good morning, Rose. Eat breakfast? Set alarm?

I hadn't responded yet. But he could see that I'd read each one. I jerked away from the screen when Mateo swung open the door.

"Hey, Rosita! We need your opinion on display space for the gift tins."

I followed Mateo into the hall, instructing myself: *do not look, do not look, do not look into the roastery.* I didn't want to acknowledge the Rafe-sized hole there.

Well, there, and at home, in my bed, on walks with Pirate…in my heart.

Shaking my head, I emerged into the noisy café. My vision instantly blurred, and I blinked hard to clear the wet. *Are you going to cry all day here too?*

My head finally caught up to my heart. *Ahhh, not Rafe-related this time—at least, not entirely.*

When Mateo, Jen, Liliana and the kids realized my holiday spirit had packed up and left town—literally—they'd stepped into the breach.

Rows of shiny garland tinsel lined the café walls from baseboard to ceiling. Dog and cat ornaments of every size and sparkle hung from the garlands, looking for new homes on trees around the neighborhood.

Our Howl-o-ween dog skeletons had reappeared all through the café, now decked out with Santa hats and mini-wreaths around their necks.

Our new Chocolate Lab gift tins ran rampant down one counter. Mateo's pup from conception to roll-out, the giant tins were waiting to be stuffed with all manner of branded gear, coffee mugs, bags of beans, dog treats, coffee-making equipment and chocolate goodies.

The final shout-out to holiday spirit? On windows, doors, walls and counters (the bathroom, too, I suspected), Mateo had posted colorful signs announcing our annual event:

CHRISTMAS EVE–EVE MAGIC ALL DAY LONG
AT THE CHOCOLATE LAB CAFÉ

BUY YOUR FAVORITE PET ORNAMENT FOR $5 OR ?
(ALL PROCEEDS TO THE OREGON HUMANE SOCIETY)

LAST CHANCE FOR STUFF–IT–YOURSELF CHOCOLATE LAB GIFT TINS
(DISCOUNTED 10%, PLUS FREE DRINK COUPONS)

HOT CHOCOLATE & MARSHMALLOWS FOR KIDDIES 18 & UNDER
(PLENTY OF HOT BEVVIES FOR OLDER KIDS TOO)

SIGN UP FOR KARAOKE KAROLING
(6 P.M. TO 9 P.M., BUT KAROLING ENCOURAGED ALL DAY)

"It's the shih tzu, Mateo!" That got a laugh and an eye roll. I gave a giggle in return, my first in a while.

My phone rang with "A Little Less Conversation." I glanced at the number and picked up. "Hello, Miss Ada. Yes, this is a good time. Yes, I've got you confirmed for…"

Friday * 8:43 p.m.

RHR:

Goodnight, Rose. Sleep tight.

Friday * 9:02 p.m.

Me

Goodnight, Rafe. You too. A kiss for Princess.

Chapter 42

Rafe

Saturday * 8:37 a.m.

Me

Good morning, Rose. Eat
breakfast? Set alarm?

Me

Snowed here overnight. P. barked, never seen
white stuff before. Belly rub for your pup.

Shit. Couldn't keep it short and simple. What are you doing,
man?

Saturday * 8:48 a.m.

Rose

Good morning, Rafe. LOL wish
I had video. Yes, 8 eggs, need
energy for DW Buy Local Days. Yes,
altho ctr called bc Pi tripped alarm.
Somehow. Kiss for HRH.

Radio silence was broken. Between her and her son, I was gonna need that translator sooner than later. Had to admit, though, HRH was easy.

Saturday * 11:16 a.m.

Finn

Don't knock ursf like that. Mom wouldn't like it. Yr good for her

Saturday * 11:20 a.m.

Me

That's a matter of opinion.

Saturday * 11:23 a.m.

Finn

Duh. I trust her, Mom knows best

Finn

Dude, I ALWAYS watch out for my mom

Finn

Got 2 go, deadweek started, balls2wall 4 finals. Lookg 4ward to home 4 mo

Saturday * 11:28 a.m.

Me

Now you're just messing with me.

Saturday * 11:30 a.m.

Finn

BET. LMAO

Smart-ass kid.

Saturday * 4:26 p.m.

Rose

Couldn't resist sending pics of Pi with
Santa Paws. Good thing Joe is big.

What a goof. All hundred pounds plus sitting bolt upright on
some poor guy's lap, head turned, tongue reaching out for a big lick
on the ear. Second photo, Rose peeking between Pirate's and Santa's
heads, all three grinning at the camera. How could I save these photos? Didn't want them to disappear. Maybe one of the kids at Bean
Love could help me.

Hmm. I shoved my face closer to the phone. *Dark smudges
under her eyes, creases at the corners. Smile doesn't quite reach her eyes.*

Saturday * 4:38 p.m.

Me

Thanks for sharing. Showed them to Princess,
she cocked her head. Can dogs see photos?
How's the buy local weekend going?

Saturday * 4:41 p.m.

Rose

GR8! Gift tins are a hit. Doing a biz
in hot coffee/choc. Fully booked for
Santa Paws. Oops, got to go—Archie
just took off after Colette. Later.

Saturday * 4:43 p.m.

Me

Later.

Later, Rose. Babe.

Saturday * 10:02 p.m.

Mateo

Could've used you @CLC today! Ran our asses off. Sharing a pitcher w/J-L.

Mateo

Caught Rosita smiling couple of times. Looking at her phone. More color in her cheeks.

Saturday * 10:14 p.m.

Jean-Luc

Missed your footie skills last Th. Sign up for Jan indoor session starts next wk.

Saturday * 10:20 p.m.

Me

Subtle, guys, subtle. Don't close the place down. Again.

Me

Good to hear she's happier. Thanks.

The eyes worry me though.

Saturday * 11:37 p.m.

Me

Know it's too late, you're sleeping now. But had to know—did you catch up with Archie & Colette? Kids, adults, dogs or ?

Me

Played in snow at park today. Fun but cold for single-coat dog.

Me

HRH curled up on bed under her blankets. Drew line at having her under my covers even tho she tried it on for size.

Fuck. Too much. Guessed it came from doing nothing much all day. I'd run tomorrow morning, go in and do some roasts. Take baby girl to the park again. Call Pete, see if he had any action on my next gig. See if there was any news on other fronts.

Saturday * 11:42 p.m.

Rose

Not too late, not sleeping. Boxer Archie spotted poodle Colette waiting in Santa Paws line, chased her. Think they're engaged now LOL.

Rose

Goodnight, Rafe. Sleep tight. Keep warm. Kiss for HRH.

Saturday * 11:45 p.m.

Me

Goodnight, Rose. Sleep tight. Belly rub for Pi.

Keep warm. Kisses for you. *Always on my mind.*

Chapter 43

Rose

"You did *not*!" Lauren gasped.

"We did too!" I claimed. Pirate grumbled where he slept, stretched down my lower legs—luckily, head, not heinie, pointed toward my face.

He'd stayed extra close—some might've called it *clingy*—since Rafe and Princess had left. He was kinda like my protection detail slash fur comforter. Except for this last weekend, I'd even been parking the big boy in the café's meeting room while I worked.

"Yep, we'd sold more than half the tins by Sunday afternoon," I said, gently stroking between Pi's eyes. "The kids were busy all day today filling online orders. I've already talked to Kenzo about more truffles and to Pete and Mike about more mini-bags of the Santa Paws blend."

"What about your branded mugs and beanies? Oh, and don't you have Chocolate Lab dog bandannas?"

"Mateo was on top of all that too. He bought extra back in September so we'd have plenty to last the entire holiday season. He's stepped up to help me since Mom passed."

Lauren sucked in a big breath. "Oh, girl, forgive me. This is going to be your first Christmas without your mom. With all my stupid drama, I forgot."

"Don't even, girl," I said firmly. "To have you move here, to have Finn home for an entire month, to celebrate with dear friends and neighbors—Mom would be happy that I'm surrounded by so much love and support. In fact, near the end, she *told* me she was happy for me. I couldn't hear her until now."

I changed the subject so we wouldn't start crying, and so I could put off why I'd *really* called.

"So it's settled? Finn's last final is Thursday afternoon, and you guys are driving up Friday?"

"That's the plan, unless it gets super snowy in the passes. Then we might leave Thursday and stay somewhere overnight." She laugh-snorted. "Although, with all my clothes and stuff crammed in the trunk and backseat, we should get pretty good traction. At least I won't have to worry about Baby's safety. It's a mixed blessing that she's staying with Oliver for the dog show."

We'd catch up when she got here. Our convo about her toxic marriage, even more toxic divorce, and custody battle would resume over Manhattans at Fay's.

I couldn't wait any longer.

I burst out, "We've been talking."

"Uh, yeahhhh, Rose," she drawled. "For about the last fifteen minutes."

"No. I mean, yes, *we* have. But I mean Rafe and I have been talking, texting actually, for the past several days."

There was a beat. Trust Lauren to come out with "texting, not sexting?" as her first comeback.

"No. I mean, yes, Rafe and I have been *texting*." I whisper-shouted, disturbing the dog, who decided to stand on my tender bits and jump down.

"Nothing sexy, just somewhat short and pretty sweet." I swung my legs from the couch to sit up.

"That's too bad."

"Lauren!" I huffed in exasperation. "You remember—I was short and *snarky* when he'd texted me they'd made it safely to Boise. Of course, Rafe being Rafe, he had to take it one step further and check on my eating and alarm-setting habits."

"I do remember, girl—you were still at the mad-and-crying phase before you moved on to sad-and-crying."

And sleepless, I added to myself. We didn't do video calls, normally, so Lauren hadn't seen how run-down I looked. Another reason for text-only with Rafe, so far.

"Rafe hasn't given up, Lauren. He hasn't given up," I said softly, arms on my knees as I stared at the rug where Pirate had resettled on his back, all four legs in the air. "He's kept on with the *good mornings* and the *good nights.* The oh-so-innocent *inquiries* about my nutrition and safety."

I snickered. "And he's gotten downright chatty in text mode—for him. He goes on and on about Princess and her fascination with snow—the white stuff not being a thing in Afghanistan. He complains about rattling around the owners' ginormous house, but then claims he's grateful for the free roof over his head. He shares funny stories about the kids who work at Bean Love—says they remind him of our kid crew."

"Okay, Rose, okay." My friend stopped me in my blathering. "It's me. I know you too well. You were heartbroken when Rafe left. But you're too kind to leave the man hanging. When did you…reengage?"

"He seemed lonely. He needed someone to talk to."

"When, girl?"

"Friday, I guess. He'd texted a *good night.* Although Saturday, I texted him during the day about Santa Paws and sent some photos. We may have texted that evening too."

"What? Four days after he left?" She lost it and started laughing out of control.

Pirate righted himself and followed her lead, barking his fool head off.

I put the phone on speaker and clapped my hands. "Everyone—that's enough! I've come to a decision."

Lauren quieted down to the occasional giggle, but Pi continued to grumble.

"Shush now. Lie down." For once, he did what I told him and jumped back on the couch.

"What *did* you decide?" she got out.

"I decided that *I* get to decide if we give love a chance. I decided to fight for Rafe. I'm going to show him he *is* the best man for me. I'll start by telling him I need him. Then I'll ask, no, *demand* that he come back home—come back home to me."

"Get it, girl!" Lauren shouted.

I laughed and clapped again. I *knew* my bestie would cheer me on.

Wait. What was this….? I picked up my phone and squinted at the screen.

"I'm getting a call from an unknown number with a San Francisco area code. Talk to you later—fingers and paws crossed."

I ended our call and answered the new one. "Hello. How may I help you?" I went for neutral in case it was spam or a café vendor or Finn with a new number or…

"Hello," came a deep male voice. "This is Antonio Amato. I'm trying to reach Rose Connolly."

"Yes, I'm Rose. Thank you so much for calling, Mr. Amato. Are you Angelina's father?"

"Yes, I'm her papa." A pause. "She's named after my older sister."

Oh!

I must've said that out loud because he asked, "Is this a good time to talk?"

Chapter 44

Rose

I sat at my dining table, Pirate at my feet, beaming at Rafe on the laptop screen. Or at least, the Rafe of eight, ten years from now.

Next to him was a lovely blue-eyed woman in her mid-twenties. Both were looking at me like I was crazy, probably because my smile was so big my cheeks hurt. A handsome guy with dark hair in a man bun came up behind Tony and dipped his head down to peer at me.

"Is she okay, Papa? She seems stuck that way."

"Nico!" his sister pleaded. "Stop it. You're being rude."

The trouble was, Nico, man bun aside, looked like my imagined Rafe of fifteen or twenty years ago.

My Zoom with the Amato family was off to a great start.

Yesterday, after a few minutes on the phone, Tony (*please call me "Tony"—Mr. Amato was my father*) had suggested we set up a video call.

"It'll be better to talk face-to-face. I have questions, many questions. I'd also like my daughter to be on the call, if that's all right with you." He'd shared in the introductions that he was a widower with three children.

"Will Raphael be joining us?"

I'd figured this was coming. "He goes by Rafe now. And he won't be joining us for this first call. He's working in Boise at the moment—a temporary coffee-roasting job." For two months...or maybe forever.

"We can still invite him to the call. Angelina knows how to do that."

"I'm sorry, Tony. Rafe doesn't know yet that I've contacted you. Please let me explain tomorrow."

Gentleman that he was, Tony had agreed to wait to hear my story. We'd exchanged emails for Angelina to schedule the Zoom call.

Now she took the lead in breaking the ice.

"Ms. Connolly..."

"Rose, please."

"Rose, thanks for messaging me originally. I'm sorry it took so long to get back to you. I wanted to show Papa your café's website and social media pages. I have one question before we get started on all our *other* questions."

She grinned and leaned closer to the screen. "Do you have any pictures of Rafe where he's *not* wearing a tiara?"

"Sure." I was prepared, hitting the *share screen* icon at the bottom of the Zoom page. "He's camera shy, but here's a couple of my favorites from when he took us to the beach in October."

All three leaned close this time. And all three started smiling and nodding and glancing at each other. The family resemblance was unmistakable.

The next question was a surprise though.

"So Rafe's okay with having dogs around?" Nico asked.

"Oh, more than okay." I laughed. "He's pretty buttoned up, but he adores his pup, Princess. She was a camp dog, and he arranged for her to come all the way from Afghanistan."

Tap. Tap. Tap. All of a sudden, a dainty dog with a long slender muzzle slipped her head under Angelina's arm and crawled partway onto her lap. She settled and stared at me.

"This is Bella, our Italian Greyhound," Nico said, reaching down to stroke her neck. "The latest in a line of greyhounds since we were little."

Pirate was sitting up now, crowding close to look at the screen. "Must run in the family," I declared, looping my arm around his neck. "We've had chocolate Labs all my life. My son Finn grew up with Pirate here."

Tony's eyes lit up. "Glad to hear it. My parents were strict—nothing to mess up, or warm up, the house. They never allowed us to have any pets. I was determined it'd be different for my kids."

Ah, so now to the heart of the matter.

Tony went on, "Rafe was in the military before he became a coffee roaster?"

"Yes, he enlisted out of high school and served for over twenty years, both here and in the Middle East, before he took retirement," I said. Yesterday, I'd already shared how Rafe and I had met when he arrived for the temporary roaster job at the Chocolate Lab.

"Rose, I tried to find him." Tony looked pained. "I tell you—and I'll tell it to Rafe's face if I get a chance to meet him—I tried to find him."

"Tony, you were so young yourself. You gotta know you did the best you could." I tried to console him while Angelina and Nico patted his shoulders.

He said in a rush, "I was nine when my parents found out Angelina was pregnant. Abortion was out of the question, and they—and the priest—wanted her to give up the baby for adoption. So much crying and slammed doors. They tried to hide it from me, but I overheard enough."

He shook his head like he was still in disbelief, all these years later. "She refused, and my father kicked her out. They weren't going to allow her to see me. She pushed into my bedroom anyway and hugged me so hard. She told me she had some money from our grandmother and that a cousin was going to help her. That was the last time I saw her."

Tony picked up some envelopes and waved them. "I got some letters from her—at least the ones my mother didn't intercept—and some photos too. Nothing about her struggles, all about Raphael. When I was about fifteen, the letters stopped. I was old enough to figure out how to take the bus to where they lived in Oakland. They were gone, and nobody was around to answer any questions."

Closing his eyes, he grimaced. "My father was quick with the slap, and my mother had no say in our house. I got out of there when I turned eighteen and never looked back. I was a hard worker, and eventually my wife and I opened a deli and grocery. With her support, I ran down my sister's death certificate *and* Raphael's birth certificate—but no trace of my nephew himself. We think the system lost any records."

"I take it your parents were never involved in the search?" I asked gently.

"No," Tony said shortly. "And they're no longer living."

Nico put his hands on his dad's shoulders, and Angelina leaned into his side. They knew something bad was coming.

"Rose, what happened to Raphael after my sister died?"

There was no way to sugarcoat it. But I did try to soften it.

"Please know that Rafe is safe now. He's healthy and fit. He's a hard worker." Here I smiled at Tony. "His experiences in the army, and maybe before, have made him over-the-top protective of the people he...cares for. He has the respect—and affection, whether he believes it or not—of my son, my friends and everyone at the Chocolate Lab."

"Rose, just tell us," Tony urged.

"Okay." I was overstepping, but I swallowed over the lump in my throat and gave in. Wanting to spare them pain, I sketched in broad strokes, while glossing over details, the story of Rafe's life with his mom, his placement in foster care after her death, and his decision to enlist after high school.

By the time I finished, tears were running down the faces on the other side of the screen. Whether it was my somber look or my halting words, Rafe's family got the untold story.

"Last week, when Rafe was getting ready to leave for his job in Boise, I pushed him, Tony."

"What do you mean, Rose?"

"I pushed him into telling me *why* he wouldn't return to Portland, to me. He told me I deserved better. He told me to find a better man. Despite how he cared for his mom, despite all his years in military service, despite all he's done for me, he didn't want anyone relying on him."

I was determined *not* to spill all the details about the teen gang and fighting and bloodshed to his new family. Those parts of his past had given me pause before I'd gotten my head—and heart—together. That was Rafe's story and his alone to share.

Instead, I finally zipped my lip. "Anyway, he decided to shut me out. I got mad and told him to go. We've reconnected since then, and I think he's forgiven me. But still…"

I was the one sobbing now. *Why was I spilling even some of this private stuff, worse yet, all these…feelings to relative strangers?*

"Rose. Rose, mia cara." Tony had the kindest look on his face. "We're going to make this right—we're all in this together."

That right there was the reason why. Because there were actually good people all around (as I knew living in Dogwood) and because I needed their help. I nodded, scrubbing my face with my palms. Pirate whimpered and stuck his head in my lap.

"Now tell me about your friend—Lauren?—who tracked me down through Angelina's Instagram postings. She lives here in San Francisco?"

"North of you in Sonoma County, actually, but she's moving here. In fact, next week she's picking up my son from college in the Bay area, and they're driving up to Portland together."

"Do you think she'd be willing to come into the city to our place before they leave?" I was nodding again—and grinning again—before Tony could finish talking. "There are some family things I'd like to send with her so you could give them to Raphael. To smooth the way for an introduction."

"Yes, I know Lauren would be delighted to come see you. I'll put you two in touch by email after this call." I laughed, remembering. "She's one of Rafe's biggest fans. Get her to tell you how she helped my son wrangle Rafe into living in my garage apartment."

Nico chimed in, "You've mentioned your son a couple of times now. Is there a Mr. Connolly?"

"Nico, stop it!" his sister demanded. "You're being too personal."

I grinned bigger. "That's okay, Angelina. *Mr. Connolly* was my dear dad. Finn's father is not in the picture. He was *never* in the picture."

Tony had the last word. "Rose, bring our Rafe home."

Chapter 45

Rafe

Me

Good morning, Rose. Thinking about my mamma lately. Don't know why. Been meaning to ask. How are you doing this first Christmas without your mom?

Monday * 7:11 a.m.

Rose

Good morning, Rafe. Thanks for asking. Have my moments—get all weepy, and I go sit on the couch with one of our old photo albums. Missing the Finn boy too—first holiday season when he's not here all the time. Can hardly wait until he arrives this Friday. Saving the tree to decorate with him. He's driving up with Lauren—did I tell you that already?

Rose

What do you remember about
Christmas when you were a kid? I
mean with your mom—or were you
too young to have any memories?

Rose

Sorry, sorry. Don't answer if
this is too hard.

I stood in the middle of the roastery, rubbing my chest. Like I
could erase the ache that'd taken up permanent residence there. *This
woman.*

Monday * 7:22 a.m.

Me

Yeah, some memories. I was probably 4 when
they started. Mamma made me believe there
was a Santa Claus. Told me he delivered all
the gifts—probably because she only had
money for a couple things. He parked on the
roof & climbed in our window. Had to leave it
unlocked that one night only.

Rose

Did you have a tree?

Me

Yep. My height, so small. Not real, of course—
bet Mamma got it on sale. We made paper
chains & a foil star for the top.

Rose

Other things you remember about
Christmas with your mom?

Me

Cookies & singing.

Monday * 7:33 a.m.

Rose

Still there? Tell me more.

Monday * 7:41 a.m.

Me

Yeah. Sorry. Had to check on a roast. On
Christmas Eve, we sang—mostly carols—
while we made sugar cookies out of the box.
Cut them in shapes, frosted them green & red.
Ate them on the spot.

Rose

LOL sugar high. How did
you ever fall asleep?

Me

Don't know. Remember putting out 1 cookie on
a plate, water for the reindeer. Conked by the
window. Waiting for Santa.

Rose

Good memories, right, Rafe?

275

Monday * 7:53 a.m.

Me

Yes. More than good. After that, Christmas was hit or miss. Didn't believe any longer. So no expectations.

Me

Babe, know it's hard without your mom. Trusting you to take care of yourself, warm yourself with your memories.

Rose

That's lovely, Rafe. Thank you. And, yes, big strong army-boxer-soccer-roaster guys can be lovely. Get over it.

Me

Rose. Babe. Gotta go deal with the roaster. Later tonight?

Me

Later. That's a promise.

Wish I could be there to keep you warm. *Except you fucking fucked it up, didn't you?*

Monday * 11:42 p.m.

Me

> Sorry I couldn't text earlier. Minor prob with roaster, had to find part, catch up on roasts. Hope your day was better than mine. Good night, Rose. Talk tomorrow. Sleep tight.

Rose

> That dog won't hunt. I know a way to make your day better. Pick up, Rafe.

Eight seconds later...

"Rose? Is everything okay?"

"Yes, unless you know someone else who's wearing only stilettos. And yes, everything's okay, or will be when you push Princess off the bed."

"What the fuck?"

"I already kicked Pi out—he's grumbling in the corner. Keep up, sweetheart."

"Babe, what the hell?"

"Time's a-wastin'—and I turn into a truffle at midnight. Oh, wait. You're one hour ahead. Guess we just have fifteen minutes. Or we *could* go by Pacific Standard Time."

"Grrr..."

"I'll take that as a *yes*. What are *you* wearing in bed tonight?"

Chapter 46

Rose

I was grinning, probably with squinty-crazy-eyes, at the roll-up sandwiches I'd prepped for Katt and Liliana. Because all was good—better than good—I added a scoop of our house-made pasta salad and popped a bonus truffle on each plate.

I'd just gotten off the phone with Lauren. This morning, she'd met with Tony at his deli-grocery in the North Beach neighborhood of San Francisco. He'd given her some letters, pictures and other family mementos to bring to me when she and Finn drove up here tomorrow.

"Such a sweet and generous man!" my bestie had raved. "They had some Italian pastries waiting for me and made me a macchiato the minute I walked in the door."

She let out a long sigh. "I got to meet Angelina and her two brothers too. That Nico is a scamp for sure. And all the guys look like your Rafe."

Not mine—not yet, I'd reminded her.

She'd described what Tony had given her. The best part? Apparently, they'd *each* written a letter and tucked them all in a big envelope for me to send (*they'd said* give, *Rose*) to Rafe.

I grabbed the two plates and walked over to the table by the front window. It was a little crowded, what with their mochas, Katt's tablet, Liliana's notepad and pen—real paper, real writing instrument—and three or four cat ornaments from the walls. But we made it work.

"How's the planning coming along?" I asked. Ana was getting her long-wished-for kitten as a surprise for Christmas. Experienced cat staff Katt was giving Liliana pointers on the Humane Society's adoption process and the welcome-to-your-new-home essentials.

"Sit, sit for a moment," Liliana urged.

I dropped down to the extra chair, and she pushed out, "I never realized how much one tiny kitty needed. Perrito's huge, and I don't remember him requiring this much."

Katt and I glanced at each other and looked away, hiding our smiles. The real question was how their talkative, playful husky was going to take to the miniature new member of their family.

Katt turned back to me and narrowed her eyes. "You look… happy. Kinda bright and sparkly and, yes, happy."

Of course, being a photographer and an artist, she'd see how my face reflected my mood.

"Is that a question or a statement?" I stalled.

"Ha! Definitely a statement. Spill the tea!" Both Katt and Liliana focused their laser-like stares in my direction.

"Okay, okay, I give up. Rafe and I have been texting for the past two weeks. More recently, talking." As one, they started smiling and nodding.

"We knew you two couldn't stay away from each other," Liliana declared.

I held one hand up. "Hold on. We're just talking at this point, keeping the channels open. Nothing about him coming back here. I haven't even asked him yet."

They frowned a little at that. It hit me, and I sat up straight in my chair.

"I need your help," I said.

"Anything!" they cried in unison.

"I want to send Rafe some gifts and some photos and…some messages about how much I miss him. Maybe how much we *all* miss him."

They nodded again, and Liliana said, "Oh, like a care package. I used to mail those to Mateo when he was deployed overseas. He *loved* getting them."

"Yeah, he's even mentioned them to me a time or three," said Katt, blushing a bright pink. *Hmm…what is that all about?* "I bet Rafe'd love getting one again."

"I don't think he ever received care packages back then," I commented. "No family, you know."

"Oh, Rose," Liliana said sadly.

I clapped my hands. "Okay. We're going to change all that. First, let's make a list of things to send him."

Liliana pulled her notepad in front of her, flipped to a new page and picked up her pen.

"Oh, fido." I reached over to her. "Here, please give me those. Let *me* take notes while you both eat."

She patted my arm. "Rosita, I can eat, talk and write all at the same time. We moms are good at multitasking, right?"

We jumped into brainstorming goodies for the care package—now grown into a care *box*—until only smears of pesto from the salad were left on their plates.

I turned to Katt. "Could you possibly come over to my house tomorrow evening to take some photos? And make prints by Saturday morning? I know it's a quick turnaround."

She nodded and added, "I'll make prints of other photos Rafe's in too."

"I want to drop off the care box at the post office by Saturday noon. I imagine I'll pay a bundle to get it to him by Christmas Eve day. But it'll be worth every penny..."

"You're cutting it close, girl," Katt warned.

"I know, I know," I agreed, worry creeping in. "Maybe I need to check with Pete to see if he has any recommendations for shipping companies. And any other ideas to go into the care...boxcar."

They laughed at me, and I didn't blame them one bit. I *had* gone a little overboard.

"Rosie, you don't have to say who you are. I'd recognize your voice anywhere."

"Oh, Pete, you're a sweetheart! Are you getting excited for your grandkids to come visit?"

"You'd better believe it! They and their folks are driving down this Saturday and staying for the week. We'll see you Monday night—sure looking forward to karaoke caroling at your place!"

"You may see me before then—I need your help. Can you keep a secret?"

Chapter 47

Rose

Finn positioned our old punched-tin star on top of the tree and climbed down the ladder. He folded it up and leaned it against a wall while Lauren went around turning off all the lamps.

They joined me in the middle of the living room, linking my arms on either side. We lifted our faces to bask in the glow of hundreds of tiny white lights. The strings were tucked back into the branches of the mammoth Douglas fir sitting in front of the windows.

Plaid ribbon wove in and around the tree, leaving the ends of the branches free for our ornaments. They were everywhere, with hardly a space to spare—vintage glass angels, Swedish straw goats, Irish Celtic knots, dogs of every breed and mix, foil-wrapped chocolates, and red and green paper chains made by five-year-old Finn. Some chains had two links, some had many more. All had been examined and re-glued as was our practice each year.

My cheeks hurt from grinning so big. I pulled my son and my bestie even closer to me and wallowed in the pure joy of the moment. A moment that capped my happiest day since Rafe's departure almost three weeks ago.

This morning, I'd packed, no, *stuffed* the care box with all the things I'd collected in the past two days. I'd started with one of the Chocolate Lab gift tins, but soon the goodies had spilled over into the surrounding cardboard container.

Besides holding my message and gifts—and those from Tony and his family—the box burst at the seams with items from everyone and their dog.

- *Hot pink Chocolate Lab beanie – Mateo*
- *Chocolate Lab dog bandanna – Ana*
- *Apple empanadas – Liliana*
- *Timbers soccer T-shirt– Jean-Luc*
- *Chocolate truffles – Kenzo*
- *Insulated dog jacket – Mica & her dad*
- *Elvis Love Songs CD – Lauren*
- *Dog snow booties – Jen & her twins*
- *Dog biscuits – Miss Ada & the girls*
- *Frosted cutout cookies – Finn & Pirate*
- *Silver coffee cupping spoon – Pete*

Once the box had been packed and taped up a bazillion ways, Finn and I had taken it over to Pete's friend at a north Portland shipping company. We'd sent it to the Bean Love Café, rather than the house, so Rafe would be there to sign for it. Guaranteed delivery by Christmas Eve!

Our night finished up with hot chocolate and marshmallows—and Baileys Irish Cream for the adults. Which turned out to be all three of us. Where did the time go?

We parted ways around eleven—Finn with Pi in tow and Lauren, still tired from their drive yesterday, to their rooms upstairs, and me to the garage apartment. Where I planned to spend some quality time with Rafe. Where we couldn't be heard.

"I can't do this any longer, Rose."

I was sitting back against the headboard for our customary post-phone-sex talk. Still trying to catch my breath, I blotted my face with the back of my hand. His face had a sheen to it, too, but he was speaking in more measured tones than I could manage at the moment.

"I'm sorry, I didn't quite get that. Must be all my panting."

He didn't laugh.

"Rafe, could you please repeat what you just said?"

He looked away from the screen and turned back, his lips pressed in a tight line. "I can't do this anymore, the texting, the talking, the phone sex. Seeing you this way."

Oh. Okay. I got it now. "Rafe, I feel the same. It sucks big-time that we're apart. But it's only for a couple more months. When you—"

"No, Rose." He cut me off. "I mean it will be too hard on you—and me—when I move on to my next job."

"You're not... You're not co...coming home?" I went from flushed to ice cold in an instant, numbness spreading from my face down to my fingertips. I fumbled and nearly dropped my phone.

"The reasons I left haven't changed," Rafe mumbled.

"What?" I whisper-shouted.

"The reasons—"

"No. I heard you. I just couldn't believe my ears."

"Rose, I know this hurts—"

I cut him off. "Let me get this straight. For the past two weeks, we've been texting and talking and video calling and...and...sharing even more than we had in the entire two months before that. We *finally* dealt with the reasons you left—and the reasons I let you go. All the guilt you carried, all the mistrust I suffered—we were putting that all behind us."

"Rose, babe, I know it seems—"

"Don't *babe* me. It's still my turn. So what changed your mind?"

I paused, tears pricking the inside corners of my eyes. No, not yet. I tilted my head toward the ceiling and blinked as fast as I could.

When I lowered my eyes to meet Rafe's gaze, he seemed pale under the stubble. But how could I tell? His image was small and far away.

Wait. I could still see it, which meant he could too. Every morning and night, he saw it in the bathroom mirror. That reminder, that knife scar, that fucking scar.

He started to speak, and I talked over him. "You're *still* letting the past interfere with our future. I thought we decided to leave the past behind. I thought we were building a relationship for the future *us*, for when you returned to Dogwood."

To me.

"What we've had," Rafe pushed out, "doesn't change the fact that I'm not good enough for you. I've let people down when they've needed me the most. There's no guarantee I won't do that with you. We need to end this—you need the way clear to find better."

There it was again. Rafe deciding what I needed. Telling me what I needed. And he was right.

"You're right," I informed him. "I *can't* do this any longer."

His eyes widened—in surprise or maybe shock—although I didn't know what he expected. I was tired of being the only one fighting for us.

"You're trapped in the past, and you're shutting me out—again—because you're afraid you're going to fail me."

The tears started running down my cheeks, "The thing is… The thing is…I need you and I love you *no matter what*. I love you *whoever* you are—the boy who was lost without his mom, the teen who got in with the bad crowd, the soldier who couldn't save his brothers—even the overprotective guy who tried to rescue me all the time."

I caught my sobs and drew in a big breath. "I see *you*, and I love you. Unconditionally, without judgment—you know, like how our dogs love us. But I can't fight for us alone. So you're right—we need to end this. Goodbye, Rafe."

I hit the red circle at the bottom of my screen. A few seconds later, Elvis started to sing. I declined the call and blocked the RHR number.

I cried myself to sleep, a mix of mad and sad tears clogging my nose. And tried not to think of the care box—and all it contained— speeding on its way to Boise.

Even Pirate couldn't retrieve that puppy now.

Chapter 48

Rafe

I sit bolt upright, throwing off the covers. Sunlight's shining through the window—must've stopped snowing in the night. Fuck. That means I'm late. I lean over to nuzzle Rose awake, but she's not there.

No Princess or Pirate around either, their bagel bed and its pile of blankets deserted. Grab my phone from the nightstand to check in with Rose—she's probably opening the café. It tells me I'm blocked—that can't be right. The damn thing dies—that explains why, forgot to charge it.

I can still catch her if I'm quick. Sure, it'll be cold without clothes, but gotta get going. Throw open the bedroom door and stop. I hear a woman singing, sweet and sultry at the same time. Familiar, can't make out the words yet. I follow the sound downstairs through the dining room to the kitchen.

Two spots are set at the butcher block island. Plates and forks on cute-as-shit placemats with Lab pups romping around. Before I get there, Pirate jumps up on me, licking my face, one paw on each shoulder. Where's Princess? There she is—running around the island toward me, barking like a loonball.

Rose stands at the stove, waving a spatula, singing something Elvis. No surprise. She hasn't left yet, not in that getup. Thank fuck. Got my T-shirt on—it's supersized, hanging below, but barely covering, her

287

heart-shaped ass. A little unsteady on her stilettos, but keeping her balance. As always.

She looks over her shoulder. "How do you want your truffles?"

"My what?"

"Your truffles, sweetheart. Milk, dark or caramelized?"

"I'm not sure I'm hungry right now. Rose, I need to tell you—"

"Breakfast is the most important meal of the day, Rafe!" She puts a fist on her hip and points the spatula at me. Ready to take me on.

"Okay, okay. You choose—whichever you decide to have." Maybe I'm not too late.

She motions toward a stool at the island, and I plant myself on it, Princess and Pirate settling at my feet. Hoping for a handout, but I know that chocolate is bad for dogs.

"Bacon's in the oven. It wouldn't be Christmas morning breakfast without bacon and truffles."

"And coffee." Going with the flow.

"Of course." She pours me a cup from the French press with her free hand and passes it my way.

"Your very own Santa Paws blend, Rafe."

I toast her, trying to wait patiently until she sits down. Hoping I'm not too late.

Rose flips off the burner and switches off the oven. She pulls out the bacon, piling it high on a serving dish. She struts over with the skillet to scoop out a half dozen dark chocolate truffles on each of our plates. The dogs spring up when she lands the bacon dish between us.

"Toss them some strips, Rafe, and take some for yourself."

She gets her cup off the counter and comes back to sit down.

Finally. I open my mouth to tell her I'm sorry I hurt you. I was wrong. You make me better. I want to come home.

I need you. I love you.

Before I can get my words out, she presses her fingers over my lips. Her sad smile doesn't reach her sadder eyes.

"You're right, Rafe. We can't do this again. It's too late."

Rose, the dogs, the kitchen, all melt away. I'm on my knees in front of her house. Too late, I recognize what she'd been singing—an Elvis favorite, "I'll Be Home for Christmas." If only in my dreams...

A cold nose nudged the side of my face, hard. I was flat on my back in bed, my cheeks wet. Had Princess been licking me? No. Tears had slid down onto my jaw and neck too.

A whimper had me shifting my eyes to the right. She sat on the other pillow, frowning at me with worry like dogs do.

"It's okay, baby girl." I dragged myself up to sit against the headboard and scrubbed my face with my palms. She whimpered again, and I pulled her in for a hug, twisting to the left to make sure the framed photo was still there on the nightstand.

It was normally the first thing I saw in the morning and the last thing I saw at night, but this was not a normal morning, and last night had been anything but normal.

My sleep had been fitful, at best, and I'd kept reaching over to light up my phone. No joy then—and none now—when I grabbed it to check for messages, voice mails, *anything* from Rose. My screen informed me it was Sunday, 9:22 (or 8:22 Portland time), and that was it.

Radio silence, again. I closed my eyes and slumped over for a few minutes—until the chiming started.

One alert sounded after another, after another, after another. I opened the phone to see texts from Finn, Mateo, Lauren, Jean-Luc. Hell—I was surprised I didn't see one from Pirate.

Finn's set the tone for all the others:

Sunday * 9:42 a.m.

Finn

> What The Fuck, Rafe? Why is my
> mother crying her eyes out? She
> says it was her decision. I thought
> you were going to do the right
> thing. WHAT THE FUCK?

Running downstairs, Princess on my heels, I made one last decision on my own. Then I replied to everyone's texts:

Sunday * 9:54 a.m.

Rafe

> I fucked up. I hurt the
> woman I love. I need your
> help. Please.

Before the news could work its way to Pete (Mateo to Liliana to Pete) and he called me, I called him.

"Pete, I screwed up big-time with Rose. I need your help in making it right. Can you keep a secret?"

Chapter 49

Rose & Rafe

Rose

I was huddled on the couch with Pirate, still wrapped in my old flannel robe, still planning to spend the day there. Maybe I'd get dressed, maybe not. Either way, I was keeping my fuzzy slippers on. Even if I was going tonight.

Rafe

It was dark when we got up, but the streetlights showed another six, eight inches of snow. Good thing we had plenty of layers to wear. At least I did—Princess only had two. Luckily, one was a fur coat. I'd be piling her blankets in the back too.

Rose

Pirate grumbled when I leaned over to look past our Christmas tree and out the windows. The snow falling fast and furious confirmed the forecasts on my laptop from the local stations. Several inches by evening—so early for Portland. Should I locate those studded tires? Why bother? I wasn't driving anywhere today.

Rafe

When the snow got heavier, I pulled into a truck stop and put on my chains. Probably should have done it back at the house, but I was in a hurry to get on the road. Baby girl was happy for the pee break, although I tried to prevent her from scarfing down snow. Didn't want her to get too cold.

Rose

"Coming up next, Elvis with 'Santa Bring My Baby Back To Me'," the DJ announced after cautioning listeners to stay safe in all the snow. I muted my laptop and stretched out on the couch, head on the snowman pillow. Pi crawled up my legs and settled with a groan. Heavy and warm, like a comforter. Maybe I could catch up on my sleep.

Rafe

"Blue Christmas" faded into the background as I hunched and stared through the foggy windshield. It snowed harder as we got closer— and the dark didn't help. We'd only stopped once more, for both of us to hit the head and grab lunch. I leaned back, and Princess immediately dropped her chin on my shoulder. Helping me navigate, maybe? Although her snoring put that in doubt.

Rafe

Snow powdering our heads, we climbed up the stairs to the front porch. I took a big breath and looked down. "Here we go, baby girl." Before I had a chance to knock, the door swung wide open. "Hello, son," said Pete, grinning ear to ear. "You made it in time."

Rose

I startled awake when Lauren burst through the front door, shouting, "Wake up, Rose! It's time to get down to the café!" It didn't help that Pi jumped off me and started barking. Or that it was dark, with no inside lights except for the tree.

She skidded to a halt and stared at me. "You can't go like that." I looked down at my jeans and oversized flannel shirt (actually, Rafe's shirt) and shrugged my shoulders.

"Wasn't planning to go anyway."

She pulled out the Mom card. "You can't miss it—it was your mom's favorite."

I gave in with ill grace. "Okay, but I'm still wearing my slippers."

She gasped when she saw my feet. "Oh, for the love of— Thankfully, your boy shoveled the sidewalks. And it seems like you brushed your hair."

Well, yeah, if you counted my fingers. Lauren grabbed my coat from the hall tree and tugged me out the door.

Chapter 50

Rose

The place was packed—literally standing room only—and Jen and her twins were holding the mic, leading the last round of "The Twelve Days of Christmas." Adam was behind his keyboard, clipboard in hand, ready to call the names of the next people signed up for Karaoke Karoling.

With an "Oh, nobody will notice you," Lauren dragged me through the side door into the café and headed to the front corner. Erik and his wife jumped up from a table just as we arrived, and we were lucky enough to snare their spots. I didn't feel guilty, not one bit. It'd occurred to me on the way over that I wasn't looking my best—so we could hide out in the corner.

Still, I was glad to be here for one of Mom's favorite holiday traditions.

People stood crammed together in front of us, blocking the view. Then two sweet voices—Liliana and Ana?—started "White Christmas" amid general laughter. Soon they were leading the audience in the chorus, and everyone was singing at the top of their lungs.

The front door opened to my left, letting in a swoosh of chilly air. Pete and his family hurried in, all bundled up against the cold. He saw me and gave a big smile and thumbs-up. *So happy for him that he can spend the holidays with his grandkids.* He led them toward the front counter and all that hot-chocolate-and-marshmallow goodness.

Finn and a couple of the kids on our crew were weaving through the crowd, delivering food, drinks and treats to the tables. I gave a little wave, but I didn't think they saw us. Mateo must've been going crazy behind the counter, but he'd laughed when I called earlier to offer to come in to work. "Thanks, Rosita, but we're all good here."

I was leaning close to Lauren to shout, "This is the biggest turnout *ever* in the history of Karaoke Karoling" when Adam tapped the mic. The crowd hushed instantly. Even the kiddos were quiet, except for Liam's Meggie, who squealed, "What's going on, Daddy?"

That started a wave of laughter, but soon Adam got everyone's attention again. "We have a late sign-up for our event tonight, and"—there were muffled sounds like he'd covered the mic and was talking with someone—"and apparently, the mic and my keyboard backup are surplus to requirements."

He added, "Let me warn you, folks—this is not your typical Christmas carol. I think you'll agree, though, that the opening line fits the season perfectly."

The hush again, and then—*Wise men say...*

I recognized the first words of "Can't Help Falling in Love," sounding in a deep baritone from the hallway to the roastery.

I surged up, knocking my chair back. Trying to see over the heads of everyone standing in my way. I flicked my eyes down to Lauren, and she widened hers in return. No help there.

The strong voice continued the song alone, no backup required or wanted.

I strained on my tiptoes, craning my neck to look. Sure seemed like the singer was getting closer. I started to push forward, and—miracle—the crowd parted, making a path.

Rafe at one end, moving this way. Me at the other end, standing frozen now.

He reached me, held out his hand and sang the ending lines about a love fated-to-be.

Not *quite* the ending though. Because I took his hand, and we sang that very last line, again, together.

Another miracle unfolded—or maybe just some help from family and friends. The crowd, still quiet, closed and parted again, creating a path to where my son was pulling the side door open.

Rafe brought his other hand up to cup my chin, leaning down to touch his lips to mine. We smiled into each other's eyes for a long moment and turned to walk down the path. When we got to the door, he looked outside at the snow drifting over the sidewalk and down at my feet. My slipper-covered-not-ready-for-winter-weather feet.

"Rose. Babe," he growled and shook his head. A second later, I was caught up in his arms, and we headed toward home.

The crowd in the café made noise now, clapping and cheering and singing as the door closed behind us.

Chapter 51

Rafe

Rose was light in my arms, even lighter than before, it seemed. *Had she been getting enough to eat since I left?*

I gripped her closer as I navigated the now slick-as-shit sidewalk. She wrapped her arms around my neck and rubbed her warm cheek against my cold one, humming the chorus again and again.

"Oh!" Rose interrupted herself when we were partway up the steps to her front porch. She was gawking over my shoulder, and I used the moment to bury my face in her hair. *Yeah, still smelling like flowers, like roses. Like Rose.*

"When did you park your pickup in the driveway? It wasn't there when we left."

And, "Is Princess here too?"

Finally, "Are you both here to stay?"

By this time, the loonballs were barking up a storm and throwing themselves against the other side of the door. I let Rose slide down my body—so soft where I was hard—and looked her in the eye.

"Yes and yes. Eventually. If you'll have us. But first, there are things I need to say. If you'll let me."

She nodded and stood on her tiptoes to give me her mouth. This time, we kissed deeply, our tongues twisting in their own dance.

Before the dogs could break down the door, I picked Rose up again and pushed into the front hall. Princess and Pirate were leaping on us, but I fended them off to carry her through the living room, past the dining table and into the kitchen. Where I balanced her carefully on one of the stools at the island and stepped back.

"First," I informed her, "I'm going to make you—actually, both of us—something to eat. I only grabbed a sandwich at Hood River today."

Rose gasped in mock horror. *How could I forget her smart-ass ways?*

"We'll talk while we're eating. We have all night. Assuming you have eggs and bacon, how does breakfast for dinner sound?" *Maybe with a side of chocolate truffles.*

She smiled and then frowned. "Won't Finn and Lauren be coming home after the café closes?"

I reached for the note tucked under the French press and handed it to her. She read aloud what I already knew, *"Our Gift to You Both—24 Hours Together—House to Yourselves—See You Christmas Eve—Love, Finn & Lauren—P.S. Mateo & Pete Say No Café Visits Tomorrow."*

Rose grinned this time. "Oh, how wonderful! We're so lucky to have such good friends and family."

Then she sobered and said, "Rafe, I have things *I* need to share with *you*, things to show you too."

Reaching up, she gently brushed her fingers along my jawline, over my scar, back and forth, back and forth. My eyes drifted shut, and I took a long breath. *Home at last. Hopefully.*

After a few moments, I slipped from her touch to start breakfast and put the kettle on. Later, over crispy bacon, scrambled eggs and strong coffee sugared up for her—the dogs settled at our feet for scraps—I asked Rose to forgive me. Well, not right at first.

At first, I told her, "I fucked up. I'm so sorry I hurt you. I was wrong—wrong to leave, wrong to not trust your judgment, wrong to tell you that you needed a better man."

By this time, my heart was thumping out of my chest. "You make *me* a better man. You make me believe my rough past doesn't matter because you see me for who I am *now*. I love you, and I want to spend every minute of every day, the rest of my life, showing you just how much. I can't live without you."

Then, and only then, did I ask, "Rose, can you forgive me? Can you give me a second chance?"

She didn't answer right away. She'd sat listening the entire time, meeting my eyes, not saying a word, eating a forkful here and there, sipping from her mug.

Finally, I couldn't stand it.

"Rose? Babe?"

Still silent, she stood and walked over to the pantry. She came back with a blue folder stuffed with papers and put it down between us.

Spreading both hands on top of the folder, Rose whispered, "I hope *you* can forgive *me*, Rafe."

When I raised my eyebrows, she went on. "Before I tell you what I did, please know that I love you. That's not going to stop even if you don't forgive me."

"Rose, what did you do?" I was getting alarmed.

She swallowed hard and started to blink more quickly. I didn't want to scare her, so I backed off, repeating more softly, "Rose, babe, what did you do?"

"I found your family, Rafe," she said in a rush. "With Lauren's help, I found your family in San Francisco. Your uncle Tony, your cousins Nico and Enzo, your cousin *Angelina*. I've talked with them, and they want to meet you."

I opened my mouth and closed it again, shaking my head.

Rose tapped the folder between us. "Sweetheart, they've each written a letter to you, welcoming you to the family. Tony searched for you when he was younger and couldn't find you. He was estranged from his parents, and they're now gone. His kids grew up hearing about you...and their aunt."

Standing again, she tugged me to my feet. "We—meaning me, Finn, Mateo, Jean-Luc, my girls and all our friends from the Chocolate Lab—put together a care package—box, actually—to send to you. Just in time, Lauren brought up the letters and more items to add. Off it went, guaranteed to arrive in Boise by tomorrow, by Christmas Eve."

She giggled. "In fact, you probably passed the truck on the interstate driving here."

Taking me by one hand, she headed out of the kitchen, back through the dining room and into the living room. She gripped my shoulders so I faced her.

I still hadn't said a word. Maybe because Rose being Rose, she hadn't let me get a word in edgewise. Maybe because I was stunned into silence.

"Anyway. The thing is—I made copies to send you and kept all the originals. I didn't want to chance losing anything. The letters are in the folder, but the photos are here."

With that, she turned me around to face the bookshelves. Now crowded in among the Connolly family pictures were new framed photos. A young mother, with dark blue eyes and curly dark hair, holding a baby. Another picture of the same woman cuddling a toddler. Hugging a preschooler in front of a little Christmas tree. My mamma and me?

More photos...a young Angelina linking arms with a younger boy. As a high schooler, wearing a cap and gown. As a little girl holding a stuffed dog. As a toddler herself.

A group shot of an older man, two young guys and a beautiful young woman, all smiling behind a birthday cake. All looking like each other, all looking like me. Or maybe it was the other way around.

I moved closer to peer at one photo, different from the others. It was a picture of Rose standing in front of the shelves, holding another frame. This time a message, not a photo.

RAFE, COME HOME. COME HOME TO ME.

I swung around and pulled Rose tight to me. Fuck…turned out I was a crier too.

Chapter 52

Rose

Rafe was taking his second shower of the day, alone this time, while I was pulling goodies out of the fridge for our annual Christmas Eve smorgasbord.

Smoked salmon, cheeses, pickled herring, meats, crab dip, crackers, mini-rolls, veggies, olives, mixed nuts all crowded our dining table until there wasn't an inch to spare. Aquavit, wine, whiskey, a coffee carafe and, yes, water marched along the sideboard. Later, we'd fill our plates, grab napkins and drinks, and go sit in the living room before the tree and fire.

Earlier, I'd switched on every twinkly light in the place—the tree, the mantle, the stair railings, the front porch, the back patio. Rafe had put up the rest of the lights outside while I'd worked on the food. Finn and Lauren would be back home any minute now. She'd asked me if she could bring Jean-Luc and Cab, and I'd said of course, *of course.* Made me wonder where she'd spent Christmas Eve *Eve.*

I was distracting myself so I wouldn't join Rafe. I'd already taken my second shower, and we didn't have time for a repeat of what happened after our first shower that morning.

Last night, after…everything…we'd settled on the couch, me on Rafe's lap, arms wrapped around each other, and talked and kissed for hours. We'd both fallen sound asleep, exhausted, dogs snuggling on the floor below us. Rafe had roused enough to carry me up to bed.

This morning had been a different story. I smiled as I remembered...

My eyes drifted open. The room was darker than a dog's mouth. Not even an inkling of dawn out the window. Why was I waking up this early? Mateo and Finn had assured me the café was covered—they'd been picking up the slack for a few days now. I could sleep in....

I started to roll over onto my back...and I couldn't. I froze. Nope— the opposite, in fact. My entire backside was roasty-toasty from my head to my heels. And not the heels of the stiletto type, but the heels of the naked type.

I was pushing back against an equally clothing-optional Rafe, who was nestled all up in my business. Face in my hair, arms pulling me flush to his furred chest, packed abs, velvet length, thick thighs and bent knees. Everything—and I meant everything—was hard, yet heated. No doubt about it. Rafe was warm for my form.

Last evening hadn't been a dream.

When I tried to sit up, he rolled me over to face him, pressing every inch to naked inch of our fronts together. I slid my free arm around his ribs to run my palm up and down his spine, my fingernails scraping over his bunched back muscles. Turning my cheek to his throat, I squeezed even closer—if that were possible—and started to lick the tattoos covering the delts on his right arm.

Rafe groaned as I dragged my body down his, pulling his arm out straight, and continuing to lick—and, yes, bite—the winding images of his black ink sleeve. Then I stopped.

On the inside of his wrist, where it'd been blank, there was an intricate rose. A swirl of countless petals in hot pink, delicately edged in black, a couple of inches in diameter. Was there a matching one on his other wrist? I didn't check to see, instead gently touching my lips to the tattoo before sliding my face over to his core to continue my licking journey.

Just as I was about to take him deep, Rafe growled "my turn" and reached to pull me up his body. Shifting me to my back, he weighed me down with his warmth and took my mouth in a ferocious kiss. We stayed in a luscious wet tangle before he started moving down my body, intent on making his own explorations.

By the time we made it to the shower, we'd exchanged three orgasms (me) and two orgasms (him). Shuddering, shattering, shouting... Good thing we were alone in the house. And those didn't count the ones Rafe gifted me after drying and patting me all over and taking me right back to our bed. We made sweet, slower love that time around. Still as shattering, just not as loud.

That howling must have been the dogs.

Between showers, sexy times and general fooling around, we'd made three decisions. Together. Well, mostly. And I'd captured them on green Post-its, now lined up on our butcher block island. Rafe's were still there, just moved over.

Post-it Number One: I was going to drive back to Boise with Rafe and Princess the day after Christmas. I'd stay the week and fly back home after New Year's. Mateo and Finn would hold the fort down, trading openings and closings, and Pete would keep up with the roasting. Confirmed by a flurry of texts—and, in Pete's case, a quick call.

Post-it Number Two: After Rafe returned from Boise early-February-ish, he'd reenter the house, our bedroom, our bed—no waiting required or allowed. He'd already reentered my heart... In truth, he'd never left it.

Post-it Number Three: Rafe would resume his roaster and production manager role at the Chocolate Lab, with Mike as occasional backup. He'd refused any pay, though, and insisted on putting some of his savings into the café's growth and Finn's college needs. *That's investing in our future, babe,* he'd growled.

Later, after a break for lunch—to build up our strength, of course—Rafe had phoned his uncle. Moving away to give them some privacy, I'd been pulled back to Rafe's chest where he'd hung on to me for the duration of the call. I'd hugged his forearm and listened as they'd grumbled through their men-of-few-words introductions, appreciation and wonderment. They ended the call after making plans to Zoom tomorrow when the whole family was over at Tony's for Christmas dinner.

Rafe was singing in the shower now—a new thing—and his voice filtered all the way down from our bathroom. *When we were alone, doors stayed open.*

Except for our front door, where a commotion of laughter, barking and shouts of merriment heralded the start of Christmas Eve festivities. I was heading through the living room to let everybody in when…what the fido? W*as that* another *new photo on the bookshelves?*

Nope—just an old one from our trip to the beach. Back in a place of pride, front and center on the middle shelf. Rafe, the dogs and me—we were all grinning at the camera. Or rather, the pic showed Rafe in profile as he smiled down at the rest of us.

What's that in the corner of the frame?

Finn and the rest were surging through the door, so I hurried over to lean close. It was a bit of duct tape peeking out from behind a perfectly round, unbroken, unchipped sand dollar. With a five-pointed star in the middle.

Epilogue
Rafe

Nine weeks on...

She jammed her chin down on my shoulder—hard—and huffed. The wipers were clearing the windshield in double time, but the going was still slow.

"I'm driving as fast as I can, baby girl." Somebody was impatient to get home. That made two of us.

I was wearing the hot pink beanie—yeah, I got side glances, but nobody dared to say shit. Princess burrowed in her new jacket, but had kicked off her booties the first chance she'd gotten. She was not amused.

We passed the exit to Troutdale, only about an hour left now. Less if this snow let up.

During her week with me in Boise and every day and night since, Rose and I had made plans. Sure, we'd made love plenty, too— even got intense on the phone, although the distance thing still sucked. But the plans were for the future, our future.

First mission was to get married. Not if, but when.

Fuck waiting.

We'd probably do it during Finn's spring break. He'd escort his mamma down the aisle and step over to be one of my best men.

He'd join Mateo, Jean-Luc and Tony (if he agreed after our visit next month). Rose's girls would be at her side. We'd asked Pete to officiate, and—after he'd recovered from the shock of "you can get ordained online?"—he'd said an enthusiastic "you betcha."

Rose claimed Pirate and Princess wanted to be in the ceremony too. Something about ring-bearer and flower girl. She'd have her way, no doubt. Always would with me.

Kinda fitting though. We wanted to hold the whole she-bang—wedding and reception—in the Chocolate Lab. And invite everyone and their dog.

Hmmm. Which Portland exit to take? Duh…the one that will get your ass there the fastest, as Finn would say. Or text. The kid was back at school now. He'd taken his mamma's car since we'd have my pickup for wheels. That was until I could lay my hands on another beater ready for my DIY skills.

"Princess! Quiet the fuck down!" When I turned on our street, she started running back and forth in the crowded cab space, still barking her fool head off. There was some kind of long sign—banner?—strung high between the two side doors of the café, but she was making too much of a racket for me to pay attention.

I pulled into the driveway and decided to leave my stuff where it was in my rush to get to Rose. Baby girl beat me to the punch and jumped over the seat and out my door. Yipping all the way, she headed around to the front of the house.

I followed her down the sidewalk, ready to thunder up the porch steps and pound on the front door. Ready to kiss the living daylights out of…

WELCOME HOME, RAFE!

The front door burst open, and Rose raced under the banner and down the front steps. She leaped onto me, arms around my neck, legs around my waist. I wrapped my arms around her, supporting her, and hung on for all I was worth.

"Rafe. Sweetheart. You're finally here. I've got you. You're safe now," she whispered in my ear. And again. "I've got you."

The End

THANK YOU FOR READING
Red Hot Roaster!

WANT THE LATEST TALES & TREATS?

Jump on my website and sign up for my email newsletter where you'll find new release alerts, exclusive bonus content and real life love stories when pets turn matchmakers or join the wedding party.

WANT MORE *Red Hot Roaster?*

Sign up for the newsletter and grab your **FREE BONUS EPILOGUE**—from the pups' point of view! Princess and Pirate share the scoop on Rose, Rafe and family four years later!

Website: kristinjeffries.com
Instagram: @kristinjeffriesauthor
Facebook: kristinjeffriesauthor

Acknowledgements

Mom, thank you for encouraging my reading right from the start. Dad, thank you for building bookcases in my bedroom to hold all my childhood favorites.

Morane, your insights and feedback on my early draft of *Red Hot Roaster* were invaluable. Thanks for taking time out of your crazy schedule to devote to me.

Margy, I appreciate your enthusiastic support for this venture—and only you know which parts of our bestie outings found their way into the book.

Ethan, you're in the tale too. Although you'll never find out since you admit to admiring the cover, but refuse to read anything spicy by your mom.

Rob, you understand when I disappear into my dog den to write for hours on end. You're my go-to-guy for all things coffee-tasting and coffee-roasting and café-running. For those and so many other reasons, I'm still crazy (about you) after all these years.

Bonny Lass, you're our very good baby girl.

About Kristin

Come sit at my table, and let's talk romance. If you're anything like me, you're looking for a little break, a little treat, a little escape from reality. Right?

Reading has been that escape for me—mystery, fantasy, science fiction and romance, always romance. So after decades as a health marketing consultant, I decided to create my own dose of healthy escape to offer you and other readers like us.

I built on these in-real-life inspirations for my contemporary romance series set in the fictional Portland neighborhood of Dogwood: my family's adventures in running the original Chocolate Lab Café in a small Wisconsin town; my love for the red hot—yet not roaming—coffee roaster who heats up my heart and home; and my affection for a long line of smouchy pups, starting with Bix, Frisky, Perky and Schnitzel in my youth and continuing with Hildy, Pirate—yes, there was an IRL Pirate!—and today's Bonny Lass.

When I'm not reading or writing, I'm indulging in my other escapes—whether they be my morning two-shot mocha, my daily walk with my black Lab girl, or my evening rye Manhattan with my husband.

Here's hoping you find your daily escapes…in romance.